MOBILE TALES

MOBILE TALES

Short Stories for
Positive Change

KAREN LAMANTIA

ARPress
45 Dan Road Suite 36
Canton MA 02021

Hotline: 1(800) 220-7660
Fax: 1(855) 752-6001

Ordering Information:
Quantity Sales. Special discounts are available on quantity purchases by corporations, associations, and others. For details, contact the publisher at the address above.

Printed in the United States of America.

ISBN-13   Paperback   979-8-89389-909-2
               eBook   979-8-89389-910-8

Library of Congress Control Number: 2024923857

This book is dedicated to the Ancestors.
May their Compassion, Love and Wisdom continue
to guide us to their Vision of Earth Healed.

AN INTRODUCTION

In the Year of Christ, the Carpenter Employed, 2020 AD, the world known as Planet Earth hears The Message. Everyone and everything hear and understands it, and all are reminded that Planet Earth is a place for Tigers. Humans learn that everything is here for the benefit of Tigers and that humanity has not only overstayed their welcome but has messed the place up something terrible. Tigers can barely survive on Earth and mankind needs to do something about that fast, before there are no Tigers left at all.

The Message gets humans in gear but could not have changed a thing if people were not ready to hear and understand it. It would mean nothing if people had no ability to make the cleanup happen. ***The End Game*** is a book about how the human effort to clean up Planet Earth starts. Many of the people who make ***The End Game*** so much fun are back in ***Mobile Tales*** and Betsy Ross Jackson has this introduction to share about the second book in The Message series.

"***Mobile Tales*** are stories about before and after the Message is heard. They are tales of a Mobile transformation that begins one heart, one mind and one Neighborhood at a time. Neighbors, just like you and me, create these stories that help change a world."

You can find ***The End Game*** at: **http://www.earthneighborhood.com,** but that is another story. Now, read these Mobile Tales, have Fun and Be Kind."

TABLE OF CONTENTS

The Sound of Beauty, on Page __1__ tells how a cafeteria lady, creates change from the discarded and discounted. Line up for a serving of herstory.

Listen up, as **I Hear Music** sounds off about one young man's journey toward his heart's desire. Join him **on Page __14__**, as he follows his ears to get there.

A Fair Tale is one of the many just stories about The Message, that opens the eyes, minds, and hearts of humanity. Turn to **Page __25__** to find out what happens Once Upon That Time, according to the Way Scans.

The Coupon Lady shares what she does best and changes the world for the better. Read from **Page __32__** and learn how a switch board operator helps feed humanity on a minimum wage.

Savor this story on **Page __44__** and learn how **A Piece of The Pie** can dispel fear and nourish understanding.

Changing Places is a story about people who share their best ideas when the world is ready to listen. Get online at **Page __54__** for this tale.

The Bidewell Mansion gives us entry to a Neighborhood where positive change is the status quo. Read on from **Page __65__** and see what helps Earth Neighbors inside and outside their 'hood.

The Puzzle Box tells how Ed finally breaks out of jail, with a little help from a Planet transformed by The Message. Liberate yourself with this story on **Page   71   .**

Open Poker decides victory in war by the turn of a card. Get in the game on **Page   80   ** and examine some new ways to settle old conflicts and Be Peace.

Join the **Grandmother Brigade** on **Page   87   ** to cooperate, using innovative ways to share and be fair, worldwide.

It's A Wonderful Country takes you into new territory on **Page   92   .** What starts out as a scam ends up creating heaven on Earth. Read all about it as the world's biggest con artist realizes his wildest dreams.

On **Page   103   ** you can get involved with their story as **Ma-Ree K!** mobilizes a group of neighbors to pay for the high costs of WWWIII, the War that ends all Wars.

Be there, on **Page   111   ,** and be Love as **Building** creates a world that is the best it can be.

Freemont and the Tomato Millionaires grow a world economy to help everyone, rich and poor, starting with seeds planted in the Mobile financial District. How'd ya' like them tomatoes? Find out on **Page   121   .**

FBI-CAN tells the tale of the Federal Bureau of Crimes Against Nature on **Page   131   .** Learn creative ways to bust polluters by using weapons of mass instruction. Now, who you gonna' call?

Catch **The Great American Review** on **Page   149   ,** to learn how a group of prostitutes and a singing waitress go on tour, to help educate Americans about the ways of the world.

Don't be afraid to look **Behind the Veil,** on **Page** _164_, for the under-cover story of the woman who sings to help the peace process in the Middle East.

On **Page** _170_, immerse yourself in this the story of **The Fish Man,** a Wanderer whose special knowledge of underwater worlds helps fish and those of us left high and dry.

Pray (or play) all over Planet Earth as **The Holy Roaming Empire** visits lands known and owned by all—International Zones of the Human Spirit. Your trip begins on **Page** _176_.

Dream on with **Dreaming Clean**, on **Page** _185_, for a tale about remaking the present by rethinking the past.

Welcome to **the Way Scan School** when the Mobile Unified School District is transformed by playing games. Read all about it and do the math on **Page** _195_.

On **Page** _212_ you can realize your dreams with **The Star Quilt,** to dare to dream!

Some humans become part of a place, even a Wild place. **Son of The Land,** on **Page** _222_, tells the story of LeRoy Fryer and a place that would not be the same without him, Planet Earth.

THE SOUND OF BEAUTY

It is her life in a densely forested area on the subcontinent of India, which makes it virtually impossible for Betsy Ross Jackson to see anything as trash. There, food that people throw away is food for something else, like flies, ants, or worms. Americans call such things garbage. Betsy calls them opportunities. She has a hard time understanding why Americans throw away so many wonderful opportunities.

Betsy's name is the first thing thrown away by Avery Winslow, the Peace Corps worker who finds her family when Tiger Country is destroyed by a chemical spill. Everything there is turned into green goo and Betsy, her husband and child are the only ones to survive. Their Tiger Country names do not.

Her adult name, given to her by women of her group, means 'the sound plants make when they grow after a rain'. Such a name must go because it cannot be spelled out or written down in any alphabet, except the one used by trees as they write leaf patterns against the sky. This alphabet will not fill the empty spaces on the many US Immigration papers and Visa applications, so Avery gives the Tiger Country citizen a new name to complete those forms.

Unfortunately, there is no way for humans to invent a rainforest to fill in the blank on the landscape left by that chemical spill. All that remains of the land is a memory of Tiger Country in the hearts and minds of Betsy Ross and her family.

When told she is to be called after a famous textile artist, Betsy Ross does not mind taking the new name. Artists of any kind are revered in Tiger Country and Betsy Ross knows that names can and do change all the time. Her husband often calls Betsy Ross 'Mae', as part of the 'Lou-Mae' or Beloved One. Such a relationship, shared by two people whose Becoming is more complete because of the other, is rare even in Tiger Country. She values that name highly. Her daughter calls Betsy Ross 'mother' in several languages and she never tires of hearing it, no matter how it sounds. Other people call her a whole host of other names, some of which Betsy Ross suspects are not all that flattering.

Being labeled an 'alien' is the name Betsy Ross finds most accurate, when told it means someone from another planet. Her life in the U.S. is so different from anything in Tiger Country, it often seems like life on another planet to her. Betsy is never sure if she is the strange one or if the land where she now lives is so alienated from the rest of the world, it is the spaced-out place.

"Ways of doing things here are so different from most ways, most humans live, for most of the time we've been on Earth." Betsy shares with Winston Brightfoot, a youth of fifteen years who is quizzing her about Tiger Country.

"How is it different?" Winston asks, as always, fascinated by ways people live and solve problems in different cultures.

"The biggest difference is that humans here identify so many things as their private property. In Tiger Country everything belongs to the Tiger."

"Even the humans?" Winston asks, trying to imagine himself the pet of a big cat. "Your people live in that forest for eons and yet you still see yourselves as guests?"

"We're all just visiting and everything that humans use is on loan to us from Tigers."

"Kind of them." Winston observes, recalling a legend among his own People–that their homeland belongs to the Swamp Panthers who kindly allow humans to remain in the sloughs and bayous around Mobile for the past ten thousand years.

"Tigers are very gracious hosts; I'll give them that." Betsy Ross concedes. "They give all we need and never make us feel the least unwelcome. Their manners are impeccable."

"So, your People never saw things in Tiger Country as their own." Winston marvels. "That must have cut down on greed and desire a lot."

"It also upped the gratitude and appreciation factor quite a bit." Betsy admits. "It helps many species get along well together, too. We share things and try to live in as much harmony as possible. If we have problems with anyone or anything else, we work them out."

"Your art shows that." Winston comments as he views the sculpture Betsy Ross is making from a pile of trash, gathered in Mobile's parks and playgrounds. "What you create is a harmonious mix of elements that is both dynamic and exciting. I've never seen anything quite like it."

The piece Betsy Ross is working on looks like a big dragonfly and seems to contain all the excitement and fun of a playground, the frenzy of a street fair and the gusto of a sports event.

"Somebody has fun here!" is the message the piece exudes.

The sculpture is energized by a spirit of play from each recreation spot and play place where Betsy Ross found its parts. Looking at her creation, Winston wonders why anyone threw away any part of it. Each bit looks as though one could have gone on having a barrel of fun with it.

"How'd you do it?" Winston asks, looking up at her creation.

"I had help." Betsy Ross assures him. "Kind people left such intriguing things behind for me to use. Such give and take are the most important part of the art, the magic of a creation. In the English language you call it 'sharing'."

"Sharing is magic?" Winston asks. "How so?"

"It connects the ones who share, through the object they share." Betsy explains. "That moves both beyond their usual time, space and idea of self. That's magic."

"Is that why people like museums?" Winston wonders. "Do people share time through things used or made in the past?"

"We have no museums in Tiger Country." Betsy explains. "We just use what we have or remake it, like I do here with my sculptures. If another human can't use something, we give it to another species or return it to the Earth. Other creatures around us share with humans in the same ways."

"Is it sharing if people think they're just throwing this stuff out?"

"They share information. What I find teaches me so much about this place. That's why I like working with objects like these. I guess what they are and how they are used, and from the way they look, feel, sound and smell, I see this world with new eyes."

"I'm seeing this junk with new eyes." Winston admits as he looks up at the sculpture swaying in the breeze from an open window.

Some of what he sees is familiar to him but is being used in ways that Winston can hardly recognize. Above him is a fantastic insect created from old bicycle tires, with dozens of plastic six-pack holders as its gossamer wings. Betsy Ross wove the plastic to form intricate geometric patterns that refract the light as the sun shines through the wings, to create a moving rainbow on their surface.

"But nothing looks the same." Winston claims. "You take junk and make it into something beautiful. Nothing is the way it was before."

"One of our wise ones taught: 'Nothing is ever created or destroyed. Things only change their form'." Betsy Ross replies.

"Albert Einstein?" Winston asks.

"That may have been her name." Betsy responds. "She lived a thousand generations ago in Tiger Country, so we don't know what people living then called her. We speak of her as 'The One Who Sees With Tiger Eyes'."

"Great view." Winston concedes then goes silent, listening, as he sways to the sound the wings make when the wind moves through them.

The piece chimes, rings, and whistles when the wind hits it. Peals of laughter and the roar of a cheering crowd can be heard, faintly, if one listens hard enough and a breeze flows around the sculpture just right.

"Great sound, too." Winston voices.

"The school must hang it in the playgro und so the children can both see and hear it. That sound is its most important feature and will provide music for the children's laughter." Betsy Ross explains.

"It's going to a school?" Winston asks, unaware that Betsy Ross sends all her completed artwork to elementary and middle schools as soon as she finishes a piece.

"Most schools need something like this." Betsy explains. "The dragonfly will accompany students in an area of enhanced Beauty. Dragonfly music and the children's music are the hum of Beauty, which is an essential part of any learning environment."

"Sounds pretty complicated."

"No more complicated than a flower and a bee, Winston. It's the bee's hum that makes the fruit we need to live. The flower attracts the bee, but the hum is the lively part. Most schools are desperately in need of the hum of Beauty. Then the egg can drop."

"The egg?"

"The new idea, the seed, or whatever you want to call what happens when the time and place are ripe for growth and change."

"How do you decide which school gets this?" Winston asks.

"I work in school cafeterias, filling in when someone on the regular crew is sick." Betsy explains. "I see a lot of schools and they could all benefit from more Beauty. Some need helps more than others."

"Here, here." Winston agrees, thinking how much like prisons most Mobile schools look and sound.

"Robert E. Lee Junior High School is in serious trouble. That's where this one is going." Betsy Ross continues as the dragonfly nods its head in the breeze. "I don't know how those children can show up there day after day."

"That place is kind of a bummer." Winston admits, familiar with the school whose reputation is so bad, city police roam the halls to keep order. "A lot of trouble is created there on a regular basis. You think the kids at that school are going to laugh near this? More like fight near it, from what I hear."

Betsy Ross smiles. "I'm sure those students are no different from anyone else. They'll know beauty when the see and hear it. The one I'm worried about is that Principal, Una Prentice. I tried to tell her about sprucing the place up a little and she told me that beauty is something people earn by hard work and determination. That poor woman, I shudder to think how she was taught such a strange notion."

"She's new there, isn't she?" asks Winston.

"She used to run a penitentiary, but she kept getting in trouble for violating prisoners' Constitutional Rights. Una quit the prison system and came to work for the School District." Betsy explains. "Since kids don't have any rights, she is right at home there."

"What is she doing about that school's problems?" Winston wonders.

"She started at Robert E. Lee last September and about half the student body have either quit school or been arrested." Betsy shares. "She may take out two-thirds of the remaining students by the end of the year. Then they'll close that school."

"That's one way of addressing a school's problems, get rid of all the students." Winston muses. "If they close the school, no more problem school."

"The problem does not go away, though, it just becomes someone else's problem."Betsy Ross points out. "Let's think of a better solution."

"Like this sculpture. What if Principal Una's beauty police won't let you put it up?"

"I have an idea that will get my sculpture just where it needs to be." Betsy Ross shares, as she picks up the phone and dials the school.

To Winston's surprise, she speaks with an upper-class British accent when her call is connected.

"The Director of the Smythington-Smythington Fisk Foundation here, to speak with your school principal. Our Foundation wishes to donate a work of art to your school."

"Some accent." Winston tells Betsy as she waits to be put through to Ms. Prentice. "You sound like Queen Elizabeth."

"I was actually going for the Queen Mother." Betsy whispers. "No one can say no to her."

Winston cannot hear what is said at the other end of the conservation, but from what Betsy says to Una, it sounds like the Principal agrees to accept the gift.

"There will be a presentation ceremony a few days after the sculpture is in place." Betsy tells Una. "The set-up crew will install the piece at a prominent spot, where your young citizens can see it."

Betsy Ross hangs up the phone, before Una can say no.

"That was some talking." Winston admits. "How'd you learn to do that accent?"

"I speak both hummingbird and hawk." Betsy explains. "If I can speak to other species, human dialects can't be all that difficult."

"I guess not." Winston admits, beginning to see the problems he has in his high school German class as minor ones.

Winston volunteers to help Betsy Ross install the sculpture, with a little help from the Way Scans. His friends are called Way Scans because of the dark glasses they wear and because they see what is on the horizon for the future.

The Way Scans have a good, working relationships with the other 'youth groups' in their city and Winston figures they can get

Betsy Ross in and out of the school's tough Neighborhood safely. Way Scan involvement will also help assure that the sculpture stays in place, unharmed, once it is put up. To make this certain, the Way Scans hold a meeting with leaders of the various gangs that operate in that part of the city, the day before they install the piece.

❋ ❋ ❋ ❋

"It's a kind of experiment to see if making the school more Beautiful will help the kids there." Winston tells representatives from the Man-Rays, the Swords of Islam, the New Aryan Brotherhood, the Asian Masters, La Raza Rio, and the Aztlan Goddesses. Those in attendance are the older brothers and sisters of many of the young people who attended the school.

"We want to see if these kids can finish school, so they have a couple of choices besides gangs in their future." Winston tells the gathering. "After all, you guys need family to run your businesses and neighborhood organizations. You either got to educate these young ones or go back to school yourselves."

The Way Scans have been talking to gang members about this kind of stuff for a while and they are well aware that poor schools are the biggest block to realizing their own Neighborhood improvement plans. None the less, there is a murmur of startled concern from many of the representatives when the idea of return to a public school is mentioned.

"Ho! How do you think this thing will make Robert E. Lee a better school?" Sami Chung Montez asks. "I left that place without graduatin' and I'd rather go to the joint than back there."

"You've hit it on the head, Sami." Winston concedes "That school needs help so bad, almost anything is worth a try."

❋ ❋ ❋ ❋

With assistance from the Ways Scans and the blessings of local Youth groups, Betsy Ross mounts the sculpture in the schoolyard.

As the wind moves through the dragonfly's giant wings, the Way Scans admit that both the sight and its sound make the sculpture compelling.

"It reminds me of the far-off cheering you hear from outside a football stadium, on the day of the big game." Bobbie Turner observes.

"I think it sounds like a church choir from about a block away." Emaline Purcell voices.

"Or maybe it's the laughter of plants." Toni Leonardo jokes.

"I think it's the sound of the eternal fire." Ruth 'The Flame' Feinstein says reflectively.

"I think it's the sound of the Planet at Peace." Winston shares. "It's the sound we'll hear when people get smart enough to stop having wars to settle their differences."

"Mission accomplished!" Betsy Ross exclaims, as she surveys the faces of the young people looking up at the work of art.

The next school day, Winston drops by the Jr. High School to see how the young people are reacting to Beauty in their midst. The students of Robert E. Lee are leaving school for the day and, much to Winston's surprise, they pass beneath it and do not even look up. Teachers going past barely take note of it either.

When Winston sees Betsy Ross coming across the school playground, dressed for her job in the school cafeteria, he waves to her and she joins him.

"Nobody notices your art." Winston says.

"Of course, they notice." Betsy assures him. "They just don't know it, yet. They've been turned off to what's around them. They ignore the world for their own protection, and it will take a while for them to be aware of this change. It's a survival thing."

"Survival?" Winston asks. "By not noticing stuff? I thought survival depends on being alert and aware."

"If you are in a family, a school, or a group that tells you that you're trash all the time, how much would you pay attention? You have to turn off or you perish. Unfortunately, when that happens your capacity for seeing and believing a lot of the good stuff, the exciting and wonderful stuff, gets put on the back burner, too."

Winston is worried. He wonders if the years of put downs and shutdowns create young people who turn themselves back on with noise, violence, or pain. He knows plenty of people who try to turn on with drugs or alcohol. He hopes for other turn-on options for young people, like this Beauty option in their schoolyard.

"Don't worry." Betsy Ross assures Winston. "They are aware of the difference. Watch their feet."

Winston looks down but it takes a while before he begins to notice that everyone walking by moves with the same rhythm. Paying close attention, he sees that the rhythm of their steps matches the hum made by the sculpture. When the wind changes the music, the pattern of their beat changes, too.

"No one can resist the sound of Beauty." Betsy Ross tells Winston. "People try to drown it out with noise and fear, but Beauty always sings to young ones in undeniable ways. That's the Beauty of it."

"But how do you know the way it should sound?" Winston asks, never having heard anything quite like the hum coming from the work of art.

"I just worked with the materials until they make the noise I hear when wind moves through the trees in Tiger Country." Betsy explains. "That is the first sound that creatures we call human ever heard. Human ears are made for that sound. We tune with it."

✳ ✳ ✳ ✳

Weeks's pass and Winston drops by the school whenever he has a chance. As Betsy Ross predicts, it takes a while for the effects of Beauty to become apparent. The first sign is the gathering of students under the sculpture, which brings out the school security team to break up any congregation of more than three young people. Then the guards, themselves, move into the area and let the young people stay for brief periods, before they insist the Youth move on. The longer the guards hang around, the longer they let the students hang out there, too. Soon, people begin making their own sounds there.

It starts with humming and whistling and then some of the kids start singing; mostly songs they learned as tiny kids or ones they make up themselves. One of the guards, Sargent Minnesota Wilbright, is an amateur vocalist with the Mobile Lamplighters, a local chapter of an international singing organization. Minnesota hears a song sung by student Tyrell Ortiz and knows, at once, that the song could be a winner in his team's upcoming, Lamplighter Regional Songfest. He persuades Tyrell to teach him the song and brings a tape recorder for an audio copy of Tyrell's concert under the dragonfly. Winston is visiting that day and witnesses the event, which he later describes to Betsy Ross.

"There are dozens of kids around and when Tyrell begins to sing, some of them bring out their own instruments to play along." Winston tells the artist. "Some have harmonicas and finger symbols, but most playthings like a half-empty box of hard candy or an empty soda cans with rocks inside. A couple of guys play pocket combs covered with paper and some of the girls shake their earrings and bangle bracelets or make stuff in their purses into rattles. A few take sticks and scrape them across the chain link fence or tap steel-toed shoes against stuff like waste cans and wooden benches. Some play themselves like drums."

It is hard for Winston to describe the intricate clapping and slapping patterns that are made by those with no other instrument than the first instrument ever used by humans; the ultimate in portable percussion, the human body. Betsy Ross knows what Winston means, as body drumming is an art form in Tiger Country.

"They sound great." Winston explains. "Then, during the third chorus of the song the dragonfly drops its egg, right in the middle of that circle of singing and dancing students. It falls out and hits Minnesota on the head."

"Human song always could open doors," Betsy Ross allows. "and an egg on the scene is a sure sign that good things are about to happen. What happened next?"

"The music stops, and Becky Lin Chow picks up the egg. It is one of those plastic things that hold women's panty hose. She opens it and your message is inside."

"My message?" asks Betsy Ross.

"Didn't you put it in there?"

"No," Betsy Ross informs him. "I found that egg and I had a feeling is had something to share, but I never looked inside. That would have spoiled the surprise for me. What did it say?"

"It read,'Your world is any way you make it'." Winston shares. "Becky read it aloud and then looked around and told the others 'This place is a real dump. We should do something about that.'"

✹ ✹ ✹ ✹

The large number of after-school groups meeting beneath the dragonfly are the first thing Winston notices when he next stops by Robert E. Lee. Some groups are making music, and some are working on dance routines. Others make mobiles from found objects, to adorn school hallways and the cafeteria area. Another group is planning murals for the schoolyard and hallways, to cover the graffiti that abounds there. They find plenty of positive stuff to portray just looking around their own school to get the picture.

A school orchestra is started, using mostly traditional musical instruments. The young people get their equipment from their grandparents, as the only musical instruments available to students since the Mobile School District Music Program was stripped of its funds, decades ago. Neighborhood grandparents also join the Robert E Lee students after school to teach the kids to play. Though their homelands are varied, there are a surprising number of bowed, string instruments from the mix of cultures represented at the school;

fiddles from China, Ethiopia, Brazil, Afghanistan, India, or Ireland and one fiddler from the Yaki Nation.

"We can hardly tell when someone from India or Appalachia is playing, and the tunes from Ethiopia sound just like the ones from Thailand." Minnesota tells the Mobile Sentinel's youngest freelance reporter, Stillpoint Sommes, as she listens to a tape of the Robert E. Lee School Band and Traditional Orchestra.

"Folks with fiddles have been movers throughout human history and the music from your school proves it." Stillpoint agrees.

"That school is sure a harmonious place, these days. Music is just part of it." Minnesota explains and goes on to tell Stillpoint about the middle school's other self-improvement projects. "The kids who were truant are returning to class and there have even been some drop-ins, instead of the usual drop-outs."

When the school Principal gets a call from Stillpoint, as a follow-up to Minnesota's story, Una Prentice is clueless about the reasons for the positive transformation at her school.

"Attendance is up and teachers tell me the students seem to be listening more." Principal Una admits reluctantly. "There in no longer a need for the police here and our Chief of Security is now an employee of the City Department of Recreation–the Music Director for Robert E. Lee's after-school programs."

"What made the change?" Stillpoint inquires.

"My program of discipline and order has finally paid off?" the Principal guesses, then holds the telephone receiver away from her ear to listen to an unusual sound- one she cannot quite place.

Una thinks she remembers such a sound from a time long ago, or perhaps it was once heard in a dream.

"I got to go now." Una tells the reporter. "I hear something, and I need to go find out what it is... It sounds just like ... I don't know what it sounds like, but it sure sounds beautiful."

You never know when something most people see as a problem turns out to be a solution.

-Howard Beau Brightfoot

I HEAR MUSIC

Bobby Rae VanDee is the worst student in the 8th Grade Graduating class of 1969, at Robert E. Lee Middle School. That is what his teacher and his Principal say when he does not succeed in the classes set up for the 'specially challenged'. He does not fit in anywhere else, either–perhaps because his ears are so big. Other students do not call Bobby Rae 'The Ear' because of the size of his auditory appendages. He gets his nickname because he can hear things better than almost anyone else alive can.

When it rains, teachers teach their students to be smart enough to come in out of it. Adults can never imagine where Bobby Rae gets to at these times, but the kids know, as they listen for the most unusual sounds and find Bobby Rae there listening, too.

"I hear music." is what Bobby Rae says to the one sent to locate him.

Howard Beau Brightfoot, in school with Bobby Rae since kindergarten, is best at finding The Ear. So as not to unfairly jeopardize his friend's academic progress, the boys develop a set of signals for Howard Beau to track Bobby Rae, before they miss too much class time. Howard blows a dog whistle, which only dogs and Bobby Rae are able to hear, and Bobby Rae responds to it by 'playing' the room.

The Ear uses whatever is around him—pipes, roof tiles, walls, and furniture and often his own body; to harmonize, resonate, reflect, or embellish these musical compositions. Howard Beau listens and follows the sounds to Bobby Rae. He learns a lot during these adventures but, unfortunately for both boys, no one gives elementary school credit for auditory excellence.

"I get to hear some pretty cool music," Howard Beau explains to his mother when she voices concern about her son's declining grades. "but it seems like Bobby Rae is going off on his sound trips more and more, and I'm missing a lot of class time."

As they speak, they hear their front doorbell play a surprisingly beautiful tune, considering the limitations of that two-note instrument. Nothing like it has ever been heard in the Brightfoot home before.

"That could be Bobby Rae, now." Anna Marie Brightfoot guesses, as she goes to the door.

"My ears are itching." Bobby Rae explains when she opens it. "You must be talking about me."

As Anna Marie invites Bobby Rae in, she sees by the way he is dressed that his family is still as poor as dirt. The tattered clothes and the shoes that look too big for him do not seem to bother Bobby Rae. He is too busy listening to their home.

"You got a nice harmony in this place." Bobby Rae tells them, paying them his highest compliment. "It's amazing for a family with seven children." he adds.

"Thank you, Bobby Rae." Anna Marie responds. "What can we do for you?"

"I came to say good-bye." Bobby Rae tells them. "I found out today that I can't go on to the place with all the instruments, next year."

"He means the high school." Howard Beau explains to his mother.

"You won't graduate 8th Grade?" Anne Marie asks, concerned.

"I guess not." Bobby Rae admits. "The only thing I read are the music scores in the band room, so I guess they think I'm not qualified to graduate."

"What will you do if you don't go to high school?" Howard Beau asks, imagining Bobby Rae wandering all over town each day, listening to things.

Howard Beau is old enough to know that Bobby Rae could get into big trouble doing something like that. People might think he is plain crazy.

"I plan to keep playing my instrument." Bobby Rae responds.

"What instrument?" Anna Marie asks. She knows that Bobby's family is too poor to afford a comb with a piece of waxed paper over it.

Anna Marie had tried giving Bobby Rae flutes, drums and other traditional InDios instruments, out of respect for his great talent and lifelong desire to make music. When Bobby Rae took them home, someone in his household got them and pawned or sold them for cash.

"My instrument," Bobby Rae explains, looking around, "the Earth."

Howard Beau knows there is no denying Bobby Rae plays earth, water, and air. He has no doubt his friend has ways of playing fire, too.

"Why leave? We are part of Earth, here in Mobile, just like any place else." Anna Marie points out.

"I have to go to find my People. I heard a song about them yesterday!" Bobby Rae exclaims, as his face lights up. "A guy was singing about, The Ones Who Sang the First Songs and Are Singing Still."

"But People have always sung and hummed." Anna Marie reminds Bobby Rae. "We used our voice boxes to make noises, even before people had complex speech. We always made music with our bodies and used things around us for instruments."

"But these Ones have almost nothing else but music." Bobby Rae explains. "That calls to me."

Anna Marie never fit in with her family of birth and left home to look for her People when she was seventeen years old. She can see that Bobbie Rae is terribly excited by the prospect of a whole society that operates on nothing but the sounds, as he does.

"You must go on and find them." Anna Marie agrees, understanding. "How will you do it?"

"I'm going to find the man who sang the song I heard." Bobby Rae explains. "Maybe he knows where the First Singers live."

Most mothers would have called Bobby Rae's parents at once, to tell them their thirteen-year-old son is about to run away from home. Anna Marie knows that the VanDees have no phone and she doubts they even have a home. When she last checked, the family was moving from one abandoned house to another, in a condemned neighborhood of the city. It is hard for Anna Marie to imagine Bobby Rae in a place more dangerous to him than a life of extreme poverty in his own hometown.

"You call us if you need help." Anna Marie tells Bobby Rae, looking into the boy's eyes to make sure he hears her. "I don't care where you are, or what time it is, if you need help you call us. OK?"

Bobby Rae nods his head and Anna Marie adds "On the telephone, Bobby Rae. I'm not talking about singing really loud."

"Oh!" Bobby Rae responds, surprised. "That is a good idea. I promise."

Bobby Rae leaves town the next day, with their telephone number and a quarter in his shoe. Anna Marie does not give him more money, hoping he will either make it out there on his own, or call them for help before he gets too far away. The next time they hear from Bobby Rae Is in the year 2020, shortly after the Message.

❋ ❋ ❋ ❋

How does he manage? The music played by Bobby Rae's cells knows nothing about money and pays no attention to lyrics about jobs, wealth, or security, which distract most of the rest of the world from the harmony of their Being. Bobby Rae stays attuned with the music and when he gets hungry, one way or another, he finds something to eat. When he gets cold, he finds more to wear. When he is tired, he rests. Bobby Rae moves on, as best he can, but wherever he travels, works, stops and even where he sleeps, Bobby Rae hears music. He does more than listen. He also makes music of his own and acquires a collection of small instruments, most of which he makes himself.

Bobby Rae earns enough to live on when he stops on street corners and starts to play to hear how a place sounds with his music in it. He often finds money people leave to thank him and the idea that you can get paid for playing is a pleasant surprise to Bobby Rae. Before he started his journey, he thought people played because they had to, like he does.

The rest of the details of his life are irrelevant to him, so will not be mentioned here.

Bobby Rae is enchanted by the music of the Pacific Ocean when it stops his progress west. He thinks it sounds spectacular; despite the barrier it presents to his progress toward the sunset. Fortunately, dockside at a Pacific port, he hears music from a cruise ship and boards the vessel when its passengers return from their time ashore. It is a few days before ship authorities discover Bobby Rae below deck, when he brings a sound to the attention of the ship's Chief Mechanic, Angus McDermott, tapping Angus on the shoulder amid the roar of the engine room.

"Something is wrong with that number 2 engine." Bobby Rae shouts to Angus. "It sounds different from the way it did when the ship left port. I think something is broken inside."

Angus has been listening to engines most of his adult life and hears what Bobby Rae hears, right away. Grateful that the problem is identified before it causes serious harm to his equipment, the Chief Mechanic hires Bobby Rae for his maintenance crew.

In the years that follow, Bobby is befriended by many who look after engines on the high seas. As Angus promises, in a letter of recommendation he gives the youth, Bobby Rae is able to hear a problem before it becomes critical and really saves some bait on his many sea voyages.

When he reaches Hawaii Bobby, Rae follows his ears until he locates a group of people on a beach, singing and playing their days and nights away. The group consists of artists, dancers and many musicians who come and go from a hut erected under palm trees. There, day or night, someone is making music and dancing. Years pass and Bobby Rae does not find the Ones Who Sang the First Song and are Singing Still but while he listens and waits, he learns to dance.

"The body is singing, even if there are no sounds. You hear the music with your eyes." the young man marvels.

New worlds open up for Bobby Rae, who incorporates a vast dance repertoire to go with the music he learns. He even picks up a few dolphin songs and dances. All the while he has his ear open for the song about the Ones Who Sang the First Song and Are Singing Still. Bobby Rae is sure that if he spends enough time in a place like the music hut, eventually One will show up there.

"You ever heard a song about these Ones?' Bobby Rae asks musicians and dancers from all parts of the world who do come.

All answer 'no' until an eight-year-old boy, Mana Tikituo, finally old enough to leave his home compound and follow his ears to the music hut, arrives.

"My grandfather sings a song about them." Mana tells Bobby Rae.

Eager to meet this elder, Bobby accompanies Mana home to see the grandfather and finds an elder Polynesian music Master. Now too old and too weak to play and sing at the music hut, he rarely speaks- choosing to listen to the music of the Earth, these days, rather than making noise of own.

The old Master does not respond to Bobby Rae's questions about the song until the visitor plays the music that started his journey, recalling it exactly as he heard it. The Youth even sounds like the old Master, when he recorded the tune with an anthropologist in 1952. The Master musician smiles when he hears Bobby Rae—it is like hearing himself young again.

"I want to know about these Ones." Bobby Rae tells the Master. "I want to go and learn their music. I want to hear if they are singing, still."

The Master sits up with some difficulty and clears his throat. "You must keep going toward the setting sun to find them. My people parted from the Ones; at the time they moved their land away from those who had no interest in music–away from those only interested in things. The First Singers no longer wanted to be around others who did not share their love of the Song."

"They moved their land?" Bobby Rae asks.

"They moved it; the Mother Earth moved it. Who knows why it danced away from the old land? The Ones separated and their land moved South. It now rests in the middle of the Southern Pacific."

"Surely there are ways to reach them these days?"

The old Master laughs. "Of course, there are ways! The place they live now is called Australia. Almost anyone can go there, though finding the Ones may be harder than getting to their island. Listen well and you'll be able to sound them out."

"Have you ever sung with them?" Bobby Rae asks, in awe of the Master's knowledge and experience.

"Not personally. Their music is in our music, though. It traveled with us, like a seed when we parted from their land, countless generations ago. We took that music in all directions. That is why music sounds similar, even though it comes from very different parts of the Planet."

"All are variations on the One's music?" Bobby Rae asks.

"I call it music of the Kingdom–Ethiopian, Celtic, Korean or Basque, Arabic, Mayan or Thai. All comes from the same seed. But try this." the old Master proposes as he hands Bobby Rae what looks like a large sea shell. "It is an instrument once played by the Ones you look for. My People took it with them when they left the Ones. We call it 'Who cares about time and space?' You blow into it."

Bobby Rae blows and hears a sound like a rainbow. "Global!" Bobby Rae claims.

"Keep it." the old Master says. "Others who've tried to play it sound like they're farting through a cooked sweet potato."

Bobby Rae blew on the instrument again and birds stopped singing to listen.

"Play it when you get to their land." the Master suggests. "It will be music to their ears."

Bobby Rae keeps playing and the music gets better and better. The old Master sinks back to rest, listening to the beautiful sounds with his whole being.

It is said that dolphins come up out of the water to listen to the sound and then began to sing back.

It is said a nearby volcano begins to emit puffs of smoke in time to the music, and the ground beneath the island rumbles a base note to compliment Bobby Rae's tune.

It is said that the Old Master dies and travels to the next world on the notes of Bobby Rae's music. Aloha, Master.

Bobby Rae says Aloha, too, and leaves on the next ship out of port. He catches at least a hundred rides and at least ten thousand tunes, on fishing boats and tramp steamers that trade between the many islands that dot the Pacific. On each island, Bobbie Rae stops to learn more music, song, and dance before moving on. Years pass and there are times when Bobby Rae is actually farther away from Australia than before he left Mobile. He is not unhappy about that. Music, that only he can hear, sings that he needs to learn more to be able to harmonize with the Singing One's when he finally reaches them.

Bobby Rae is on a fishing boat, off an island on the West Coast of Alaska, at the time The Message is heard. Most people in his hometown have all but forgotten Bobby Rae, but he never forgot his old friend, Howard Beau Brightfoot. Bobby Rae recognizes Howard Beau's voice in a broadcast of a Press conference for the Tiger Preservation Project, the day after The Message. When Bobby Rae hears Howard Beau's call for help with the world's efforts to clean-up Planet Earth for Tigers and everything else, he decides to give his old friend a call back.

"Hi! Howard Beau. This is Bobby Rae Van Dee." the Wanderer states when he leaves a message on the Friends of the Planet answering machine. "I just wanted to tell your mom I'm fine. I still have her number and her quarter, but I'm headed to Australia now to find the Ones Who Are Singing, Still. I heard the Message and it's about time."

"Won't that be some family reunion?" Howard Beau muses when he checks his messages. "I hope he has better luck finding them than I did."

Howard Beau tries, unsuccessfully, to reach the InDios people of Australia, to invite them to an International Conference of Religious Leaders in Jerusalem. None of his contacts in the land down under seem able to find a One of them.

All Bobby Rae finds, when he moves out of the Sydney Urban Population Center and walks into the outback, is a lot of open and seemingly empty space. There are plants and animals in great numbers, but the humans have gone. Bobby Rae walks for days without seeing anyone as he passes through abandoned towns and outposts, farms, and way stations.

After The Message, the majority of the human population of Australia moves to the few areas of the island that are most suitable for agriculture and to their nation's large, urban areas. The rest of the island is returned to the kangaroos and the dingoes, the emu, and the koala bears, with a polite "Thank you, it's been fun." from their human Neighbors.

As Bobby Rae walks on into the Wild, he listens. Sometimes he fills the silence with music and sometimes he just lets the silence echo around him. As the Wanderer surveys the barren-looking landscape, he breaks the immense silence that surrounds him by playing his instruments. The music comforts Bobby Rae and seems to take all the loneliness out of that vast emptiness, filling its silence with the sound of possibility.

After a time, Bobby Rae begins to hear things and wonders if it is possible to experience auditory mirages–to hear sounds reflected off layers of air, that are not actually within hearing distance. In some spots the music he hears is very faint but in others it is quite loud and clear, as though he is in a space or a place that allows him to receive the sounds. By keeping to the right path Bobby Rae hears human voices but even on the loudest paths, he sees no one.

Bobbie Rae has been studying the ways sound reflects off surfaces, from walls to layers of air, since he was a kid. He can hear the echo of the Earth's sound off a full moon and knows an echo when he hears one.

"That sound is not an echo." Bobby Rae muses. "Unless it's an echo through time."

Since he has an instrument called "Who Cares About Space and Time", when Bobbie Rae picks it up and begins to play along, the music he hears gets louder and clearer. Then a door opens, right in the middle of the air, and out comes the Ones Who are Singing Still. They are dancing, as well.

Bobby Rae can understand them through their music and learns that, besides the drums, whistles, and other unique instruments they play, the land is part of their musical composition. Its paths sing and hum to the sounds they make and guide them from place to place, to what is needed for their physical survival in a harsh land. Their music is also their spiritual Path to the DreamTime.

"Now that's some playing." Bobby Rae acknowledges. "Why come back, now?"

Their songs tell Bobby Rae that The Ones are back for a meeting with other Holy People."

"Will there be music?" Bobby Rae asks eagerly.

He knows that humans make their best music about that which they worship, be it love, money or Christ the Carpenter Employed, and does not want to miss a concerted effort for Peace.

"We go now to play the Holy Ones to Union." he hears.

"Can I come, too?" Bobby Rae asks.

"We need your music to make our sound hole." the Ones sing in response.

Bobby Rae does not hesitate to accept the invitation and responds with a resounding "Let us play!"

Around the time of The Message, fairy tales and stories begin to change. This is one of the many stories told about how The Message is heard on Planet Earth.

- Betsy Ross Jackson

A FAIR TALE

'The Message'

It is Winston Brightfoot's turn to tell a bedtime story to his littlest brother, Lucius Clay. The two-year-old loves hearing about the adventures of Winston and his friends, the Way Scans. This is the Fair Tale Winston tells Lucius Clay one night, about the time the Message is heard:

"Once upon a time in a land much blessed, lived numerous princes and princesses, kings and queens. There were so many, so elevated and so blessed, that they lost sight of the fact that they were fabulously wealthy and fabulously lucky, compared to the rest of the world.

They lived in a land that has not suffered from the disruption of war, firsthand, for centuries. They have virtually everything they need to live; clean water, enough food, and more resources around them than others can even imagine. The highest born in the greatest kingdoms of the past; history's Emperors, Pharaohs, Kings and Queens, never lived as well as did these numerous men, women, and children. All are mighty lucky folks.

There is, however, a strange spell cast over these royal citizens at birth. The spell causes most of them to doubt their very good luck and to be dissatisfied with their tremendous, good fortune. As a result, they are never quite happy with their many blessings and opportunities and often have the idea that there must be something wrong with their life. This same spell is worked on people who come to stay in their kingdom, too. Sooner or later, though they know they are in the land of the incredibly favored and that they are incredibly blessed to be there, these newcomers begin to feel dissatisfied, too.

The one who casts this spell is a wicked trickster named Capitalizmo. This sorcerer has the ability to pull the wool over almost everyone's eyes, from cradle to grave. In spite of the fact that the lives of people in the Kingdom are pretty darn good (it had been a heck of a century for most of them), Capitalizmo is able to promote dissatisfaction there.

Capitalismo's spell takes the form of a fear that keeps most people of the Kingdom of Luck and Good Fortune from looking beyond their private lives to see how the rest of the world lives. That trickster knows if they take a look, they could never be dissatisfied or desire more and more of everything for themselves. They would see, clearly, that they already have all they need. They would also want him to share the giant share that Capitalismo takes from them and others, for himself and those like him.

Capitalismo has managed to corner the lion's share of wealth, resources, and power, making all that those in the land of good fortune have a mere drop in the ocean of his wealth. Sharing his wealth and power with everyone would never use all he has socked away but would create a world of justice and peace, Capitalismo's greatest enemy.

"Who can make loads of easy money in a world of justice and peace?" Capitalismo asks. "Not me, so forget it! Creating unrest, dissatisfaction, prejudice, and hatred are what my spells are for. Only then will people turn to things, instead of to each other and Planet Earth, for real satisfaction."

Despite the power of Capitalismo's spells, some of the Royal Youth can open their eyes wide enough, for long enough, to see beyond their privilege. Often this view of reality is as near as the poor neighborhoods in their own city. This is not the kind of viewpoint Capitalismo likes to see. Instead of wanting more and more for themselves, these clear-sighted Youth see how the Kingdom of Luck and Fortune takes advantage of some, for the benefit of others. This view of their kingdom shocks and disturbs them because they see how it is used all over the world, as well as close to home.

One especially spell-resistant Youth group lives in the royal city of Mobile. They call themselves the Way Scans and this royally awesome group never lets anything stop them from learning or seeing their world clearly. They do not have to look far to see the results of Capitalismo's illusions at work.

It may be the sunglasses they wear that shield them from harmful misinformation and keep out the blinding light of Capitalismo's spells and illusions, but most likely it is their good sense and their excellent teachers that allow them to envision another future for all.

Here's what they see when they get that picture:

The Way Scans see how Capitalismo works in their community to make sure that certain people are made to matter less than others. This determination is made because of their race, sex, their family of origin, or where they live. These factors this limit the kind of education made available to them and the money they are paid, as adults, for the work they do. In turn, this limit where they live and work and ways political systems work, often to their detriment.

The ones chosen not to matter often have less voice in what happens in the operation of their community, even if they have the most voters in a city or a state. In some locations crime and violence is allowed to disrupt their community, when it would never be tolerated anywhere else in their city. The police force are almost never members of their group and, in this way, many of these citizens leave their area only to go to jail. When they go to jail, they lose their right to vote. Without this voting power they lose their last chance for a voice to change their situation, short of violent revolution.

Their labor in prisons is supported by taxpayers so is virtually free to their employers and undercuts the bargaining power of other laborers, assuring they, too, will never have the economic stability to move beyond the boundaries of the culture, economy or society that limits them.

The Way Scans can also see how Capitalismo uses these same tactics in his dealings with the have-not world outside the land of the incredibly lucky. Armies and militia units are used to enforce business as usual, instead of the police doing so. In this way, Capitalismo is often able to get people of other nations to fight among themselves, just as he is able to get people from poor neighborhoods to fight among themselves.

When all this starts coming clear to the Way Scans, they begin teaching other Youth and become a weapon of mass instruction for the Youth of Mobile. These young people start to take actions for their own, against Capitalismo's plans and dreams for their kind. Some of their plans involve their parents and families, some involve other Youth groups, and this helps young people see past the illusions and the strange ideas that Capitalismo still churns out like crazy.

Fortunately for the purpose of truth, one of Capitalismo's newest diversions is the computer. Computers let people find out anything they want to know about anything, anywhere. These same machines also let them talk to one another, all over the Planet. It is not long before Youth around the world make plans to revolutionize how things are done, worldwide. The Way Scans help get their Message out, assisted by Youth in other parts of the world:

"If we work it right, we can broadcast The Message everywhere on Earth, at the same time, and in the local language of each area, using the Internet." Princess Emaline tells the other Ways Scans.

The group thinks this is a global idea but is still not sure what the Message should be.

"I vote for something to protect the environment." Prince Winston Brightfoot suggests. "We all live on the same Planet. That Message will appeal to everyone and Creator knows, Earth needs all the help She can get."

"Why will people think the Message is for them?" Prince Bobbie Turner asks.

"We'll need to personalize it, so people can see they are part of a Planet-wide solution." Winston proposes.

"We better tell them a story then." Princess Toni suggests. "The funnier the better, so people will listen to it."

"What is funny in one place, is sometimes tragic in another." Princess Ruth "The Flame" Feinstein points out.

"Let's ask Abel for suggestions."

Abel Rebinowitz has a news kiosk near the Mobile Stock Exchange and is an expert on the state of the world and its human citizens. He has made an extensive study of modern politics and other human systems and knows what does and does not work in this day and age.

"Make it a game. People will go through no end of trouble, if you say something is a game." suggests Abel. "But give people an important part to play. Say they are on the team chosen to clean up the world, or some such. Who knows, they might actually pull together and do it."

"That approach could be a real motivation for the end of the world as we know it." Princess Toni jokes.

"We should make it fun, with Rules to follow and nobody has to play if they don't want to." Princess Emaline voices. "Otherwise, it could get mean. People hate that."

"With a limited time for the cleanup. Otherwise, people will keep putting off changes they need to make." Prince Bobbie adds. "People often procrastinate when it comes to change. They are afraid of it."

"Have people do something for themselves and their own family, while saving the world and give them a reward for playing, like a prize–something everyone wants." Abel suggests.

"That could be part of The Message." Princess Ruth agrees. "The Prize should give all people involved something they need, like a Union contract does for workers and management."

The Flame's father, Leonard Feinstein, just negotiated a deal with the International Garment Workers Union that stipulates he will pay living wages to all workers in all his factories, inside and outside the USA. He is one of the first, North American businessmen to an initiate living wage program for all his employees, both foreign and domestic.

"A Union of Earth's people, working together to make the planet a better place for all." Princess Emaline pronounces. "Sounds like fun, an important factor in any human game. Let's give players extra points for being kind."

"Don't forget the other creatures that live here, too.

I'm sure we can count on those aardvarks to do their fair share. Count the plants in, too. We couldn't do this without them." Princess Toni adds."

Lucius Clay laughs, as Winston finishes his story:

"I will not tell you how the Way Scans managed to get The Message to everyone on Earth. Let it be said, one Friday evening at 6PM Eastern Standard Time, everyone on Earth gets The Message, the aardvarks and plants included. Everyone hears it and everyone understands it. The End."

"Global." Lucius Clay tells Winston. "Does everyone play, even the aardvarks?"

"If they want to. Each begins to take action in the place where they live and work. The biggest changes happen one neighborhood at a time."

"What happens to that Capitalizmo guy?" Lucius Clay asks, sleepily.

"One of the first things Youth do is stop fighting the wars Capitalismo tries to continue all over planet Earth. Eventually he gives up, retires and moves to Florida." Winston tells his brother.

Then Howard Beau pulls the covers up around the small boy's chin, to let him sleep and dream fair stories of his own. All Lucius Clay's dreams that night is about the Earth healed, as The Message is heard and understood by all.

If necessity is the mother of invention, then those in need are the ones to come up with the best solutions.

- E. Power "Sunny" Leonardo

THE COUPON LADY

Addie McCraken, receptionist at the Mobile office of the International Food Exchange, thinks her boss proposes a plan that is way out of her league. He wants to put her in charge of a program to distribute food, worldwide. The mother of five, Addie has enough on her plate just keeping her own family fed.

"I was hired to answer the phones and I don't think ending world hunger is in my job description. My own family is job enough, thank you."

"That's just why I thought of you." Billie Joe points out. "You feed, clothe and house a family of six on a minimum wage salary. The way you use those coupons of yours, brand name companies pay you folks to eat. Not many can pull off something like that."

"No choice. It's the only way I can make ends meet." Addie admits.

"Who else, least of all the rich, could do what you do?" Billie Joe asks. "Heck, without their money to fall back on they'd all starve to death in a week. My bet would be on you, Addie, if money disappears from Planet Earth tomorrow."

The employees of the International Food Exchange are actually planning to make money disappear from the global food equation; to see if they can find ways to distribute all food that is grown, harvested and stored, to the planet's human population. The IFE's distribution plan also includes distribution of feed for domestic stock animals for the human food supply.

"It's all just theoretical, of course." Billie Joe tells Addie. "It's a computerized simulation, to see if there really is enough food to go around, and adequate resources to get it where needed if we take money out of the picture."

The Mobile Division of the IFE can do that. It is part of a world-wide corporation that keeps track of food and how it is grown, sold, shipped, trucked, flown, or carried, to where it is bought, stored, or in some cases, destroyed. The Mobile office keeps track of virtually all commercial food crops grown in the American heartland and is a major part of IFE's international data network to other, regional offices, so IFE employees are connected, electronically, to most of the whole world's food supplies.

Mobile IFE is located in the 'Big Old Ear of Corn Building' and is part of the reason the Maison building has this nickname. This IFE affiliate keeps tabs on the billions of ears of corn, and millions of bushels of wheat produced the USA, Canada, and Mexico. That means they keep track of a big part of food for sale on Planet Earth.

"And now we are tied into a Global Watch Satellite Tracking System, so we can also track food that never sees a marketplace." Billie Joe explains. "We can see what most of the world's small farmers are growing and we can keep track of what subsistence farmers grow for themselves and their immediate Neighbors."

"As people develop food production systems in urban Neighborhoods all over the world, they will produce more food locally and less will be sent into each city or urban area." Lynda

Preto, IFE employee and head of the Mobile Chapter of End World Hunger NOW! points out. "Our satellite view, with reports from Urban Food Production Programs on the ground, will help us make sure the right amount of food gets to people in each community."

Lynda is the one who thought of using IFE resources to see if a barter-based worldwide food distribution system might work. Such a plan is End World Hunger NOW's dream come true.

"Who's going to' pay for all that?" Evanston DiFreto, head of the IFE accounting department, asks. Food and fuel not paid for are his worst nightmare.

"None of our business." Lynda responds. "We are just playing a game to see if the world has enough food for everyone. That's where Addie comes in."

"But what if the food people get is not what they want to eat?" Addie asks.

This is a personally relevant question for Addie, as her growing children are beginning to balk at the strange foods her barter in coupons and rebates, specials, bargain- priced offers and giveaways, brings to their table. That morning at her breakfast table everyone had enough to eat, and Addie had covered most of the basic food groups, but her kids complained when she served them the following.

sample-size cans of cocktail weenies, green apples picked off a tree on her walk home the evening before, cheese-type food sprayed from a can onto the wheat crackers she got for a product test, and water, mixed with a packet of juice mix she bought at the supermarket. Addie will send for a rebate on the juice mix that will pay for it, the stamp she uses to send for it, and make her a 25-cent profit on the meal.

"Why can't we eat regular food, like other people do?" her daughter, Kendra, asks as she looks into her lunch bag. She sees: a cheese and cracker sample that Addie sent for in the mail, a free serving of freeze dried peaches, like the astronauts eat on the space shuttle (given away free at a NASA lecture on the space program, because there are so few space guys and gals to eat it and they have to get rid of the backlog food before it goes bad) a packet of bean dip, a free sample from the grocery store, and a miniature can of spaghetti, with a product survey for Kendra to fill out to tell the company what she thinks of their food in a can.

No matter what Kendra thinks of what she eats, she knows the answer to the question she asks her mother. They cannot afford to buy food and pay rent at the same time, so they eat like this, like it or not.

Her mother refuses to go on any kind of welfare, even food stamps, because handouts are against her religion. Addie agrees with her elected government representatives about this. They are handing out less and less food to women and their children every day. Helping hungry people with food is apparently against their religion, too.

"Stop complaining." Addie's oldest child, Seth, tells his sister. "You know tons of kids at school want your lunch. Most of them go to school with zip and are supposed to eat that cafeteria junk!"

Addie's children collectively shudder at the thought of what they see offered at their school cafeteria. Their unusual lunches are gourmet treats compared to a school lunch food programs that serves kids ketchup as a member of the fruit and vegetable food group. Kendra's words serve to remind Addie that others may not be as easy to feed as are her five children.

"Some people do not have the flexibility about diet that we have, because of religious taboos and cultural preferences." Addie explains to Billie Joe. "Sometimes diet is dictated by climate or by environment, or by long-established customs, like having turkey at Thanksgiving. The world cannot be fed without considering such things and I will need some help to find out what people in different countries like to eat. Then, maybe, we could give this worldwide barter thing a try."

"I know just the person to help out." Lynda Preto shares. "She is head chef at the International restaurant and Betsy Ross Jackson knows about every kind of food on the Planet. I heard she planned an Inuit menu last week- a caribou and ptarmigan buffet. They don't call her the Food Lady for nothing."

Betsy Ross is called the Food Lady because she gives the neighborhood homeless shelter and the local AIDS meals-on-wheels program the same food the International cooks for its wealthy patrons. She made a food sharing program part of her contract and the restaurant managers were willing to offer her anything to sign on as their head chef.

Betsy learned her international culinary skills locally, by working at every kind of restaurant in Mobile, since her move there from Tiger Country. She begins work as a dishwasher then, by learning as much as possible about the culture, ingredients, foods, and cooking methods at each place, works her way up to head chef. Betsy Ross knows food, Aborigine to Zionist, abalone to zabaglione, and plans the menus for The International, a world-famous restaurant that specializes in a different food item each day.

"I ate at the International once." Evanston DiFreto admits. "The place was expensive, and it took six months to get a reservation there, but it was worth it. I went on bean night. It was miraculous!"

Evanston still recalls the sight of the dozens of bean dishes from every part of the world, gracing the buffet tables at the International that evening.

"There are beans from every nation and culture. A few were old family recipes—sometimes thousands of years old." Evanston told the group. "My favorite dish was red *Ugali,* from East Africa. It is made with mashed potatoes, beans, and large kernels of white corn. It tastes like heaven."

"Sounds good but is it good for you?" jokes Billy Joe.

"Chef Betsy gave me the recipe and told me that *Ugali* is made with a combination of ingredients that is almost perfect for the human body. It tastes like heaven but it's definitely people food. Get her on board for the IFE program."

"She helps out whenever she can, and she especially likes games." Lynda shares.

"Games?" Billie Joe asks. "I don't know how you can call this a game. It is a vital part of the human effort to clean up Planet Earth. If people don't have food, they won't be able to do what needs to be done and the fear of hunger makes people very reluctant to change anything. It makes them downright mean to each other, too."

"But this is a game." Lynda insists. "It's always been a game, even when we use money to pay for food. Ask Evanston, our man in the accounting office, if you don't believe me."

Their chief accountant must agree with Lynda. He knows that the world of a balance sheet is, in truth, just a game and is best operated that way. He explains:

"Has anyone in this food distribution system ever seen cash money paid out for anything the IFE keeps track of?" Evanston asks the group. "Every cent 'farmers' get for their crops is moved around by computers. Every cent paid out to ship, store and process the stuff is handled by computers, too. Even employees like us are paid using computerized banking systems. Who knows what value any of this food has, even the way we are doing it now? Lynda's right, it's all just a big game we play with food, and with most of our other resources like timber, metals and fuels."

"I guess you're right." Billie Joe concedes.

"The real death blow to the possibility of a fiscally responsible world fell in Spring 1998, when the United States' General Accounting Office completed an audit of all US government agencies." Evanston admits. "That audit showed that billions of dollars are unaccounted for and that many government agencies just keep operating on the world's faith in our system. Faith is the primary reason our government's checks are honored at banks in the USA and around the world."

"A barter system to feed the world's people does not sound like such a wild idea when you consider that." Addie observes.

"It could work." Evanston concedes. "At least, this way, people will get beans in exchange for their potatoes. The way the world economy operates these days, with foreign loans to pay off, their potatoes get most world citizens only a partial payment on interest for a loan their government received twenty-five years ago. The ones who grow the potatoes get almost nothing for them, they no longer have potatoes to eat themselves and they get no beans at all."

"We could even up that odd situation with a food swap." Addie admits. "I'll do it."

"Hold on, Addie. We will try it. We take the idea of money out of the world food game and see how that plays out." Billie Joe states. "If we that see everyone's basic food needs get met, then we let others worry about money."

"I'll play, too." Evanston offers. "The team will need to consider costs of food production, transportation and processing, as well as storage in this game plan."

"What about the cost of fuel to cook the food?" Addie asks. "If people don't have energy to cook food or to process it for storage, sending them food might be a big waste."

Addie still has nightmares about the time she did not have enough money to pay her household utility bill and the power company cut them off. They cooked everything on a hibachi for months, scrounging for wood wherever they could find it. For a while, Addie was cooking the way that most of the world's people cook. It may have looked like a Bar-B-Que, but it was no picnic.

"While we're at it, let's try to figure out where food processing plants could be located in each region." Lynda suggests. "If small factories can operate near places where the food is grown, that will help an area produce enough food for its people, year-round. Drying, dehydrating, or canning food can cut down on losses to pests and spoilage, too. All that will help assure a food supply when crops can't grow."

"Could solar powered dehydration factories and food canneries work for that?" Billie Joe asks.

Billie Joe's brother-in-law, Hernando, invented a solar powered cooker and food dehydrator but Hernando is currently living in a one-bedroom unit over Billie Joe's garage. He is willing to do almost anything to help his wife's husband make a success of his invention.

"I got to get Hernando into a home of his own, before he invents something else that makes a big mess." Billie Joe tells himself, recalling the nightmare of the compost bio-heat generator that Hernando insisted would do away with their need for a household water heater.

Billie Joe has no idea what Hernando will come up with to drive him nuts, but his mental health necessity is the mother of the invention of the worldwide, Food First Food Processing Program. The program equips Neighborhoods with solar-powered food processing plants that provide local jobs and a reliable food supply for most of the world's people, within a decade.

IFE employees like Billie Joe, Evanston, Addie, and Lynda work out the details of many of the programs that fulfill the wildest dreams of End World Hunger NOW! and the simplest dream–that of having enough to eat- for Earth's human population. Then comes the hard part–paying for all that.

❉ ❉ ❉ ❉

"Leave money out of the picture and feeding the world's people is a snap." Lynda Preto testifies before the U.S. Senate Agriculture Committee, headed by Senator Sterlin Sommes.

"How do we make sure the rest of the world isn't stealing us blind in this barter deal?" Senator Obdurate Cadman asks.

"We barter according to a formula." Lynda explains. "First, we consider food needs of the local population and what kind of a toll it takes on the environment to produce each crop they need. Then we assign each food a value, based on a formula that considers a food's caloric and nutritional value and how much energy, water, soil nutrients, time, and labor, it takes to produce it, process it and transport it." Lynda explains. "Then we add or subtract points for that food's cultural and social importance. In that way we can figure out what it's worth in a swap."

"Huh?" the Senators say to themselves and nod in agreement, as if they understand what she said.

"The IFE system seems to cover all the bases, as far as human need," Senator Sommes states. "but does it take into account human greed?"

Senator Sterlin is a Senator because he understands stuff like that.

"Greed has been a big factor in commercial Agriculture for the past 100 years." Lynda admits. "Some agricultural projects are heavily subsidized by the government. This cost is borne by the taxpayers and often makes small-scale production of food non-competitive. For example, many California rice-growers plant rice in dry areas, where no rice should be grown. This crop makes the huge water-guzzling rice plantations a lot of money, but takes water away from wild areas, at an incalculable cost to the environment."

The Senator from California jumps up. One of his biggest campaign contributors is California's Agribusiness industry and plenty of those farmers grow rice in what was once desert. Before he can say a thing, Senator Sterlin Sommes intervenes with a comment.

"Since this meeting is closed to the Press, we can mention how much a pound of that rice would cost if we stopped subsidizing rice growers with cheap water, and all the other kinds of incentives they get for putting those rice seeds in the ground."

The Senator from California sits down at once, hoping this subject will be dropped before that information gets out, even to the other Senators. He doubts even they would support the actual cost of a pound of California rice. At last calculation it cost the state $4.50 in supports and subsidies.

"So, using this Food Distribution Swap of yours, the IFDC is able to figure out what food is needed and how to best get that need met?" the Senator asks.

"We can." Lynda acknowledges. "Our barter expert helps bring everything together in a workable plan."

"Some world-famous economists, or agricultural expert helping you with that, no doubt." Senator Sommes guesses.

"She is our office receptionist," Lynda tells the lawmakers "but we showed her how to use the computer and the IFE team did the rest."

"What?" the Senator screams. "We're supposed to change world food supply systems because your office receptionist says so?"

"Her plans have been checked and double checked by agriculturists, nutritionists, economists and commodities brokers, as well as environmentalists, farmers, and with the people who have to sell, buy and eat the food. No one can find anything wrong with what Addie's plans. In this field, she's an expert." Lynda assures the committee members.

"What about natural disasters?" Senator Obdurate asks.

"No doubt there will be problems, droughts or floods, or other kinds of emergencies. We hope that having such an accurate picture of the worldwide food supply will help in those times of trouble. We'll know where we can get food for people in need and will have systems set up to get food and fuel there as soon as the need is identified." Billie Joe assures the gathered lawmakers.

The Senate Committee recommends the trial of a regional IFE Food Barter Plan and, within weeks, it is passed in both the US Senate and House of Representatives. Soon treaties are signed to begin the food production and barter programs in North America, with Mexico, Canada and Caribbean Nations joining in. Other regions are given information on how the IFE system works and have the option of joining the 'Big Swap Meet' with the USA or starting one of their own.

"Wishes come true for the world's farmers, once they begin selling food according to an international formula for its value." Senator Sommes tells a meeting of the End World Hunger NOW! Mobile

Chapter, at their annual 'Bite It! Award' dinner. Senator Sommes is their keynote speaker.

"Once a pound of rice costs the same in Beijing as it does in Berkeley, there is no longer an incentive to sell food to the highest bidder." the Senator explains. "In fact, the biggest incentive is to sell food as close to where it's grown as possible, so you don't have to hassle with carting it all over creation."

Sterlin looks out over his audience and is happy to see some of his biggest campaign contributors. They are at the Awards Dinner, too, and with good reason.

"Most of the food exported from the US, these days, is over-production that goes out to fill a need somewhere else. In fact, American farmers are busier and are making more profits than ever before." Sterlin adds.

"U.S. consumers now buy more food grown locally." Rebecca Rebinowitz, the Club Vice-Chairwoman, points out when she gets up to give the Bite It! Award to Addie McCracken, the IFE receptionist. "That makes for cheaper food and frees up a lot of disposable income so consumers can buy other things they need; like shelter, clothing, medicine and education. This plan makes wishes come true for more than farmers."

"I got my wish." Billie Joe thinks to himself, as he ponders the success of Hernando's solar cookers and food dehydrators.

The Food First Program would have made Hernando a billionaire had he not given patents for his inventions to the United Nations, to allow for cheap manufacture of his solar ovens and drying units in small workshops all over the world. Hernando kept only one patent, for a clip used to seal his solar oven. The clip costs a penny and makes the cost of the oven, which is made from common, recycled materials, so low that everyone can afford to make one or buy one. Sales of the clip make Hernando a millionaire and he and his family move out of Billie Joe's garage apartment into a co-housing project across town where their compost-heated water heaters do not bother Billie Jo a bit.

In addition to making Billie Jo happy, Addie and several billion other people get their wish and never have to worry about power for cooking food again. The sun supplies it, free.

"I got my wish." Addie McCracken comments in her Bite- It Award acceptance speech. "I'm able to stop depending on coupons and giveaways to feed my family. Instead, we get free food for helping out at the roof garden on top of our apartment house. The rest I buy from my Neighborhood garden project, at what was once the parking lot of Mobile's largest shopping mall. There, we get our produce and small livestock cheaply enough for me to afford it and we're eating better than ever."

Addie does not mention that she sometimes has cravings for astronaut ice cream or for a tiny can of macaroni and cheese. The cravings pass when Addie realizes she misses the game she once played to feed her family, not the food they ate and that now she plays that game, worldwide, as an IFE Trader.

A PEACE OF THE PIE

LeRoy is only six years old when he sees a man, he thinks is his Uncle Lucius, out on the bayou. LeRoy has heard tales of his Uncle's exploits; how Lucius hunts, fishes, and traps for his living, is said to live on his own in the swaps, way back beyond the Fryer farm. LeRoy has never seen Uncle Lucius but is sure the wild-looking man must be that consummate explorer, that all-around outdoorsman whose wild and untamed figure is crouched on the banks of the river, not far from their farmhouse.

The man's clothes are torn and dirty and his shoes a wreck. He is no camper or environmentalist, like the ones who sometimes find their way into the channel that takes them past the Fryer homestead. This man looks wild and acts different from anyone LeRoy knows, talking to himself, as he works in the mud of the riverbank.

LeRoy wonders why the man's skin is such an odd color, bright red under the layer of mud smeared over the parts that show through his tattered clothing. LeRoy does not know anyone who needs to cover their skin with mud to look like the dark rich Earth of the swamp. LeRoy's family all have skin that color to begin with.

"Just call me the Swamp Fox." he hears the man say. The man looks like a fox LeRoy's daddy once caught in their hen houses. That creature was bright red, too. LeRoy creeps closer, keeping out of sight to observe the man and what he is making on the muddy bank.

"Maybe that's why Uncle Lucius left the family and is hiding out in the Wild." LeRoy thinks. "Maybe he feels bad because his skin is not beautiful and dark, like the rest of the Fryers."

Daniel and Calypso Fryer, LeRoy's parents, pride themselves on the beauty of their people and celebrate how each of their offspring reflects the rainbow of human possibility inherent in their African past. LeRoy's mama tells him that people of Africa come in all shades, shapes and sizes and their family proves it. Her youngest has the deep brown skin and the golden eyes of their ancestors from the upper regions of the Nile River.

"But maybe Uncle Lucius is part fox, too." LeRoy considers. "My God Daddy Stonewall swears he spends a good part of his life as a swamp panther when he comes out here to visit."

Stonewall Brightfoot tells his God Son that people can become animals and vise-versa in a wild place like the swamps so LeRoy sees no reason why Uncle Lucius cannot be a swamp fox, if he chooses.

"Maybe that's some kind of den he's building." LeRoy guesses, climbing out on a tree limb to get a better look at the construction on the riverbank below.

He edges himself directly over the spot where the man is working and is delighted by the model city he sees when he looks down. The child has never seen a city before, but he knows about models. LeRoy's brothers and sisters make models of their farm, complete with tiny clay animals, for him to play with. They also make models of the farm and the swamps, showing paths and landmarks, to help him find his way home from the river, the farthest he can go by himself at his age.

LeRoy surveys the model built of mud, rocks, and bits of green. There are office buildings, like some he has seen in picture books, and one that looks like a Big Ear of Corn, set right in the middle of it all.

"Can I play, too?" LeRoy asks, unable to contain his desire for a closer look.

The Man reacts to the voice from above with such surprise he falls on his ass, sitting down heavily on a newly designed Neighborhood of his tiny community. Merriweather looks up to see the golden eyes of a treed creature staring down at him. He has not seen another person for several weeks, so it takes him a moment to recognize the boy above him as a human child.

"What you are doing out here in the Wild, boy?" Merriweather asks.

"I live on the farm, Uncle Lucius. I'm Daniel's youngest son."

"I'm not your Uncle, not kin to you at all. Name is Merriweather Marion Jenkins. I'm named after the Swamp Fox, Francis Marion. Ever hear of him?"

"No." LeRoy responds, coming down out of the tree. "Did he make cities, too?"

"He helped build this whole Nation—helped fight the Redcoats for it. Hid by day as a farmer, but by night he caused all kinds of trouble for those he didn't want in his Neighborhood." Merriweather tells the child. "You go on away and leave me in peace, boy."

Merriweather has been in the Wild since his escape from The Abiding Light Sanitarium for the mentally ill, sent there by Court Order for trying to kill the President of the USA. His attempt on the President's life was made at the Tiger Summit, a few days after The Message, and he has been on his own in the Wild since his escape from the guards escorting him to the nut house.

Merriweather is now living among the only group he can tolerate; he, him, and himself, and does not welcome any other, especially when that other is a person of color. The possibility of mixing with colored folks is the reason Merriweather tried to kill the President and stop the Tiger Summit in its tracks.

"Leave me in peace." Merriweather tells the child.

"I only have one piece, but I'll share it with you if you let me look at what you've done." LeRoy proposes, taking out a piece of homemade berry pie he has wrapped in oilcloth in the front pocket of his overalls.

The piece is a little squished, but LeRoy knows it will taste fine. As much as he loves pie, he will give it up for a closer look at the man's creation.

"I'm not about to eat Niggrah food." Merriweather responds, eyeing the pie that looks just like the ones their cook, Ms. Fuscia, made for him when he was a kid.

Merriweather can mentally taste that berry pie–its rich flaky crust melting on his tongue, and it brings to mind the cook and housekeeper who raised him, fed him, and kept the Jenkins' family home running for almost all his years there.

Ms. Fuscia worked at the old Bidewell family mansion on into the 1960s, after he brought his own bride to live in the house that had been in his mama's family for six generations. Merriweather has not seen the likes of her culinary skills since he banished Ms. Fuscia from his household in 1965, after the Voting Rights Act was passed as Federal law. Asking Ms. Fuscia to leave his family home was the hardest thing Merriweather ever had to do. It was like asking his own mama to get out and never return.

For months after he did this, Merriweather had dreams he is starving and would wake up in a sweat, so hungry that no matter what he ate he never felt satisfied. He finally moved his family out of the Bidewell Mansion, unable to tolerate the memories that plagued him there.

Despite Merriweather's resolve to ignore the pie now offered, visions of Ms. Fuscia, as she cooks, pass before his mind's eye. A big part of his hunger is the memory of the times spent with her in their big old kitchen. He was able to talk to this wise, kind woman there; telling her his worries and concerns–things he told no one else in the world. Their talk is as nourishing as Ms. Fuscia's rich barbecue, the fried catfish she made, her potato salad and the fresh greens and vegetables she grew in their back garden. The memory of that food has Merriweather longing for a past he had been trying, for years, to forget.

As much as he craves it, Merriweather knows he has to refuse the pie the boy offers him now. He knows he cannot stand tasting the love and human concern cooked into each bite of a pie such as that. One taste and he would never be able to tolerate his present diet; the food he takes from abandoned cabins and hunting lodges, left behind after The Message when people get out of the Wild and go to live in Urban Centers. This food keeps him fed but is as barren of human feeling as his life is of human contact.

His longing is visible in Merriweather's face and the child sees it and holds the pie out to him. "You can have this, Mister, even if you don't want me lookin' at your city."

"No. No." Merriweather declines. "Wouldn't be right, me taking food from you, but you can have a look at what I've done."

Down from the tree, LeRoy is so fascinated by what he sees he hands Merriweather the pie to keep both his hands free to examine the diorama. He bends down for a closer look at a scale model of a marketplace located next to tiny a railroad station.

"Why wouldn't it be right?" the child asks.

"I can't take favors from those I wrong." Merriweather explains, as he recalls making this same explanation to Ms. Fuscia at the time, he let her go.

She understands his need to fire her, after he joins with the forces that work against Civil Rights for her people. Ms. Fuscia understands how his politics make it impossible for him to accept her help in his home. She has that kind of integrity herself and expects no less from Merriweather, the boy she raised.

"You haven't wronged me. I never seen you before." LeRoy states as he moves on to examine what appears to be a large parking lot turned into acres of greenhouses, like the one his mama has for starting plants in the winter months.

"The wrongs were wrought by me and by those who came before me." Merriweather admits. "I have added to them in my lifetime, by not addressing their injustice, then or now."

"But you've done me no wrong." the child insists. "Why feel bad?"

"Feel bad? I don't feel bad. I'm proud of the way my people have taken care of our own. Generations of my kin have worked hard to survive and doing' it meant keeping' your people down in all kinds of ways. The things I do diminish others. That's how it works for me and my kind."

"How can you diminish me? My mama says I grow an inch a month." LeRoy asks.

"Lordy, we have been clever at it- had a lot of help from the powers that be, of course. I'm criticized for making my views known but plenty act just like me, every day of their lives, then pretend its history—something finished and done with. I'm living proof of our nation's legacy of fear and hate and I'm not afraid to admit it."

"You're afraid of a piece of pie?" LeRoy asks.

"It's a fear of not having enough if your people are given their due."

"There's enough. My mama always makes plenty and she wouldn't want anyone going hungry at her door. We're known for our hospitality."

Merriweather looks at the pie one last time, then gives it back to the child and gestures toward the model city at their feet.

"See this beautiful place, boy? I'm the biggest urban developer in the South and I want to build a place just like this- a place with enough for all the people who live there. If it were up to me, there'd be no place for the likes of you. That's my hospitality—a white town for white folks."

"Don't care." LeRoy responds. "Fryers got their own place, and we have good pie here!"

The child studies the pie in his hand and is about to take a bite, when he sees a look of such longing flash across the man's face, he stops. He holds the pie out to Merriweather, again.

"You come over to my place for pie, if you want." LeRoy offers.

Merriweather closes his eyes and waves the pie away.

"My kind been doing that for too long, living off the likes of you. I got to forget that pie." he tells the child. "I got to remember that your people and your pie should not be part of my future, here." he adds as he gestures toward the city at his feet.

"It's a mighty nice place." LeRoy admits, looking down.

"I'll build my city and keep it pure." Merriweather explains as he contemplates a life as far away from good pie as possible.

LeRoy often hears his daddy tell the story of how his own great-great-grandpa built their farm in the Wild, after the Civil War, to get as far away from white folks as possible. The man's idea does not seem so strange. In fact, Fryers pride themselves on the way they wrested their farm from the bayou, generations ago, and have kept it productive through hard work and ingenuity.

"No white man could build a farm like this in the middle of the Wild, or work to keep it going like we do." LeRoy often hears his daddy say.

The boy knows how hard his own family works to keep their house in repair and their farm running. Big as the man is, he does not look like he could do half the work of one Fryer. Building his city out of sticks and mud is all that the raggedy-looking white man looks capable of doing.

"Who will build that city for you?" LeRoy asks. "You got folks to help you out?"

The boy's question gives Merriweather pause. He can identify a few men of his own racial background in his large construction company, but he usually promotes them to supervise the Hispanic workers, the Africans, the Native Americans and, in recent years, the Asian men and women who make up his current work crews. To Merriweather's knowledge, there is no one like him left doing the actual construction work, these days.

"That could be a problem." Merriweather admits. "Maybe I could just hire folks to build the place an' then tell them all to go on home."

"Then who would keep it runnin'?" LeRoy asks.

LeRoy's family has been short-handed since his biggest brother, Jessup, went off to agricultural college. Aware of the difference the loss of one worker makes to the farm, LeRoy tries to do his part, but is still too small to do much work.

"Good point." Merriweather concedes as he watches the boy. "The need for human labor will be intensive in such a community."

Merriweather plucks a weed from the middle of the roadway that runs through his tiny metropolis to connect each Neighborhood. In his model community he plans to turn the parking lots back into paradise, as side streets become gardens and playgrounds and private cars no longer have more space devoted to them than do humans.

"Think you'll find enough folks like you who want to live out in the Wild?" LeRoy asks. "My sister, Peaches, says we're all supposed to live in an Urban Center now, but my daddy says he's not about to go."

After The Message, LeRoy's brothers and sisters talk of little else but making a move to the city. They do not share their father's desire to keep the family farm.

"See, your pa doesn't want to integrate any more than I do. Watch out, child! You almost stepped on the Bidewell Mansion." Merriweather warns.

LeRoy looks down to see a residential area with tiny homes, set amid green crops, bisected by orchards and ponds. The community center, next to LeRoy's right foot, is in the middle of the Neighborhood with paths leading to it from each side. There are several outbuildings near the big house.

Merriweather watches the boy intently studying the diorama and wonders if his own grandson, Jefferson, would ever want to live in his model city, if it were segregated. Jefferson's current best friend is a boy who looks a lot like the one he sees before him, the son of a well-to-do neighbor of his daughter, Jasmine. Merriweather has not been able to talk Jeff out of that friendship, try as he might.

"My own kids are not about to join me in any kind of segregated community." Merriweather admits, aloud. "They say they don't believe in segregation. Why should they? They never even knew any colored folks except rich ones–they never had to. I saw to that."

"What's seg-re-gate?" asks LeRoy.

"These days it's what separates those who have from those who have not. Folks like my children deny their prejudice because segregation is not spoken of in polite society. They just keep to their own kind–those that have." Merriweather admits. "My generation allowed them that luxury."

"Can't you make amends?" LeRoy asks.

"To make amends I, and those like me, have to stop taking such a big piece of the pie." Merriweather explains. "Few will admit they segregate anything, these days, but they live in ways and in places that others can't afford. Then they make sure they and their own have the best schools and services. Tough luck for the rest, they think, if they ever think about the rest at all."

"How would others having pie hurt them?" LeRoy asks.

"Entitlement is just another name for fear, boy. They are afraid of losing what they have. In my younger days we used to live with the results of our fear and prejudice, saw it every day of our lives. We faced up to it and what it does to us and to others. My kids live so separate from those in need, they have no idea the harm they do. I have done my job too well."

"If you help to build this great place for everyone maybe you can all have good pie there." LeRoy points out. "There will be enough for everyone."

Merriweather looks down on his model for one of the oldest and now one of the poorest Neighborhoods in Mobile, the Bidewell Estates. His design for the outbuilding near the big house is for a learning center for both children and adults, the likes of which he heard discussed at the Tiger Summit. Merriweather wants to help build a just and sustainable neighborhood near his old family home but knows that his own children would stop his grandkids going there, if it was not situated in their exclusive, gated community. They would never consider sending their kids to a poor part of town to share resources.

"My kids would never live there, no matter how good it is. They already have everything they need. Why should they change a thing?"

"You want to change." LeRoy reminds Merriweather "Can't they change, too, if they stop being afraid?"

"It's true that rich folks have always done what they want to do, no matter what. Who knows, maybe someday we'll have enough heart to share our piece of the pie." the old man muses.

LeRoy holds out the pie to his elder. "Please take this. We have lots more at home–more than enough to give you some."

"Not, yet." Merriweather responds. "You've given me food for thought, instead. I'm going on back home to help make the Bidewell Mansion Neighborhood the best it can be."

"I'll come visit sometime," the boy calls out to Merriweather, as the man climbs into his rowboat at the water's edge, "and I'll bring pie!"

Not everything that helps change a world happens at once. Often, the biggest changes happen a little at a time.

-Susie Porter Carmen

CHANGING PLACES

"God knows what Belly is going to do with a degree in Social Work, these days." Preston Sommes, Jr. remarks to his wife, Cora May, as they watch Betty Lou walk toward the Dean of the School of Clinical Social Work to receive her diploma.

A few days after The Message, most others she schooled with give up on the idea of social work as a career. Betty Lou, Belly to all who know her, is one of the few graduates who show up for the ceremony.

"Belly always wanted to help people." Cora May comments. "Message or no Message, she is not one to give up on a dream."

"People are finding help everywhere they turn these days." Preston notes. "They don't seem to need social workers to give them a hand."

"Belly said she wasn't about to let all those years of education go to waste." shares Belly's younger sister, Stillpoint.

"She can always help me out at Press International." Preston proposes. "My advice column helps solve community environment problems, rather than personal ones, but it's keeping me busier than ever."

"I thought I'd be the one to lend you a hand with the Preston Report." Stillpoint volunteers. "I want to be a journalist. Let Belly go find her own problems."

"Maybe she can sign on at the Mobile Care Center." Cora May puts in. "A lot of mental health therapists are working there now, heading up work crews to revitalize our Neighborhoods."

"Belly on a work crew?" Stillpoint laughs. "That will be the day. She's too hooked on minding other folk's business to stop seeing them once they finish work on a construction project. She's into long term therapy."

"You're right." Cora Mae agrees. "Belly's still giving advice to people she met in nursery school. Half the folks she's ever known think Belly is their best friend and most intimate confidant. It's her gift."

"And I've got the phone bills to prove it." Preston agrees. "Thank God for E-mail or we'd never have been able to pay for social work school."

"Belly should run for political office, Senator." Stillpoint tells her Uncle Sterlin, when he stops shaking hands and greeting people long enough to join the rest of the family to watch the ceremony.

"Who'd run my local campaigns, then?" Sterlin asks, looking worried. "Belly gets me more votes than sugar gets ants. I just' hope she never runs against me."

"Don't panic, Sterlin." his brother reassures the Senator. "Belly has no more interest in a political career than I do. She has a job interview out at the Abiding Light Sanitarium tomorrow."

"I can't believe the Abiding Light is still open." Stillpoint says and shudders at the thought of the place. "I can't imagine why anyone would want to stay there, after The Message."

"A few patients are still in residence, but I had a call from the Head Nurse, yesterday. Those working there want to keep the sanitarium open." Sterlin shares.

"Surely there are more creative, supportive places for people to go for help, these days?" Cora May asks.

Having been out to the Abiding Light a couple of times with her church group, she has nightmares about the place for weeks afterward.

"That staff say they got folks there will never move on. Personally, I think they're the ones they're talking about." Sterlin explains.

"I bet they think by hiring Belly, you'll put in a word for them with the Governor and keep the place open." Stillpoint suggests.

"Heck no!" Senator Sommes responds. "You ask me, it's about time that old Sommes place returned to the Wild. It was once our family plantation, but Lord knows it's seen its day. Let the place go back to the wild if you ask me."

✴ ✴ ✴ ✴

The next morning, as Belly gets off the train at the station outside the gates of The Abiding Light, she wonders if the Sanitarium has been abandoned and left to return to the Wild. There is no one to be seen inside the walled garden and the land around the compound looks deserted. Brush and trees are closing in on its perimeter, as though embracing the facility in healing arms.

"Anybody home?" Belly calls, as she enters the once grand foyer of the old Sommes plantation home. The hall is deserted, and Belly thinks she hears strains of piano music, an ancient waltz, from beyond the doors of what was once the grand ballroom of their family mansion.

"Must be genetic memory." Belly muses as she recalls the stories of the balls and parties Sommes ancestors once held in the old place. "Genetic nightmare is more like it. God knows what injustices my family did to others here."

✴ ✴ ✴ ✴

People speculate that Belly, born Betty Lou Sommes, got her nickname because she is always acting the perfect Southern belle. Belly thinks her nickname comes from the fact that most of what

Sommes family did in the past makes her feel sick to her stomach. She knows that Sommes' kin are not one big, happy family.

Betty Lou researched her family tree as part of a school project when she was in the fourth grade. Her study showed her she is related to just about everyone in Mobile, in one way or another, be they black, white or InDios. European and African Sommes kin live in or near Mobile for more than three hundred years before her birth and her InDios ancestors have been in the neighborhood for more than three millennia.

Belly recognizes that her ancestors are smart enough not to discriminate when it comes to making babies. They all recognize obviously good breeding material, no matter how it is packaged, and act on that knowledge to produce a long-lived and prolific family. The reason Belly tries to help so many Mobile Neighbors is because they are all her relatives, and she has a strong sense of family obligation.

"Doesn't mean those who carry the name of Sommes treated all my kin right." Belly admits. "Just about the whole town of Mobile is my family, in one way or another, but most of them were just plain exploited, if and when they had anything to do with folks that do have the Sommes surname."

"I was damn lucky to be born a Sommes." Belly tells her mother when she is ten years old. "That means I'll always have everything I need. I just better get busy making sure other family members have what they need, too."

Belly keeps busy doing her best to make up for generations of ethnic cleansing, slavery and economic exploitation done in the name of the Sommes family. Cora May does not argue with her daughter, who voices the basic premise upon which rests the creed of all, true Southern gentility. It is the creed by which Cora May lives, and it is impossible for her to be rude, uncaring, or unkind to anyone she meets, no matter who they are. Belly is her mother's daughter.

Belly's father is the consummate Southern gentleman and Preston never tolerates bigotry or prejudice against anyone. He extends the scope of those he recognizes as his equal to the entire human population of Mobile and is happy to throw in any other humans on Planet Earth, for good measure. In this, Belly is her father's daughter.

* * * *

"I've been a community activist for as long as I can recall." Belly tells Dr. Brainburn, the Psychiatrist at the Abiding Light. "I began organizing to benefit people in need when I was in grade school. Social work is a perfect career choice for me. I'm glad The Message turned everyone toward kindness as a way of life but that does not change what I need to do with my time here one bit."

"Can't fault that." Dr. Brainburn points out. "Sorry we have so little for you to do, these days. After the Message, most of our Residents left."

"Could I help those who remain to get well enough to leave?"

"We aren't hiring you to work with all our Residents." Dr. Brainburn explains. "Just for one of them- Freda Tarkle Phillips."

"You're hiring me to work with only one person? Is she dangerous?"

"What she does never hurt anyone, to my knowledge." the Psychiatrist admits. "It might even have helped a few."

"Then why don't you just discharge her?" Belly asks.

"Look at her chart and you'll see why getting her out of here is not so easy." Dr. Brainburn admits, handing Belly three volumes of medical records.

Like most of her ancestors, Belly is not a person who runs from a challenge. She is intrigued by the idea of working with a woman whose case has everyone else stumped. When she sits down to have a look Belly discovers that Freda has been at the Sanitarium for only one year.

"I expected to see the history of someone who's been in hospitals their whole life." Belly tells Prunella Cantrell, when the Head Nurse gives her a tour of the building on the way to introduce her to Freda.

"Seems like centuries to me." Prunella shares. "Freda set up shop in the Recreation Therapy Department, about a week after she arrived, and we haven't been able to get her out since. You saw her record and read for yourself what happens when we try to discharge her."

"But why?" Belly asks, as she looks down the dim hallways and to the even sadder-looking community rooms. "Who would want to stay here, if they didn't have to."

"You've got to admit, that is pretty crazy." Nurse Prunella points out. "Freda also scores as severely delusional on our impairment indicator scales, so we get paid for her. If someone wants to give us bucks to keep her here, we keep her."

"But is there anything wrong with her?" Belly asks.

"The jury's still out on that one." Prunella states as she opens the door to the Recreation area. "Brainburn thinks she's fine but you can judge for yourself."

As Belly enters the Recreation department she is greeted by laughter. She follows the sound to an enclave at the end of the room, to windows whose light is filtered through a network of patterns and colors—a hive-like cocoon. The fabric structure contains several Abiding Light Residents and Staff Orderly, Ramone Escobar, CNA. Freda Tarkle is there, holding court like a disheveled queen bee, seated at a computer as she taps away at the keyboard.

"Fair warning to all who enter here." Freda calls, as Belly steps inside the woven walls to join them. "Your whole world will change. We'll see to that."

"Nice soft sculpture." Belly comments. The effect of the piece, which now surrounds her, is a pleasant one from inside. "Who's the artist?"

"Mother Earth." Freda shares. "We just rearrange her things a little, as humans are wanting to do. After all, this is the recreation department."

"Nice creation." Belly comments.

"That's what we're here for." Freda informs and there are nods and smiles from the others. Belly notes that Orderly Ramone seems to agree with all that is said.

"Well, don't let me stop you." Belly advises.

"As if you could." Freda states and the group laughs.

"I am a clinical social worker." Belly tells Freda. "I'm supposed to help you... get out of here."

Their laughter stops, instantly, and even Orderly Ramone looks unhappy.

"Wait a minute." Belly tells the group. "I've read Freda's chart and I know how much you all depend on her. There was a riot here the last time they scheduled her discharge, but Freda can't stay forever."

"Why not?" asks The Blind Guy. "Forever is now if you look at it from the right point of view."

"What would you know about point of view?" Lukecia Stubs asks The Blind Guy. "You're blind."

"Not a visual point of view," the Blind Guy explains. "a temporal one."

"Temporal or otherwise, we don't want Freda to go." Roberta Lightfoot Masters explains. "Who'll weave stories for us if she leaves?"

"She weaves what for you?" Belly asks, then looks again at the intricate patterns and designs incorporated into the walls that surround them. "Do you mean these designs?"

"More than designs." Orderly Ramone explains. "Freda recreates reality."

"Recreative non-fiction." Roberta adds. "Freda weaves some great stories and sends them out on the web. Then they start to come true."

"Sort of a reverse idea of reference." Freda shares with Belly, speaking to the therapist in mentalhealtheze. "Most psychotics think the world is speaking to them. I speak to the world, and it listens. Call it a classic case of reality projection."

"Locked up in here, how do you know that your projections really make things happen?" Belly asks.

"We have television and radio, as well as the Internet. We may look like we're locked away, but we are surprisingly well-informed." Lytella Carlos explains.

"We also get many newspapers and magazines from my cousin, Abel Rebinowitz." patient Sigmund Freed informs Belly. "What else do we have to do here, but keep up with world events?"

"And help create them." Freda adds.

"We're getting our turn-around time down to an average of two weeks." Lytella advises. "Our fastest time, so far, is twenty-four hours between our release of a new story and its material realization."

"Give me an example." Belly requests. "I'm still not sure I understand what you're talking about."

"The Message." Freda explained. "We wrote a story about some young people who want to have everyone help clean up Planet Earth. Next thing, The Message is heard by everyone and their brother."

"And their third cousin, twice removed." The Blind Guy notes.

"That was the one that took only twenty-four hours." Orderly Ramone explains.

"My guess, it was a Message whose time had come." Freda admits. "They don't all work that fast."

"What story didn't work?" Belly asks.

"Wristwatch telephones." Freda answers. "Someone invented them a month after we mentioned them in one of our stories, but people look like such dorks using them, they never caught on."

"We?" Belly asked. "I thought you were the one who spins the yarns here, Freda."

"We all help." the Blind Guy puts in. "We come up with the concepts and ideas and Freda weaves them into stories."

"It's a collaborative effort." Roberta Masters adds.

"After all, we can't put just any old idea out there."

Freda explains. "We have to be responsible about it. That requires feedback from a group to get the right perspective."

"Helps us see the big picture." The Blind Guy observes.

"Is the group effort what makes your stories so powerful?" Belly asks.

"All stories are powerful." Freda answers. "All do what our stories do. Do you fault us for being aware of that and for telling only that which is positive and good?"

"Lordy, no." Belly assures them. "The world needs all the good ideas it can get."

"The folks spreading bad news and negativity, violence and hatred have had the world's attention long enough." Freda notes. "Now it's our turn."

"Half of that bad news is a manipulative distortion or misinformation." the Blind Guy proposes. "I'm an expert at spotting a bold face lie, when it's told."

"And he's The Blind Guy." Lukecia points out. "Imagine what the rest of us can do if we pay attention."

"I think I'd rather not imagine." Belly admits, feeling a bit overwhelmed.

Social work school did not prepared Belly for anything like this bunch. She was taught that the mental health profession is a science, but all this sounds more like science fiction.

"Why do you need to be in here to work together?" Belly asks. "Can't you work on these stories anywhere?"

"Ha!" Freda laughs. "You know as well as I do that the world would never give us the time, place or space to do what we're doing, if we leave here. They'd have us in job training and rehabilitation programs, to improve ourselves, before tick turns to tock."

"They'd want us to be people just like everyone else. I'd get my six kids back and there goes any chance for a complete sentence, let alone a finished story." Freda explains.

"Things are changing." Belly reminds the group. "Since The Message, all kinds of new vocational options are available to people."

"Then why are you here?" Freda asks. "Seems to me you would make an excellent Neighborhood Watch Person."

"A what?" Belly asks.

"Neighborhood Watcher." Freda explains. "The story we just finished is about a woman who helps a whole Neighborhood. Like so much that gets realized, it just makes sense that any Neighborhood would need to have a person, maybe a couple, whose job it is to coordinate Neighborhood change. You know, make sure people are using their gifts, that the Neighborhood is using its resources right, that people there are getting their needs met, that kind of stuff."

"That sounds like a great job." Belly admits. "I could do that."

"Get in on the ground floor and find some place in the city that needs you. Challenge yourself- make it the place with the least resources. See what you can do there," Freda suggests "and leave us alone."

"I'll consider it." Belly agrees. "If you consider other options, too."

"Like what?"

"You ever thought maybe the ideas you come up with are telling you the stories?" Belly asks. "You send them out on the web, and they become reality for everyone."

"Hey! You're good...." Freda admits. "But how would that change things for me? No matter how the story gets here, I still have to find a way to tell it and if I leave here, I'll never have the time to do that."

"And she won't have us to help her out." Roberta reminds Belly.

"Why don't you think up the story of a world where people value the kind of contribution you make to positive change." Belly suggests. "Shouldn't that be enough to make sure you get your basic needs met and enough time and support to tell your stories?"

"That is a great idea." Freda agrees. "You want to help us write it?"

"No thanks." Belly responds. "I'll stick with that one about the Neighborhood Watcher, myself. I have a just the Neighborhood in mind to make it come true."

Belly leaves the group kicking around ideas for their personal liberation and she drops by to see Dr. Brainburn, before leaving the Abiding Light.

"My guess is that Freda will be out of here as soon as the world heals enough to support her." Belly tells the Psychiatrist. "I take no credit for that. She's working out those details with a little help from her friends."

"That's great." Dr. Brainburn admits. "Now, if I could just find some way to get the Staff to leave."

"You can find out how that happens in Freda's next book, *The Gospels According to Reverend Ike.*" Belly tells the Psychiatrist. "Freda and her group are working on that story, too. Apparently, many of them can't leave until the staff are well enough to go."

"We'll be here for a while then." Dr. Brainburn sighs. "I sure hope they give me a decent part in that tale. I want to play, too."

"Count yourself in." Belly promises. "Count everyone else in, too."

THE BIDEWELL MANSION

The Neighborhood around the old Bidewell Mansion was going to pot for years before The Message. Most Neighbors are far too busy working to keep a roof over their head to worry about how that roof looks and the Bidewell Mansion, the once-stately home of the Bidewell family, is falling apart along with the rest of the Neighborhood.

The rambling old house is in the middle of a tract of homes, built in the mid-sixties when fair-housing laws make it slightly easier for people of color to get home loans. The sale of family property for the Bidewell Estates takes place when the only surviving Bidewell kin, Merriweather Marion Jenkins, sells the family land to developer Bernardo Carmen. Merriweather takes the money from the sale and starts a construction company to build gated communities for those, like him, in pursuit of a segregated dream.

Bernardo Carmen decides to keep the Bidewell Mansion for himself because the house is an historic building and cannot be torn down. Bernardo also wants to make sure no grandee ever buys the old place to lord it over the rest of the Neighborhood.

"I think my granddaddy was once a worker on this plantation." Bernardo tells his son, Fernando, when he gives the house and grounds to his boy as a wedding present. "You make sure the house is never the home of a *patrone* again. Just because your house is bigger, doesn't mean you're any better than anyone else is, son. It just means you have a bigger house."

❋ ❋ ❋ ❋

"Little to no chance anyone, elitist or not, will ever buy this place." Susie Porter Carmen, Real Estate Agent, and daughter-in-law of Bernardo, says as she looks up at the shabby building, in its shabby Neighborhood.

It is a few days after The Message and eight years since her husband, Fernando, died and left her a widow with two growing children and one on the way. In the years that follow his death, Susie has enough determination to continue to run Carmen Reality and to raise her family, but never enough time or manpower to keep the Bidewell Mansion in any decent state of repair.

Her real estate business is one of the busiest Real Estate offices in Mobile and Susie tries to sell the old house. No one wants a twelve-bedroom mansion, or much else in what is now designated neighborhood 7, District 7 of the Mobile Urban Center. Prior to The Message Susie did very little business in her own Neighborhood. More buildings were abandoned there than sold.

"I've considered walking away from this old white elephant." Susie tells her handyman, Willie Santiago. "If it wasn't for you, I would have left the Bidewell Mansion long ago."

"What you gonna do when I retire, Ms. Carmen?" Willie asks.

They laugh because both know Willie is not the kind of man that retires. Both know he will probably drop dead working and Willie guesses it will be while working on the Bidewell Mansion. He is having a harder and harder time getting up and down stairs, never mind the stepladder or scaffolding needed for proper repair of the Mansion's roof and walls.

"This place also needs a full-time gardener to deal with the jungle of growth in those back and side yards." Willie tells Susie. "You need a Game Keeper for some of those carriage houses and outbuildings. You got things livin' in 'um! Face it, the old place is getting to be too much for me."

"It's been too much for me since we moved in here." Susie admits. "I just wish something creative could be done with this big, old place."

Thanks to The Message, Susie gets her wish. Part of the answer to her prayers is a Neighborhood, self-help learning project she and Willie start, to teach neighbors how to do their own home repairs. The other part of the answer is World War III.

Shortly after The Message, all military personnel on the Planet refuse to go into combat. People figure that war is just going into battle with oneself. They tell their Presidents, Dictators, Premiers, Kings, Prime Ministers, Emperors, High Rulers and High Rollers to find other ways to settle current, pending, or future disputes, wars, civil liberation struggles or other military engagements.

"No matter what you want to call it, armed combat needs to stop." Private Ulysses Eisenhower Parnham tells his Uncle, who also happens to be the Commander In Chief of the USA.

The Private is the youngest son of the President's sister, Rose, and Ulysses is not being disrespectful to his Uncle. The President called his nephew on the phone to ask for the young soldier's honest opinion.

"Find something else for us to do, Sir!" Ulysses requests.

"It's not that the men and women of our military don't want to fight any more, Sir." Maxwell Parker, Presidential Advisor to the Joint Chiefs of Staff explains to the President after the call. "They just don't want to fight with other people. They have faith in you, Sir. They know you can come up with another kind of military engagement to keep them fighting the good fight."

The President gives it some thought and does some dreaming on it, too. Then he gets hold of an old friend, known to the world as The King of Peace, and suggests that the world wage another kind of war. World War III, known as 'The War of Construction', breaks out all over Planet Earth. The terms of this war require the UN to give any resource, money or help requested by opposing sides in a conflict, provided the help is used to assist people, repair human cities, or to heal damage done to the environment.

Footing the bill for all this are governments, private industry and some world citizens who are richer than God and have nothing better to do with their money than save a Planet in need. Nations do not have to be at war to request help but those who insist on fighting are assigned different parts of their disputed territory to restore and renovate for the better.

"Let's get busy!" respond governors and government wannabes.

"Show me a well-organized group, who can give people what they need for a decent life, who don't wreck the environment doing so." citizens all over the world tell their leaders and proceed to back the ones who do the best job for them and their Planet.

Not all combat takes place between political groups. On the advice of the former owner of the Bidewell Mansion, Susie and other leaders of Neighborhood 7 & 7 cite as their enemy the US Military-Industrial-Prison Complex. One of the biggest builders of prisons and military bases in the South, Merriweather Marion Jenkins knows the toll taken on people like 7&7 Neighbors by such institutions. He accurately names their enemy for them, for he saw that enemy and it was he.

"Prisons been housing your men and women and decimating your families, the military have been taking your sons and daughters for cannon fodder and industry been polluting your environment for decades. I won't even go into how drugs come into your communities through all those channels." Merriweather explains. "It's time to go war against your real enemies."

Then Merriweather pulls in every favor he can to help 7& 7 Neighbors apply for UN funds to remake their 'hood.

The resources they command are used to expand existing housing units to accommodate a doubling of their current population. After The Message, when people leave the Wild to settle in urban areas, 7 & 7 makes them welcome. Neighborhood 7&7 also welcomes the skills the new arrivals bring and their help to execute a battle plan that is an example for their city and for the rest of the world.

"Leave the Wild Places to the birds and the butterflies, the moose and the marmosets, the caribou and the crickets." the 7 & 7 folks tell one another. "We can make cities green and wonderful places for people to live. Yes, we can!"

Not only do they do so, but they also show others how to do so, too. Susie Carmen, Merriweather, and the 7&7 Neighbors help the Bidewell Mansion become the focal point for multiple Neighborhood projects that include temporary housing for new arrivals, a community garden, a community learning center, a food processing plant, and an urban agricultural research center.

❋ ❋ ❋ ❋

"Neighborhood 7&7 is a perfect example of the way people work together creatively." Susie states, smiling for the TV cameras that tape the first episode of the Home Repair Show.

Their show, begun as a program for their local cable access channel, turns out to be so funny and informative it is picked up by their local TV network. When national broadcasters see it, they syndicate it across the USA. UN officials view the show when it is broadcast nationally, and it is not long before UNESCO Information Network distributes it to TV stations around the world.

"Keep making those shows about projects that people can do in their homes or gardens, and as part of their Neighborhood development schemes." Bookbinder Mohammed, their UNESCO advisor tells a meeting of the 7&7 Home Repair Show crew. "And keep making those shows funny."

"That won't be hard." Susie assures him. "Few of us know what we're doing, but we don't care if we look silly figuring it out. I'm the poster child for how not to do almost anything."

"The show must be doing something right." Bookbinder replies. "It's one of the most popular shows in North America and it seems to be a hit in India and Indiana and most places in between."

"People, from all parts of the world, are the secret of our success." Susie states. "Even before The Message, we had a mix of people from other nations and almost every race, religion and culture. This blessing provides us with lots of different ways to solve life's problems."

"7&7 Neighbors can come up with a dozen ways to meet almost any human need, with millions of years of human history and experience to call on." Merriweather Jenkins agrees, backing Susie up. "There seem to be no end to the innovative and creative ways people can live on Planet Earth. 7&7 Neighbors know most of them and are happy to share that knowledge."

"Thank Creator the 7&7 Neighbors did not forget their old ways. Some of those ways are coming in mighty handy! You never know who, or what can help the most." Susie adds. "That's the fun part."

"If we can learn from the knowledge and experience of the whole human race and combine that knowledge with the latest in technology." Merriweather points out. "The combination of old and new helps our Neighborhood and our World. That's the Beauty part."

Susie shares part of next week's show with their UNESCO sponsors:

"We'll be showing how to plant wild rice in a Neighborhood water garden, ways to build structures from packed earth and we'll also look at Polynesian building design, to construct a roof that lets a breeze move through a building to cool it off in summer."

"Let's hope the world tunes in to have some fun with all that." Merriweather wishes. "7 & 7 is our work in progress, but everyone is welcome to join us and help Planet Earth, one Neighborhood at a time."

THE PUZZLE BOX

Ed Pedersen figures he has no chance of staying out of prison for the rest of his life, just about any way he looks at it. Sure, he maxed out on his current sentence and is due to be released, but he cannot see how his life will change much.

What gives Ed some hopes are the legitimate job skills he has at the time of his release a good teacher, in the Building and Maintenance Training Program at the Pokee Men's Correctional Center, taught Ed how to fix just about anything, from a roof to a foundation, inside or outside a building. Ed even took a correspondence course in organic gardening.

"Hell, I had enough time in there to learn to become a brain surgeon." Ed tells the Parole Board when he sits before them three years before The Message. "I could not get a physician's license in this state, so I gave up on that idea and learned plumbing instead."

The Parole Board turns Ed down at that hearing, but three years later he has served his time and they have to let him out.

Even with his release immanent Ed gives serious thought to "leaving us", the way out taken by most men and women who are incarcerated at the time of The Message. They learn from the Message that they are free to move on to any life form they chose. With this as an option, most people in jail move on right quick. Quite a few guards and prison staff 'leave us', too.

"Apparently they want to try it again in another life form, or elsewhere in the cosmos." the Prison Chaplain, Reverend Toni Smallwell, tells the few prisoners and guards left standing to attend the combined memorial service for both the departed inmates and prison staff. "Can anyone blame them for that?"

No one can. Like Ed, they know life in prison helps no one at all. All involved with the business of prisons, inmates, or prison employees, are in a big puzzle box with no observable way out for most, except death. They take death. Ed, still curious about life in his current form, decides to stick around to see if he can find another way out.

❋ ❋ ❋ ❋

Ed is put in the prison box when he is born to a poor family, with parents that have a tendency to cause trouble. Ed's father, and grandfather before him are both anarchists, so they spend a lot of time in jail as political prisoners. When Ed's mother dies, he and his brothers and sisters go to foster homes because his relatives are all incarcerated. His baby sister, Clarice, calls their foster home, "the little kid's prison."

The foster homes are not exactly prisons, because prisons are generally better staffed and more closely regulated than are foster homes. Ed's brothers and sisters, like most children who are raised in foster homes, either go insane or die from drug use, within a couple of years of leaving foster care. Many of them also go to prison.

Ed enters the juvenile justice system when he is eleven, though his time in foster homes prepares him well for those youth camps, rehabilitation centers, special schools and child detention facilities that are the actual prisons for kids in their state.

Ed is not a particularly bad kid. If he had a family life growing up, he probably would have been trained to do and be something else besides a criminal. He just never had that kind of option available to him. Ed sticks with what he knows and by the time he is eighteen, he is primed to graduate to the Adult Department of Corrections.

Ed is much too smart to be caught doing most of the stupid kinds of crimes, for which the majority of those in jails are convicted. Most people are in prison for being just plain ignorant of how things work and too poor to defend themselves in court for their drug use or for the silly things they do to survive. Ed's years in kid's prison train him for bigger things than that.

Ed is recruited in Juvenile facilities he attends and is trained to be a front man and a fall guy. Schemes and cons are their way of life and are nearly always foolproof for them, but not for those they enlist to help pull them off, the ones who do the time for their crimes. When Ed is eighteen years old, he is released from Juvenile Hall with nowhere else to go and is employed by such master con men, who operate on a grand scale, involving wealthy people and large amounts of their money.

The goal of Ed's employers is not to create career options for Youth, but to enlist Ed and those like him to take the heat while they leave town with their ill-got gains. Their scheme sells fake artworks to rich people. All their customers know they are buying from crooks but think the art they are getting is the real thing. They assume the lower price they pay is because the artwork is stolen, but they are sold fakes, instead. Furious about being swindled by "cons", these rich dupes get the law to come down heavy on Ed, the only member of the group caught in the act.

Ed serves an especially long sentence for his first conviction because his crime harmed those of wealth and power. Ed learns he should never screw rich folks, none of whom were prosecuted for attempting to buy stolen property. Apparently, it is not a crime to pay a lot of money for worthless fakes.

In ten years, Ed is out on Parole but no better suited to an 'honest' life than he was before he went in. To his credit, Ed rejected the offers of his former employers to work for them while in the joint, recruiting and training the smartest inmates for scams. Ed says "no" to that prison employment option and also declines their offer of work when he gets out.

Once released, Ed takes the first legitimate job he can find, as a telemarketer. His second criminal conviction is for fraudulent solicitation across state lines. In his defense, Ed never knew that the political party, for which he was raising funds, had no permit to have him do so. Unfortunately for Ed and the other phone operators, this political group is considered a real threat to the parties in power so, again, the justice system shows little mercy. Ed ends up at the Men's Correctional Facility at Pokee and learns never to screw with politics.

"I'm always the dupe for charlatans and crooks!" Ed complains to his Vocational Training Counselor, Mr. Web, at the Pokee Prison Facility. "I'm planning to get myself a trade, fixing things, this time in. I've decided to work for myself if I ever get out of prison again."

Ed knows the greatest challenge to his plan for self-improvement is the difficulty getting into the Prison Vocational classes. Yearly budget cuts reduce training options to almost nothing and he has to wait years for some of the courses. Ed persists in his desire to learn something constructive, no matter what it takes.

Fortunately, some of the prisoners have to be skilled enough to keep the prisons running at no cost to the system, so a few inmates are trained to do the work there. Ed learns basic plumbing, electrical wiring, simple carpentry, roof repair, welding and how to fix heating and refrigeration systems. He gets to practice dry wall and painting skills when the prison adds on to the family visiting area and 'hires' inmates, at 12 cents an hour, to do the work.

Those around Ed rarely encourage him in his pursuit of a new career.

"You'll never find a decent place to live or get a legitimate job." his former colleagues assure Ed when they come in to serve a sentence and update Ed on the gang's doings outside the joint.

"What do you know about straight life, anyway?" they chide him. "At most, you spent a couple of years of your whole life outside. You will never be able to go straight."

Ed knows these men are just trying to talk him into some plan or another that will earn him strike three. Since a third felony conviction means a life sentence, Ed is determined not to play that particular game.

"I'll find some way out of this puzzle box of life behind bars or die trying." Ed vows.

Then The Message is heard, and all are told that humanity is about to start a new game–cleaning up Planet Earth.

"I think I'll stick around and join that team." Ed decides. "The world needs me, for the first time in my life."

This need is obvious to others as it is to Ed. The Warden and his cousin, Senator Sterlin Sommes, realize that Ed is one of the few prisoners left at Pokee who can run the prison water treatment plant and local sanitation facilities, upon which the surrounding, human population rely for clean water and waste management.

The Pokee sanitation facility was built inside the prison, as a perk to the locals when the prison came to their neighborhood. With most of the other prisoner's dead, a crash of these sanitation systems is certain, without Ed's help.

"I'll sign you on as a staff member to run the water treatment plant and waste disposal system." the Warden offers Ed.

"You'll no longer be an inmate and we'll pay you $75,000 a year, with full benefits as a state employee." Senator Sommes adds, desperate for a solution to this problem.

The Senator lobbied hard for the sanitation facilities built inside prison walls. To have them fail, because all the prisoners who run them are dead, will not make the Senator look good. Senator Sommes never likes to give anyone a chance to complain about any of the projects he sponsors or supports but is sure someone will try to hold him accountable if there's a problem with Pokee's water or its sewers.

"Reliance on prison labor for essential services like clean water and garbage recycling might look like poor planning to some, if the system collapses." the Senator tells Warden Benson. "Of course, folks never complain when the service works and can be furnished dirt cheap, but let it break down and there'll be hell to pay."

The Senator's problem is not Ed's problem, but the inmate takes pity on the lawmaker and agrees to help out for a while.

"I won't spend a minute more here than I need to," Ed tells the Senator and the Warden "but I will spend the time left on my sentence teaching the prison staff how to run the water treatment systems. Otherwise, aren't they all out of jobs?"

Ed has a point. With no one left to guard any more, guards, counselors and other staff have nothing to do. Ed offers them retraining in the essential jobs once done by the prisoners. Another prisoner, Justice Turner, helps show prison employees how to keep the prison's recycling center going.

Advised by Justice, who has been running the Pokee recycling center for a decade, Pokee citizens come up with a plan to turn the former prison into a re-use center for their entire region. Their center provides work for hundreds of local people and handles recycling for half their state.

Citizens also expand the prison's water treatment capacity to clean up the wastewater from the area's poultry and pig farms that has been polluting local rivers and creeks for the past decade. All those pigs and chickens are mighty hard on the environment and animal waste had been laying waste to their watershed for years.

"Having a prison here was a waste." Pokee citizens admit. "Millions spent on keeping people there in boxes should have gone to this kind of project, a decade ago."

✳ ✳ ✳ ✳

"Wasting the facilities at Pokee by keeping people locked up there is not cost or energy-efficient." Senator Sommes tells the audience at an awards banquet, given in his honor when he is presented with the "Better Ways For Better Days Award", for the Pokee transformation plan. The plan wins are in the category: 'The most rapid transition of an outmoded institution, after The Message'.

"Prison facilities need to be making more jobs and more money for our citizens, as they help our Planet. Let's hope this idea spreads." The Senator concludes his acceptance speech.

His State follows the Senator's suggestion and turns its many prisons and detention facilities into Regional Environment Clean-up Centers. The Federal Prison System soon does the same nation-wide. Recycling and watershed cleanup work is done from places once used as human garbage dumps. These converted prison facilities are at the forefront in the cleanup of waterways and waste dumps of all kinds.

✳ ✳ ✳ ✳

After Ed trains the prison guards, counselors and forensic psychologists, parole officers and probation department employees, as well as the many others who rely on a system of putting people in boxes for their living, he thankfully gets out of Pokee.

In appreciation for Ed's help, Senator Sommes refers the ex-offender to Mobile's advocate for the homeless, T. Willie Wheelwright, with a Sterlin recommendation to help Ed find the right job, in the right Neighborhood, when he returns to society.

"Your ability to fix things will open many doors for you." T. Willie assures Ed. "You are going to get offers you won't believe."

"People want an ex-con as their Neighbor, these days?" Ed asks. "Things sure have changed."

T. Willie explains why any Neighborhood would jump at the chance to provide Ed with housing and a salary; for the help he gives on development projects and to coordinate food production in their urban gardens.

"Neighborhood repair persons, gardeners or maintenance staff are in big demand, especially if you're recommended by someone like the Senator. The rich know he takes care of his own, so you can write your own ticket to the wealthiest Neighborhoods in the city."

Ed recalls that many of the rich are the crooks who make the dime but never do the time and is reluctant to live and work among such people.

"You got a Neighborhood with people who work hard for a living and don't have too much money?" Ed asks.

Ed follows T. Willie's recommendations and applies for the position of Neighborhood Handyman at Neighborhood 7, District 7, formerly known as the Bidewell Estates. Ed sees that most of the people in 7&7 are people of color. This reminds Ed of the foster homes, youth detention facilities and the prisons where he spent most of his life, and he feels right at home there.

Other than the racial and economic makeup of its population, 7 & 7 is worlds apart from any place Ed ever lived before. Neighborhood 7&7 is bursting with life and many ideas for creative change. That suits Ed just fine, too.

The first-person Ed meets at 7&7 is a lovely young woman, Betty Lou Sommes—Belly to all who know her. Belly and Ed take one look at each other and fall in love. They are advised, years later, that they are a Lou-Mae, beloved ones who would never be the most they can be, had they not met and united. That advisement is no news to them. They knew that the minute they met.

Fortunately for the many people they help during their life together, they decided to marry the day after they meet and Senator

Sterlin Sommes', Belly's uncle, personally takes Ed home to meet the family. Sterlin gives his unconditional support for the match. He knows Ed is a great catch for his niece and for Neighborhood 7&7, where Belly has just taken a job as the Neighborhood Watcher.

"Ed is a good man." Sterlin tells his brother, Preston, and his sister-in- law, Cora May. "Besides, being smart as a whip, he has job skills that will put him in charge of that whole Neighborhood, inside a year."

"Doesn't it matter to Uncle Sterlin that Ed was a crook?" Stillpoint, Belly's younger sister, whispers to her mom.

"If your Uncle stopped hanging around with crooks, he'd have to kiss his political career good-bye." Cora May whispers back. "Sterlin sees something in this man, and he usually knows what's what."

Senator Sommes not only knows what's what, he also knows the makings of power and influence when he sees them. He sees them in both Ed and Belly.

"Together, they will help turn 7&7 into a show place for the city and for the state. Heck, for the whole world!" the Senator predicts, as he toasts the couple at their wedding reception, held at the Bidewell Mansion, now the 7 & 7 Community Center.

All the 7&7 Neighbors are there and Susie Carmen, the mansion's owner, invites Ed and Belly to move into the old house to coordinate the Neighborhood's development projects from there.

"This big old house and the rest of this Neighborhood are falling apart." Ed tells his new wife. "But I look on that as a game. It's like one big puzzle to me, with something new to figure out each day. It's also my chance to step out of that puzzle box of survival. All I got to worry about now, is how to help our Planet, right here in our own back yard."

"That survival box has held most of us tighter than prison walls, before The Message." Belly assures Ed. "There are lots of different boxes that limit humans, and they don't all have bars."

"Now we can all get out and help our Neighbors out, too." Ed agrees. "You, me and everyone else—all finally out of that old puzzle box!"

OPEN POKER

Shortly after The Message is heard, all the troops at war put down their guns and say, "Uh-uh!" to their Military Higher Ups and Generals, Commandants, Chiefs of Staff's, and Commanders in Chief.

"No more o' that." they voice, as their vision clears and they realize that the people they are trying to maim, kill and destroy are none other than themselves.

Before The Message it is getting increasingly hard to tell who is 'them' and who is 'us', in a majority of the wars in progress. A lot of the wars are civil wars, with people fighting their own countrymen, women, and children. Even in the wars between nations, the 'Who is the enemy?' question is often hard to figure out.

Maybe the enemy is dressed a little differently, eats different food, has different kinds of beauty contests, rides in different kinds of vehicles, speaks a different language and salutes a different flag, but other than that, the combatants are pretty much the same model. Each is equipped to bleed, suffer, and die, in the same way.

Most equally regret they ever let anyone talk them into showing up for the war, in the first place.

The combatants are often young people and are usually poor people who, no matter which side they are on, have very little to gain from the battles they fight.

"We have a lot more in common with each other than we do with the politicians and financial pundits, the moguls and the magnates, the wealthy and their professional arms dealers and war-makers who run these shows." the universal soldiers say, after The Message.

It also comes to their attention that even if they survive a war untouched, unmarked, whole, and physically well, they will be harmed by war in unseen ways. War is a no-win situation for the people who fight, even when they are the victors.

"Those powerful people make their plans and expect us to do the fighting and dying for them? Uh-uh! Figure out another way to settle your beef and leave us out of the death and destruction part." the military men and women of the world state.

Then young men and women in the armed services, all over the globe, put down their guns, park their tanks, bring their planes into the hangars, and drop their ships' anchors.

"We'd like to help." they all say. "Killing each other and making a mess on the Planet just destroys things and does not help at all. Give us something better to do."

What choice do political and religious leaders have but to find other ways to settle their fights and conflicts, military actions and combat engagements, strategic infiltration, surgical strikes, ethnic cleansing, and the many other ways they try to blast the heck out of anything and everything, to win a war? They have to try something else, so these leaders turn to the United Nations to find solutions.

The most popular solution is the War of Construction.

This battle option gives warring sides a chance to show which faction can help their area most, when given any resources they request to improve things in the contested territory. The land is divided, giving each side a part of it, the help of the local residents, and anything else they need. Each side has any money or material resource they ask for, to make their land a wonderful place for humans to live. People see which combatants have their act together, to work in the best interest of the human population and their Planet.

How much does it cost to make places that are wholesome for all creatures living there? The entire cost is ten times cheaper than paying for a war, even a little one.

"The more nations playing this World War III game the better!" The King of Peace tells the delegates to the War of Construction Peace Convention, held five days after The Message. "The idea of having an opposition to beat out seems to motivate people to take part in the War effort. It makes the whole thing more of a team sport and I'm sure we can get almost everyone playing this one."

Great as such a game plan sounds, there are still some warriors who are unhappy about such combat. They are usually leaders who are trained at the School of the Norte' Americos, a killer training academy at Fort Bendthem, Georgia, famous for generating human killing machines.

These warriors are trained to do virtually and practically anything to anyone, to gain and keep control in whatever conflict they are engaged. Because of their unparalleled ruthlessness, they often become heads of their nation's military. Then they become their nation's political leaders, usually by military take-over. These men and women have no clue how to do anything constructive, and all are smart enough to know they do not have a snowball's chance in hell fighting such a non-conventional war. They want no part of such a plan.

"Try something else, then." The King of Peace suggests to those who turn down the War of Construction option.

This former US President, known for his humanitarian work and international diplomacy, is at the UN to help coordinate the War of Construction efforts in the battle zones of US inner cities and rural areas. There has been war going on in those zones for over a century, with his nation's poor the casualties. The King of Peace is there to make sure the UN helps these citizens fight a war against the Military-Industrial-Prison complex that has oppressed them for so long.

Busy as he is with that, the King of Peace takes pity on leaders who can think of no alternatives to killing and destruction to settle their disputes. He has no easy answers for them, but he inspires them to new action with a brief statement of confidence:

"You are clever people, figure something out."

One duo of *Generalisimos* has a duel with pistols at a hundred paces. Each shoots the other dead. Two down, but too many to go.

Two other High Commanders, representing opposing sides in a civil war, have a boxing match and go ten rounds at the Last Stands Hotel, Las Vegas. The money each makes on the fight, from Cable TV royalties and promotional fees they are paid, earns them so much they retire from the military and give up all idea of running a country. So much the better for the people of their nation, who do not want either of them in power. Their populace elects a Methodist Minister their Premier and the man does a fine job.

One Commander challenges the Head of the opposition forces to personal combat and suggests each of them fight with water rifles, seated inside giant pairs of chattering, clacking teeth.

"They move around the battle area like big, white and pink tanks and the one who scores the most "hits" with their water gun is the winner." General Ramone Sanoma tells his opponent and instantly immobilizes her with laughter.

She concedes defeat and surrenders, much to the delight of their nation's people. They are happy to have a leader with such a great sense of humor, for a change. Most that rule cannot give or take a joke to save their life, or their nation.

Two other heads of State have a staring match to see who blinks first. While they are staring, they actually see one another for the first time. They recognize that their nations, united in the past, have been divided by nothing more than modern politics. They decide to re-unite and rebuild together and take turns running things until their combined population can elect the government of their choice.

One multi-national group of opposing forces has a foot race. The Generals from each faction are the competitors but most of these men and women are over fifty years old. Most of them are in terrible shape and many of them stroke out, have heart attacks, or collapse in mid-race. The winner is the leader of a multi-national rebel band, who has been hiding out in the mountains between these warring nations, for a decade. She is the leader deemed most fit to lead and takes over all territories in dispute.

One by one the conflicts, the wars and their revolutions, the coups and the counterrevolutions are settled. There remains only one group of men and women from five, different factions fighting over the same pitiful scrap of Planet Earth. They have been at war with one another for centuries and they are not willing to sit down and talk about other ways to settle their conflicts.

Fearful that these men and women will devise non-human ways, like nuclear or biological weapons, to fight one another, the King of Peace discusses the problem with the Queen of Peace. She always has good ideas that help a lot.

"How about a game of Open Poker?" The Queen of Peace asks.

"What's Open Poker?"

The Queen explains how Open Poker is like regular poker only all cards are shown to all players at all times.

"People have to learn skills like bluffing, when everyone can actually see what cards, you hold. I guarantee they will all agree to play. Who can resist the challenge of Open Poker?" the Queen of Peace asks the King. "It's the game of a lifetime."

The leaders accept the challenge as each think they can certainly out-play the others. The idea that they might not win is foreign to them. If they had the ability to consider losing, they would have given up on their conflict generations ago, as that war was definitely a lose-lose-lose-lose-lose situation for all concerned.

To teach them Open Poker the Queen of Peace brings in an expert, eight-year-old Ramona Star Brightfoot. Her father, Wilhelm, is the inventor of the game but Ramona is the undisputed family champion, hands up. She is also very good at teaching the game to others.

"The first thing you have to do is surrender to the future." Ramona Star explains to the five Commanders.

There is a gasp of astonished surprise from the men and women at the table, as though someone just punctured a giant, mufti balloon.

"Unless you do that, you spend all your mental energy worrying about what cards you will be dealt, and then worried about which cards you do get. All that is a useless waste of energy." the child points out. "You'll lose this game for sure, with that kind of attitude."

Each combatant is in full battle dress, as they sit around a poker table the King of Peace lent to the UN for their game. Each has a hard time imagining surrender to anything or anyone. They are convinced only after Ramona Star beats them all, in seven and a half minutes, with a pair of twos.

"The kid is good." they all admit.

The best thing about Ramona's victory is that she wins in such an amusing way, her game-mates cannot get mad at her.

"I do it by becoming the cards and making my pair of twos seem so much more important than three aces held by one and the Royal Flush held by another." the child explains.

The leaders begin to see that it is not so much what they have in their hands as what they do with what they have. Points of view start shifting, and minds begin to open to new, creative possibilities.

The players at the table forget they hate each other's guts and begin to play with each other, instead of in opposition to one another. This does not happen all at once, and some of them never quite catch on to Open Poker, but by the time Ramona Star leaves the table they get the idea that they are playing the game of many, many lifetimes.

"I got to go now." Ramona Star tells the assembled Military mighty. "The King of Peace promised to buy me ice cream."

Before she leaves, she gives each one of them a kiss on the cheek and whispers in each one's ear:

"You have a lot of kids just like me in the place you are fighting about. War kills them mighty fast. Try an' find another way."

"Ho!" the Leaders say to one another. "If we join that War of Construction plan, we can all go home and teach the children of our land to play Open Poker instead."

That is just what they do, and a good time is had by all.

THE GRANDPARENT BRIGADE

Ms. Ernestine Patton Parker first discovers the power of grandparents when she is a Unit leader in the Marine Corps, on duty in the Caribbean. The men and women of her battalion are there on maneuvers and a couple of hundred Marines, in full battle gear, are coming off amphibious landing vehicles and mounting a mock attack on a simulated enemy outpost. They are halted in mid-charge by a group of grandmothers. The old women refuse to let them proceed further than the tree line bordering the beach.

"Find somewhere else to play war." Ms. Rose Sharon Lacey, a seventy-five-year-old Afro-Caribbean woman, tells the troops quietly and with an air of such dignity, she stops the Marines in their tracks.

"There are plants beyond these trees that we harvest for our teas and medicines. You'll run over them and kill everything. You can't go there." she finishes and then lines up with a group of women, some of whom looked even older and more dignified than Ms. Rose Sharon.

Then the elders begin to sing a song that sounds like something most people hear sung to them by their own grandmother, aunt, or by someone who cares about them at sometime early in their life. The Marines have no choice but to find somewhere else to play war.

The next time Ernestine Parker sees grandmother power in action is on a peacekeeping mission to distribute food in Somalia during a famine there. A lot of the food never makes it further than the trucks of the warlords and bandits who take most of it away to sell later. If they feel generous, they give out a little of it to those in need, to assure that some customers will remain alive for future sales.

There is almost nothing the US military or the international aid workers can do about this situation. American commanders can say little, knowing that captured booty is the oldest perk known to warriors since war began. Ernestine notes that when an old woman or an elderly man approaches one of these war lords to ask for food from the truck, they are almost never refused.

Ernestine watches while an elder harangue the bandits into handing out a whole truckload of food to thousands of men, women and children who are waiting for a little of it in order to survive. As great as their human needs are, they require a champion to intercede for them. The heroes and heroines who do so are often grandparents.

"Consistently, the elders are the ones who speak for the people and the ones who listen to people when they speak their needs." Ernestine tells her father, General Maxwell Parker. "They know what is going on and they know how to get things done."

Though Ernestine is no longer in the Marines, she is trying to get her father's support for the newly proposed international food, fuel, and tool distribution plan, as part of the War of Construction. Hoping for a future for the US Military, Ernestine knows they are all out of a job if no one comes up with a plan for them to join the rest of humanity in a WW III engagement.

"I think our armed forces should join the grandmothers and grandfathers of the world, and the military of some of the other well-equipped nations, and deliver food, supplies and tools wherever people need those things." Ernestine proposes.

Her father, a powerful advisor to both the Joint Chiefs of Staff and the US President, is intrigued by this idea.

"You mean the whole Army is in logistics?" General Maxwell asks.

"Right. We find out what is needed and get those supplies in as quickly and efficiently as possible. That should keep our military busy for a while." Ernestine explains.

Maxwell Parker is a student of military history and knows that soldiers without enough to do invent wars to fight, often with their own people. Max also knows that until all military personnel can be trained and transitioned into other careers, they need something constructive to do with their time and resources.

"Otherwise, they will figure out some way to fight without human personnel, using weapons of mass destruction." General Parker reminds the President when he advises him on the IFE plan.

When Max is in touch with the leaders of each branch of the US Armed Forces, he finds that most would like nothing better than provide support for WWIII engagements. They are as sick to death of death and destruction as anyone, often more so, having seen the effects of war firsthand.

"Tell me why we need the grandmothers, again?" Head of the Joint Chiefs asks General Parker. "Won't people welcome us coming in with the food and materials they need?"

"Would you be happy seeing another nation's military units running around the USA?" Max responds. "Even if they were delivering food to the starving, I doubt Americans would stand for it. Why should any other nation?"

"Point taken, but what can we do? We have to get the food and tools to people in a reliable way and keep good records of what goes where."

"That's where the grandparents come in. We take our men and women out of uniform and have an elder along when they make a delivery. Fewer people will take offense at a stranger in the neighborhood if they are with grandma. More of the food and tools will get where they are supposed to go, too, with an elder as our guide."

"Sounds like a plan." the General responds.

"Do you think we can find enough personal in our armed services that speak the languages and know the customs of the country they are sent to?" Ernestine asks.

"Between the US military and the other UN nations who can help with this delivery system, we should be able to match the delivery crews to the nations getting the goods." Maxwell speculates. "The US army has men and women from every place on Earth, these days."

"The elders are already on site." Ernestine points out.

"I bet they are." General Max agrees as he recalls his own grandmother.

The world outside the rural community where Stella Mae Parker lived for ninety years never heard of her, but she was a healer and a mid-wife in her community. Her word was law when it came to health matters and a lot of other matters. The white people even listened to her.

"My grandma would have made a great contribution to that Grandparent Brigade." Maxwell admits. "Just let anyone try and stop her from getting food to women and children in need, or tools to those working on a community project. She would have half the town after them if they tried to interfere."

"How do we enlist the grandparents we need?" the Commander in Chief asks Max the next day at a meeting of the Joint Chiefs of Staff. "You can't exactly draft them."

"Already taken care of." Max assures the assembled representatives of the most powerful fighting force in the history of Planet Earth. "We have a meeting planned for women leaders from around the world. Each will identify local women who can recruit just the right people from each location. They will help us find elderly people who are respected and influential in their community. There's no way someone from outside can know or even guess who those elders might be."

It turns out that Stella Mae is not alone in her ability to help a community. Almost every place on the Planet has one or more elders who can take charge and make sure that deliveries of food and tools are made and that goods go where they are needed. They know the one to pay off if payoffs are necessary. They know the one to intimidate if that is needed and they also know how to blow the whistle for public response, if anyone seriously gets in the way of people getting what they require.

"We should have recruited grandparents into the Company." a shadowy character tells another, at a clandestine meeting, held in a back room of a palace of power, somewhere on the eastern seaboard. "They seem to know everything that's going on, and who's behind it, everywhere in the world."

"Never could have worked." another shadowy character answers. "Those grandparents wouldn't have let us get away with all we've been doing for the past 50 years. The Company would have been busted, faster than you can say Nana."

IT'S A WUNDERFUL COUNTRY

Books Wunder Jr. comes from a long line of con men, tricksters, and crooks. Books Sr. is the first one to admit to it, providing he is not trying to pull some kind of scam or swindle on you. Since the Wunder family steals only from the very rich, or cons vast sums of money and property out of large corporations and governments, Books Sr. always had plenty of friends listening when he tells the stories of his exploits.

His son's first memories of his father are the lavish parties his dad threw for other cons and crooks. These men and women, like Books Sr., enjoy living large and hate the idea of ever working for anything. They can party for days and spend hours sitting and listening to Books tell of his scams and cons. This is more of an education to Books Jr. than any school.

After the parties young Books also overhears his father talking to his Great Uncle Llyle. Both men berate some of the guests who, though rich as hell, do not gain their wealth by ingenuity or intrigue. They either get in on some kind of legitimate government subsidy program, or outright steal money or property from someone. The ones most despised are the characters whose jobs are considered legitimate but make millions in endeavors like the stock market or currency exchange.

"Just a day trader." Books Senior scoffs. "Might as well be a professional gambler. It doesn't take a lot of smarts to buy something and then chance it'll go up or down."

"How about that guy who just asked for money on his web site? How much smarts does that take?" Uncle Llyle sneers. "All right, so he made a couple hundred thousand bucks, but get creative, man!"

"It wasn't even illegal." Books Senior points out. "He didn't say what he wanted it for or promise to give people anything in return for their 'donation'. Begging for a living, that's what that was."

Uncle Llyle used to entertain Books Jr., for hours, with stories of the Wunder family's big deals of the past. The child's bedtime stories were about the kind of wheeling and dealing ways Wunders enriched themselves, scams that put Wunders at the top of their profession down through history.

"We never resort to force or violence." Uncle Llyle reminds his great nephew. "Useless waste of resources. The closest we'll go to selling weapons is to sell bombs that don't work to both sides in a war. You can call that our family contribution to world peace."

Great Uncle Llyle never mentioned how he got all his money, and it was not until after his death that Books Jr. discovers that Llyle did no more than be born into a rich family, for his bucks. Llyle's mother certainly had something to do with their fortunate circumstances, when she became pregnant with Llyle and got the heir to the PetroChem fortune to marry her. Llyle did help with that scam, before he was even born.

Uncle Llyle is not the first Wunder to help another member of the family out with a money-generating scheme. Wunders often work together to add to the family reputation and to their own personal fortunes. This is part of the reason that Wunders can pull off the many outrageous and creative cons that are the stuff of family legend. As often as they work together, members of the clan also try to outdo one another with each succeeding generation. Books Jr. wonders how he can possibly top the past cons of his Wunder ancestors.

"Got to learn to use the most important muscle in the human body, son." Books Sr. tells his boy. "That one between your ears. You use that brain of yours, Junior, and get good family support for your projects, you'll make the Wunders proud."

When Jr. is twelve years old, Books Sr. pulls a scam so big, it makes other Wunder ancestors look like they went straight and worked for a living, by comparison. Books Jr. is sure he will never be able to top his father's big con when, after The Message, Books Wunder Sr. invents a country, pronounces himself Head of State and declares it to be at war with three neighboring nations, two of which are also fictitious. This scam makes it possible for Books Sr. to take advantage of money and goods that flow from the United Nations War of Construction program, meant to bring about lasting, world peace.

"I want a piece of that." Books Sr. tells Uncle Llyle, as his son listens. "Warring Nations are invited to the UN to work out their conflicts and come to terms for a War of Construction over their disputed territories."

"Do tell." Llyle responds.

"I'm now the head of one of those nations and, as such, am supposed to rebuild the human cities, replant the forests and create sustainable farms in my country." Books Senior explains. "They're just handing out whatever I say I need to do that."

When Uncle Llyle grasps the concept that each warring faction will be given all the money, and all the materials and resources they want to rebuild their lands, he knows why Books Sr. cannot resist getting in on that action. Llyle agrees to help Books Sr. with the scam, even though both men see the enormous risks involved in such a venture.

"You're taking the biggest chance of your life here." Llyle warns his nephew.

"I can't let this kind of an opportunity pass me by. I wouldn't be able to live with myself." Books Sr. admits.

"Let me help." Llyle offers, feeling the same.

Books Sr. locates his fictitious nation in East Africa and calls it Watomba. He claims Watomba is at war with his neighbors; Somalia, East Lumbungo and the Kingdom of Ifi.

"Those Little African countries change their names every time they have a coup." Books Senior tells the two actors he hires to play delegates to the UN meeting, from the nations of East Lumbungo and Ifi.

"No one will figure out these places don't exist," He assures them "and Somalia has been at war with most of its neighbors for hundreds of years."

Books knows the delegate from Somalia will be far too involved in negotiations with Ethiopia, Kenya, and several islands off its coast, to pay attention to Watomba's claims to just three miles of its border.

Before they present themselves at the UN building for the peace talks, Books Sr. outfits himself and his two other "enemy" delegates in the most sumptuous flowing garments he can find. He adds a few fly whisks made from cow tail, a couple of faux cheetah skin caps and some substantial gold jewelry, to complete the picture. It is hard to tell them apart from many of the other African leaders, except those from socialist nations who are usually in military uniform.

"The whole thing was even easier than I imagined." Books Senior tells Uncles Llyle when he returns from the UN. "All the terms of combat I submitted for the War of Construction, are accepted."

The men collapse, helpless with laughter, at the size of the scam just pulled off. Then Uncle Llyle voices his only concern.

"How you gonna' collect? You can't have them send you money here, can you?"

"Most of these tiny nations keep a substantial portion of their national wealth in US banks, anyway. I just fill out these papers, tell them how much I want, and they deposit the money into an account I've opened here in New York City."

Assured that the funds they request are theirs for the taking, both men start to work on a realistic list of what they will request in the form of goods, supposedly to repair the damage of years of war and neglect visited on the nation of Watomba. By looking at other African nations they have plenty of problem scenarios to draw from.

"What you going to do with all these building materials and supplies?" Llyle asks "You obviously can't send them to people who don't exist."

"Got that covered." Books assured his uncle. "Watomba is landlocked, and its airport is a mess from years of fighting. We have all our supplies delivered to the nearest port of entry, in a neighbor nation, take the stuff from there and sell it to the highest bidder."

"Then what?"

"Then they sell it to sell to other people. It will route more supplies to Africa, where there is some of the greatest need on the Planet. I doubt anyone will notice they are getting a few more water treatment systems, more housing materials and more organic farm inputs than they ordered." Books Senior explains.

"We're lucky Watomba is so poor." Llyle notes "The kinds of things we're asking for can be used almost anywhere in the world that people are in need."

When they realize, they are starting to talk as though Watomba really exists, both men go into fits of laughter.

"I'm almost sorry this place isn't real." Books Sr. states wistfully. "We've come up with some great ideas here. With us running things, Watomba could be heaven on earth."

"Don't get carried away, Books." Llyle warns. "Your opposition in the conflict could do an even better job, win the support of the Watomban people, and put you right out of office."

Both men crack up laughing again.

Books Sr. laughs all the way to the bank when he receives his first installment, a seventeen million dollars payment to bolster the sagging Watomban economy and stabilize their currency, the Dinella, the coin of their realm named after the first lady of the nation, Dinella Watomba Mata.

Books Sr., the current Prime Minister and Commander in Chief of the Watomban armed forces, is known to the UN administration as Watsa Mata. According to his official UN biography, Watsa was born in a rural area of his nation, when it was still a colony of New Zealand, and was instrumental in the Watomban struggle for Independence. Watsa supposedly fled the country, when facing a jail term for inciting his people to revolt, and was educated in Des Moines, Iowa, USA, after entering the country on a student visa.

Watsa took his degree in computer programming and minored in international economics at the Toliver Business Academy, a private institution in downtown Des Moines. This explains Watsa's excellent English to any of the UN officials with whom he speaks.

Books Jr. observes the Watomba operation firsthand because, for a brief time, their home becomes the official Watomban Embassy and his Uncle Llyle the Watomban Secretary of the Treasury, as well as its Ambassador to the USA. Book's mom becomes the Embassy receptionist and Books Jr. pretends he is the Embassy security guard. No one gets into their official compound without the young man's scrutiny, and he is also put in charge of handling the embassy mail, to respond to those requesting visas to Watomba.

"It's an important job we're giving you son." Books Sr. tells his offspring. "You've got to write back to these people who want to visit Watomba and convince them they can't go there. God knows what we'd do if someone tried to find the place, couldn't, and then made a stink about it to someone at the US State Department. That could bring us to the attention of the UN. I can't think what we'd do if the United States decides to send us an Ambassador!"

Books Senior sidesteps that potential land mine by establishing a Watomba Consulate in the capital of the nearest, real African nation of Somalia. The Watomba Consular Officer there, Book's Cousin Freddie, gets in tight with the other Consular officers in Mogadishu by throwing lavish parties. Then he assures them that Watomba is not worthy of a diplomatic posting and that its Capital, Ratandu, is hell on earth.

Freddie's description of Ratandu, as a bastion of fundamentalist dogma, ruled with an iron hand by a band of Radical Unitarians who never let anyone have a bit of fun, helps assure that no one wants to even visit the place. They decline to mention Watomba in communications to their governments, either, in case they be considered for a transfer there. Books, Sr. also comes up with a formula for keeping out International Aide workers and Missionaries of various religions, when they request to either visit or work in Watomba.

"We tell them our own churches and other social service agencies are fully staffed by Watomban citizens and that outsiders need to look for work elsewhere. We refuse to give them work permits and send them phony letters from several, fake Watomba church and social organizations, to assure them we are taking care of our own in Watomba. We suggest they look for postings in other nations if they need a job."

"Why should we give people from other countries jobs to help us, anyway?" Ambassador Llyle agrees. "Let them help their own people."

"My thoughts exactly." Books, Jr. agrees. "We've got to protect our own in Watomba and keep our citizens fully employed."

The Wunders ability to emerge themselves so deeply into a scam is one of the reasons they have been so successful with their cons for generations. Their ability to come off as completely truthful, reliable, and sincere, while perpetrating the most outrageous frauds, often serves to protect them from detection.

The woman responsible for Books Wunder's undoing is an ex-Marine, Ms. Ernestine Patton Parker, who discovers their con when the materials requests, made on behalf of the Nation of Watomba, come to her attention. It is Ms. Ernestine who first realizes that there is no place like home if home is called Watomba.

As a former logistics officer in the US Marines, most of her military career is spent getting supplies to troops and civilians in every part of the world, at a moment's notice. After The Message, Ms. Ernestine coordinates the UN Food and Fuel Distribution Program barter system, to exchange food and materials all over the Planet.

"This country doesn't exist." Ernestine tells her boss, Lynda Preto. "No such place."

"Maybe they used to be called something else." Lynda comments. "We've been sending stuff there for months and nothing has come back to us as undeliverable."

"But why would they be requesting cotton candy-making machines?" Ernestine asks looking down the inventory of supplies the nation of Watomba has entered in the 'Vitally Essential' category of their request list.

"Says here that cotton candy is their national food." Lynda reads, under 'Reasons to Justify Request'. Watomba sounds like a fun place, to me."

"Fun or not, I'm getting on the horn to the National Geographic Society, to find out if Watomba has a place in physical reality on Planet Earth." Ernestine proposes.

It takes her a couple of days to confirm that it does not. Fortunately for the WW III effort, the Prime Minister of Watomba is making a State visit to Washington DC the week this is discovered. Watsa Mata, due to meet with the US President to discuss matters of trade, security, and cultural exchange between their two nations, is taken into custody shortly before he gets out in front of the White House Press Corps and the international news crews.

After consultation with the UN, it is decided that Books will have a speedy trial in The Hague, a zone to which most world citizens pay very little attention. More people know about the location of Watomba than know about the location of The Hague. Both UN and US officials want a quiet trial for Books Senior, alias Watsa Mata.

"A thing like this could ruin the public perception of the War of Construction." the US President comments, when told he is meeting with a delegation from the Navaho Nation, instead of the bogus Prime Minister of Watomba. "It could be mighty embarrassing to my Administration, as well."

"The Navaho have been around for more than ten thousand years." the President is assured by his Press Secretary, Llyla Prentice-Jones. "No chance of a legitimacy problem there."

Books is whisked off the White House grounds by helicopter and transported to The Hague. There he is tried for international fraud, charged with theft from the United Nations and the people of the world, of 1.3 billion dollars in funds and goods. He is also charged with wasting humanity's precious time with his nonsense. He faces a possible sentence of five years in prison and repayment of all moneys, with interest, as the penalty for the thefts. He faces a possible life sentence in jail for wasting humanity's time.

It should be said that Books Sr. puts up a brilliant defense on his own behalf. He even brings in a series of witnesses to testify they are Watomban citizens, and that Prime Minister Mata is their democratically elected leader. The team of brilliant, international prosecutors are hard-pressed to prove that no such nation exists.

"What does a nation have, a certificate that says it's real?" Books Sr. asks the somber panel of Judges hearing his case. "Everyone knows that Nations exist solely because other nations recognize that they do. Watomba was recognized by the UN, in the War of Construction, and we had diplomats from many Nations visit our

Consulate in Mogadishu. Those facts should be adequate proof of International recognition, for this court."

"But that land you say is Watomba is really part of Somalia." the Chief Prosecutor points out to Books. "How can you say it's your country?"

"That's why the territory was in dispute at the UN." Books counters. "I claim that land in the name of Watomba and the Watomban people."

Books figures if it worked for the Conquistadors, it could work for him. Then he adds:

"Everyone here knows that Somalia claims land all the way to Nairobi and halfway to the Mediterranean. Who rules most of the horn of Africa is in dispute now and has been for a couple of centuries? Why pick on Watomba as non-existent?"

Books plays his trump card when he gets the President of Somalia to appear in court to testify in support of his claim to the area.

"The area occupied by the nation of Watomba is undoubtedly the sorriest spot-on Earth." The Somali leader tells the Judges. "If this man wants it, he can have it. Perhaps he can do something with the barren soil, the starving people, and the dismal economy of the place. I have no idea how to help that forsaken spot. Let him try. I unconditionally surrender the Nation of Watomba to Prime Minister Mata."

After all this, it is hard to prove that Books is not legally within his rights to do exactly what he did, as a participant in the UN War of Construction. It is only the fact that he has no proof, whatsoever, that he has ever set foot inside the territory he calls Watomba, or anywhere near it, that finally convicts Books of a crime. The Court cannot buy him running a nation he has never been to.

Books Wunder Jr. is told about his dad's trial by his Great Uncle Llyle, who is deeply impressed by his nephew's ability to almost bring off the biggest scam in the history of Planet Earth. The old man is also deeply saddened by the trial verdict.

"They completely ruined the family when the Court sentenced your dad to a six-year term of actually running the Nation of Watomba." Llyle mourned. "Books Senior has to live there and use everything he got from the UN to improve that place."

"Why isn't that a good idea?" Books Jr. asks. "Dad had some great plans."

"No doubt he'll help Watomba," Uncle Llyle admits. "but that Court did the worse thing they could ever do to a Wunder. He's been sentenced to a fate worse than death!" Llyle cries, barely able to control his feeling of grief and shame. "They made him go legit!"

YO! MA'REE!

Applause for the women who just made their first Neighborhood score resounds in time to the hip-hop beat of a song created by Ma'Ree herself. It is the monthly motivational meeting of Ma's Mobile Regional Gangs and the room is packed with veteran Scorers and the Ma'Ree 'Virgins', as the less experienced members are called.

These new members dance up and introduce themselves to the group and get their "Shovel of Success" pin as a reward. Many look with envy at the gem-incrusted Shovel worn by the Top Regional Scorer, Polly Jean Columbus, as she hands them their jewelry. Polly Jean is a woman who can score.

Then Polly asks that those who score from $100 to $1000 a week come up for their special 'Score One For the Hood" sweat shirts; in special colors that reflected the amount of their take for the past week. Each leaves the stage after they introduce themselves and share how they made their biggest scores. There were a few innovative ideas mentioned that bring a buzz of comment and applause from the audience, as members recognized a new opportunity they had not considered before. New ideas shared at these meetings are one reason the turnout for Ma'Ree gatherings is always good.

"We'll be passing out Star Scorer Prizes a little later tonight. I'm really excited about some of the amazing Scores created this month, and when our top Scorer shares some of the secrets of her success, you will be, too!" Polly Jean adds before she turns the microphone over to the evening's presenter, Mary Ellen Motang.

The group applauds as Mary Ellen takes the microphone from Polly. She is known personally to many of those in the room and is an inspiration to most. It is said that Mary Ellen can teach a blind man how to see and when it got out that she would instruct Members in more ways to "Score some Makeovers for their Hoods", many show to the meeting to get that dope from a master.

"Rumor has it that she gives Ma'Ree tips." October Mandalay tells Rosemary Retro, next to her.

"I'm taking notes," Rosemary responds. "and she's about to start."

"I'd like to thank you all for coming out tonight," Mary Ellen begins. "With special thanks to new members who just shared their neighborhood scores with us."

The room gets quiet. "I'd also like to thank so many veteran Scorers, here tonight to share their scores and help with the special challenges our newcomers will share with us, now." Mary Ellen continues. "They probably feel hopeless about the state their hood is in, but Ma'Ree's gang can help find solutions for those problems and score the funds to pay for those solutions. What's our motto?"

"If we don't put in the time, we don't get the dime!" is the resounding call from the gathered crowd.

"Remember, if you want to Guarantee success, Ma'Ree K's 1-2-3 plan is the perfect model to follow. Now, what are the three steps to success in any plan?"

"One – ID the problem." Belly Pedersen calls from the back of the room.

"Two – Find out who benefits from the status quo, and how they can get more from a positive change." Sun Yee Mato speaks out from the first row.

"Three- Make a plan, identify its cost and find a funding source!" the group thunders in unison.

"So, let's get started!" Mary Ellen exclaims. "We've asked our new members to fill out a simple problem identification form."

She holds up a pink document and folds back its top page to reveal another page under it as new members pour over their forms and check boxes where they identify a need.

"If you turn that problem page, you'll find a list on the next that shows where you can look to score funding. This is just a starting point, and your personal sponsor will set up an individual planning appointment to help you find other ways to score for your area. Sound exciting? Let's get started with a problem and see how we can score with it. We'll find a simple solution that will bring dramatic results. Who wants to share first?"

Winnie Richardson waves her pink form in the air and shouts. "Me, please!"

Mary Ellen takes her form and looks it over. She smiles broadly as she shares, "Big problems mean big opportunities to score, and this hood got game."

Members laugh and applaud in response to the presenter's comments and then get quiet as she continues.

"Winnie has a neighborhood that is built on an old toxic dumpsite. Some really amazing goo is starting to seep through into the backyards and up under the foundations of many of the homes. Sounds like a real mess. Ideas anyone?"

"SuperFund money, if they want the site cleaned up." Polly Jean calls out.

"Tiger Preservation Project Human Relocation Program funds, if they want to leave that place." Rosemary Jamdun interjects.

"National Institute of Science funds, if they want to try new technology to clean up the site." October Mandaly shares.

"How about a Return to the Earth funding grant, if your hood decides they want to use organic systems to clean up, and then allow the place to return to the Wild when it's been made safe again?" Mary Ellen adds.

Winnie looks overwhelmed by the possibilities to remedy a situation she though hopeless, only a moment before.

"You're noticing four ways you might get resources together to score a solution for this problem. Don't you love it? Think of the chance for change and the piece of change you'll make for writing that grant application? What an opportunity to score!"

Winnie Richardson smiles broadly and waves her pink sheet as the group applauds and she sits down.

"I'm excited." Mary Ellen shares. "Makes me want to go out and find some neighborhood of my own with a toxic site nearby. Now, I'm going to share what we call a 'booster' to make those plans for constructive change happen even faster."

All ears in the room are tune to what this veteran Super – Scorer has to say. These are the ideas that help her score funds equal to the GNP of some nations and pay Mary Ellen commissions far above the salary of most Heads of State, including the US President.

"Declare War." Mary Ellen whispers into the microphone.

There are some blank stares from the troop, so she explains.

"Most places built on radioactive waste, or toxic junk of some kind, are places where poor folks are forced to live. The dumps are put underground by either the US military or some big industry, so you just declare war on the military-industrial complex. That gets you what kind of funding? Let me hear it?"

"United Nations War of Construction funds!" screams Parneth Matthews, from the back of the room.

"Score one for that woman." Mary Ellen responds. "The UN not only supplies technical assistance and advice, but they will also allocate whatever money, manpower or resources needed to do the job, immediately. One stop score, no waiting."

There is a buzz of excited comment from the group and Mary Ellen adds. "Of course, this score is for big, life-threatening problems, like the one Winnie has, but doesn't it feel good to think about what can be done? Are you as excited about this as I am?"

Mary Ellen looks out over the hopeful faces of the women in the room and can see they are jazzed. Her audience clearly has a real buzz on from the possibility of scoring on funding grants they know will fill needs in their home areas and will help the Planet, too. She doubts any of them will sleep that night, as they stay awake figuring out ways to solve the many problems humans face, for cities all over Planet Earth to become sustainable places for humans to live.

"For smaller problems; the kind most of us find in our Neighborhoods, think of yourself as the one who can score to make those things happen. Someone needs to get funding for families in need of food or shelter, for more money for our schools and to set up organic food processing centers. That fundraiser may as well be you."

Newcomers to the troop look incredulous as Mary Ellen adds, "After you've scored on a few projects you'll see how easy it is and most times the bigger the project, the easier it is to score the funds."

Ma'Ree's gangs are often referred to as the first line of finance for those Neighborhoods with the greatest need. Wealthy philanthropists, who want to give money away where it can do some real good for a change, are great supporters of Ma'Ree Gang projects. They know her members are in sync with what goes on in their 'hood and that they request funds for projects their whole Neighborhood gets behind.

"The best money I ever spent." Bigwheel Biggs says of the bucks Lomita Powell scores for the restoration of a creek going through the Neighborhood where he was born and raised. "I spent half my childhood in that creek and it about broke my heart when they channeled it and paved it over. I was glad to give those funds."

Lomita cleared a cool thirty thousand, as her one percent commission on that project. She also got fresh fish to eat when the critters returned to the creek, after it was opened to the air and cleaned up.

More stories like Lomita's are shared as the Ma'Ree Super-Scorers get up to tell tales of projects that earned them the stones that fill their Shovel pins – rubies for some, sapphires for others and emeralds and diamonds for a not a few. In total, the Regional members score over sixteen million dollars for projects in their area, in the past month. That was $160,000 in commissions for their scores, with one percent of their commission funds going to Ma'Ree's organization, to pay for their meetings and support services.

"Top Scorer Prize goes to Belly Pedersen of Neighborhood 7, District 7 of the Mobile Urban Center." Mary Ellen announces. "Belly also gets our Award for special Scores that include more homeless people in her projects than anyone else in the Region. Belly, come up and tell us what you've done this month and share your scoring secrets!"

Belly Pedersen is given a standing ovation as she takes center stage. The tips she shares are simple and straightforward.

"Find a need and then find the best way to fill it. That's what those shovels are for." Belly states. "If you are clear about what you need, you just keep asking until you score a funding answer. It works every time."

"What projects did you score on?" cries out October Mandalay. Belly is Mandalay's personal Scoring Sponsor and every month they work together she learns new ways to score.

"No one project is that big but combined they will make a big difference." Belly informs the listening women. "There is a renovation project, where two homes will be remodeled to create a third living unit. The project is coordinated by Habitat International and uses the labor of some homeless folks who will be living in the newly created third home. Part of their mortgage payments will go to the two other homeowners, seniors on fixed incomes, who can use the extra cash. That project was financed through a conventional bank that paid me a loan finder's fee for my involvement."

Murmurs of interest are heard throughout the room, as people recognize that almost every Neighborhood needs to expand its numbers of affordable housing units. They see that they can try such a plan to do it.

"Don't you love it?" Mary Ellen calls out. "Share more, Belly. This is really exciting."

"We also got Urban renewal funds for an organic waste treatment center and a water catchment pond." Belly tells the group. "That means we build a wetland area and do a gray water feed to it through a system of gravel filters. It cleans the junk out of the water and makes it safe to use in our gardens."

There is a shower of applause for that one as Scorers realize that almost every Neighborhood needs more clean water.

"We got FEMA funds for flood control for that water project, too." Belly adds. "Ponds like this help reduce flooding for the whole area when it rains."

There is an excited buzz from the crowd as they comment on the multiple sources of support for such needed work.

"Then there's the bees." Belly shares. "We got funds from the Department of Agriculture to start hives to support our local pollinator population, and to make honey for the local human population."

The buzz of her audience, in response to that score, tells Belly that more Neighborhoods will be doing the same, soon.

"The shortage of bees to pollinate crops makes this kind of program a necessity in most locations." Belly confirms. "I actually had several funding agencies come to me, to offer us money to start raising bees in 7&7. One was our local, Urban Food Production Program and the other was the Human Resources Employment Office. The funding grant I got them last year, to start a BeeKeeper training class, has students graduating soon. Those trained beekeepers need Neighborhoods to work in. Go to either of those agencies if you want bucks for bees at your local."

"Last but not least, we got a grant from the International Broadcasting Corporation to do a Youth Home Repair and Gardening Show for TV. Our 7 & 7 Neighbors decided to let Youth do our Home Repair Show productions, from now on. The adults in the Neighborhood don't have near as much fun with home and garden fix-ups as the kids do, so the shows are a lot funnier, and are more fun to watch, when our Youth produce them."

"That brought your Neighborhood total to over $500,000 dollars, in investments for Neighborhood improvements, employment generating activity and environment protection, not to mention the production of significant laughter and some useful home and garden information from your kids." Mary Ellen calls out. "What a difference some great ideas and a little money makes, when scored for the right projects! Let's hear it for Belly and the whole 7&7 Neighborhood. They all help put together these great plans for positive change!"

Scorers are on their feet for a standing ovation as Belly takes a bow. She holds her hands up for silence and the group quiets to hear her closing remarks.

"I'd like to say thanks to Ma'Ree K, for changing the focus, from makeovers for women to makeovers for our Planet. It is this kind of salesmanship and go-get-it attitude that built the MK cosmetics empire, one customer at a time. It's the use of these techniques that allow us to score the funds we need to save our Planet, one Neighborhood at a time."

"Ma'Ree always tells her followers 'I'm not in this for the money.'" Mary Ellen sums up. "These days our leader says her wealth comes from another sources, a healed Earth and a more stable world. Money can't buy that!"

"Ma'Ree! Ma'Ree! Ma'Ree!" members chant as they end their meeting dancing, clapping, and making all kinds of joyful noise.

BUILDING

Curious One Pau is feeling very frustrated, as are all the people of his village. They were taken from their homes in South China and relocated to the mountains of Tibet, there because the Chinese government must repair a monastery it previously destroyed as part of the Liberation of Tibet from its ancient ways.

Not only are the Gon Han villagers unused to the cold climate of the mountainous country, the unfamiliar foods of Tibet, and the general barrenness of the alien landscape; they are also extremely frustrated in their work as artists. Each night, since their arrival, the work they do that day crumbles to dust, reduced to a pile of rubble by the next morning.

"We do our best work each day, then find it in a million pieces at sunrise." Curious One's father explains to Area Commander Tui, sent to find out why there is no progress in the restoration of the one, small temple the Communist government is tasked to restore, under the terms of their WW III engagement with The Lama's Tibetan government in exile.

Tui is sent to investigate the reasons for their inability to repair the monastery they must rebuild. Despite their army of artists working on the monastery, they are losing the battle.

"Delays in rebuilding this monastery are beyond our control." the group's leader informs Tui. "If you don't believe me, see for yourself."

"I will." Area Commander Tui promises. "When I discover you are all lying, look forward to long prison terms as punishment."

"Is that a promise?" more than one of the artists thinks.

"At least when we do our artwork in jail, it won't disappear the next day." Glorious Pearl comments. "Our art is our life and the situation here is intolerable. I'm eighty-five years old and I don't have the time to waste on this battlefront."

"The Tibetan people have already rebuilt half the monasteries in the nation?" Area Commander Tui screams. "All we have is this one, small building to reconstruct and it looks as though you've not done a thing! What's the problem?"

"Problems, Respected Area Commander. Have a look at the photos of how this place looked in the past." Curious One's father entreats, as the spokesperson for them all. "You'll begin see what we're up against."

Commander Tui accepts a set of photos of the Monastery, taken before its destruction. The pictures show simple architecture with decorations painted on the walls and carved woodwork covering the pillars and ceilings.

"Nothing here is beyond your ability." Tui barks.

"Your people refurbished the Imperial Palaces. This is a simple task compared to that undertaking." he adds, as he hands the photos back to the artist.

"Now look at the photos again." Curious One's father responds, returning the pictures to Area Commander.

When Tui glances through the photos a second time none of them look at all familiar. They appear to be for a completely different structure. He does not believe his eyes and shuffles through the photos several more times, still never seeing the same view more than once.

"What is this?" Tui screams. "It's impossible! How can you restore anything if the photos are never the same?"

"That is the least of our problem." Glorious Pearl Chu points out. "No matter what we do, it's dust the next morning. Whether we paint a picture of the Buddha or one of Mickey Mao, nothing survives the night."

Area Commander Tui is not a stupid man. He knows when he is in over his head and that he must consider these problems well before he makes his report on the restoration project to his higher ups. A report that sounds this crazy can ruin a man's career.

"I leave you, now. Take a day off and relax. You folks all look pretty tense. I'll get back to you." he promises and leaves with the photos to have another look at them and think the problem over.

The artists of Gon Han Village are relieved for a number of reasons. Many feared they would be shot for non-performance of duty. Others feared losing their mind, trying to perform their duty. This is their first holiday since they arrived at the Morning Star Monastery three months ago and everyone is happy to have a day off to think about something besides their duty.

"The Lama said we'd need more than skill to rebuild this place." Curious One's Mother tells her son as she prepares a picnic lunch for the family to take with them to a nearby waterfall.

"Who's The Lama?" Curious One inquires.

"Religious guy." the boy's mother answers. "He used to run things here in Tibet, before we liberated it."

"What did he say we need?"

"He said these temples were built by the human spirit and must be rebuilt by the human spirit."

"Ghosts?" the child asks in wide-eyed wonder.

"Not exactly. Stop asking so many questions, or I'll never get our lunch together." she warns.

The kid shuts up. He is excited about their trip to the waterfall, having seen it from afar. Rock walls riddled with caves frame the fall that courses over a high cliff. Curious One, true to his name, wonders what is in those caves and goes to find out, heading straight up the hillside as soon as they arrive.

When Curious One reaches the nearest cave, he yells into it and makes its emptiness chime like a big bell. The child continues on, looking inside cave after empty cave, until he finds one with a painting on its rock wall that looks like a big wheel with a heart in the middle of it.

Curious One enters the cave for a closer look at the only completed work of art seen since their arrival at the Morning Star Monastery. The mural appears as though it has been there for a long, long time.

"Nice, huh?" Curious One hears as he stands studying the decoration.

The child turns to see an old man with a very big smile, who nods and grins as he approaches. The man is dressed as a Buddhist Monk, in robes that are currently against the law to wear in Tibet. Fortunately, the fashion police are not in the Neighborhood to arrest him.

"How does it stay here?" Curious One asks, never one to beat around the bush.

"It has been here since the start of time." the Old Man answers.

"When was that?" Curious One asks.

Having heard that people keep time he always wanted to know where time was before people kept it.

"When All That Is came out of the Nothing." the Old Man answers.

"Is that what this picture shows?"

"Good eye, kid. You must be a scientist. This picture shows where the material world is attached to all that is not. Sort of a belly button for the Universe as we know it. I think scientists these days call them strings, loops, or some such."

"Why does it look like a heart?" Curious One wonders.

"Because it is a heart." the Old Man answers. "Our hearts are what create a world that matters here. They allow us to have relationship with other that creates our material world."

"That's the spirit!" Curious One recalls his Mother's words.

"You are gooood." The Old Man laughs. "You must be an artist, too, and see things clearly to create Beauty."

"Why does it matter what I create?" Curious One asks. "All we make here disappears."

"Everything created appears and disappears all the time." the Old Man points out. "That's part of the loop deal. Why should that matter to you?"

"Our work should last longer than a few hours." Curious One points out. "How can it teach anything, like this picture does, if what we create goes away so fast?"

"All things humans do, have done or will do, are accomplished and are gone in an instant of galactic time." the Old Man points out. "It's no big bang, what mankind accomplishes here."

"What about this?" Curious One asks, pointing to the painting again. "How can we make art like this?"

"Ah!" the Old Man exclaims. "You mean remaking your world through the heart? Creating from the spirit? Having relationship with what you create? Yes, that is something with a bit more substance to it. It matters, so to speak. Humans do it well. Would you like to do that?"

"If it helps us get this monastery built, so we can go home?" Curious One responds.

He hears what winters are like in Tibet, a place where summer seems like winter to the people of his South China village. Curious One wants to be long gone from the place before winter comes.

"Monastery, world, whatever… You can make anything you want." the Old Man promises.

"How?"

"I'll tell you how, but you have to practice it. The more you do so the better you'll get at it."

"Tell me." Curious One agrees.

The Old Man first asks Curious One to think about something that saddens or worries him or about anything that makes him feel angry, fearful, or upset.

"Then breath that thing right inside you until it goes right to your heart."

"If I don't like it, why would I want it in my heart?" Curious One asks. "Shouldn't I get as far away from it as possible?"

"If you run from what you fear you will never work to transform it."

"How can I change it?"

"You can change your own idea of it by cherishing it and surrounding it with love, illuminating it with your caring concern. When you breathe that idea out you are newly transformed, releasing new ideas to the world."

"Breathe in what you don't want and breathe out what you do want?" Curious One asks, not sure he has it straight.

"That's it." the Old Man agrees. "You'll change anything you don't care for by caring about it. It's really quite simple."

"Can I make a picture that way?" Curious One hopes, eyeing the wall.

"You can make a universe that way." the Old Man assures him. "A picture should be a snap."

"Good." Curious One says. "Then maybe we can finish up this monastery and head South."

"You must do that." the Old Man tells Curious One. "That's what I came to tell you today. You should finish here and go on to Beijing to attend school there. You are to become a scientist of great reputation and will go to live in another country, far from China. All around you will listen to you and will respect your opinion enormously."

"Me?" Curious One asks. "Why me?"

"Because you must give permission one day." The Old Man answers as he heads for the door. "But don't worry about that now. It is not time for it to make sense. You won't even remember at all, 'till that time comes."

"Why won't I?" Curious One asks.

"Because you have a monastery to rebuild and a world to remake. Have fun doing that," the Old Man calls, as he reaches the cave opening. "and be kind."

Curious One runs for the cave entrance but cannot spot the Old Man on the cliffs outside once he reaches the opening. He sees his parents below, calling for him, and Curious One races down the cliff path, excited about what just happened.

"I've found a way to make our work last!" he exclaims.

When asked for specifics, Curious One cannot explain the process as clearly as the Old Man did, but his father is willing to give the boy the benefit of the doubt. Truth told; he is willing to try anything to finish their project.

"You probably have to be some kind of Holy Guy to explain it." his father admits. "But that doesn't mean we shouldn't try it. We meet tomorrow and you can show us."

The next day all the artists gather at a monastery wall, newly constructed that morning, upon which Curious One will paint.

"First you think of whatever you are concerned or afraid about, or anything that makes you really sad or mad." Curious One tells the watching artists. "Then you breathe that in, until it goes right to your heart."

"What?" Glorious Pearl Chu asks. "I try to ignore or forget things I don't like. Then I try to make myself believe they don't really exist."

"If you don't spend a lot of energy denying what's real you can spend that energy transforming it, right there in your heart. Then you let that new idea come out."

"Transform it?" Curious One's mother asks, curious herself.

"Into love, light, the best it can be…. to another idea about that thing…. whatever works best for you. Then you breathe that out."

"How?" Curious One's father asks, in favor of such a positive idea in theory but being a practical guy, curious about the mechanics involved.

"It comes out in your art." Curious One answers.

"Show us how." Glorious Pearl requests. "We'll see if it lasts more than 12 hours. Maybe this is how artwork needs to be done here."

Some suspect that this is how life needs to be done, here and elsewhere, too, so all watch with interest as Curious One begins to use this new approach and some paint, to apply the technique.

The child easily identifies his fears when it begins to snow. Curious One's concerns about the Tibetan winter fill his mind and he breathe of them deeply. Then he breathes out. Then he breathes in deeply, again. Then he smiles, breathes out and starts to paint. As Curious One paints, he sighs deeply from time to time and a painting of a glowing fire flows from his brush.

He works quickly, with intense concentration, and the image of a *Garuda*, the ancient symbol for reincarnation, emerges. The child's rendering of the Phoenix, as it rises from the ashes of death, is masterful—as though painted by spirit and not by the hand of a small child.

"From death comes a new beginning, as life comes forth again and again from the eternal fire." Curious One explains. "What seems like death, like winter, is just a pause for regeneration before new life begins. The winter is needed for the world's re-creation each Spring."

"We would have no Spring without winter. Both are needed." Curious One admits. "I guess winter is not so bad, after all."

Curious One works on the wall for many hours and those who watch him speak many truths. Some of them began to breathe, as the boy is doing, and to think of what they fear and dread and take those ideas to heart. As they transform the thoughts into better ideas, they get busy and begin to build, carve, and decorate other sections of the new wall. When they stop at sunset, they have completed one wall of the monastery. By that time, the artists no longer care if their artwork disappears the next day, or not.

"Everything disappears, eventually." they all agree, happy to have seen their painting and to experience the joy of their creations, even for a day.

"How do we know the artwork in this monastery ever lasted longer than a day, even before we arrived? Maybe that's how art works here." they tell one another.

"It remains to be seen if it all turns to rubble tonight." Curious One's mother remarks. "If so, we must teach Area Commander Tui this method to transform his anger and fear, or this project will be his undoing."

"The Old Man told me anyone can use this method in whatever work they do." Curious One assures his mom. "Whatever their work all can keep making and remaking their world for the better, even our government officials."

"I still hope it lasts." Curious One's father admits. "It's our best work yet and if it's still here at sunrise we can do more of it."

No one sleeps very well that night and at the sound of the first rooster's crow, the Gon Han Villagers leap from their beds to brave the snowy cold and rush to the temple building. The wall with Curious One's painting at its center is still there. The light from the rising sun seems to ignite the colors of the Phoenix' fire that glows with a warmth that comforts them as they huddle together in the chilly morning, shivering but happy.

"One problem." Area Commander Tui points out as he walks in, pleased to see a wall and something on it, but concerned about the wall's appearance. "This wall is not shown in any of the photos you gave me. You are supposed to make this temple the way it was before, and it never had the likes of this on its walls."

Area Commander pulls out the photos of the temple and hands them to Curious One's father, who flips through the pictures, greatly concerned they might have to destroy the only art their group has managed to produce.

"Here it is!" Curious One's father exclaims, holding the photo aloft for all to see. "We both must have missed this one." he adds to appease Commander Tui.

He does not recall ever having seen an image of a Phoenix in the photos, either, but Curious One's father suspects that the temple, itself, does not want to be as it was in the past. He feels it needs to be recreated and that this will cause the photos to change until they reflect its best possible future.

"We're all ready to start work, today." he tells Tui, hopefully. "We have good ideas to begin to rebuild in the best way possible."

"Get on with it, then." Area Commander Tui barks and leaves before he is presented with anything more, he cannot explain or understand.

The artists get busy and are soon breathing new life into the temple they recreate. Fortunately, the wonderful visions they make remain and are mirrored in the photos of the temple at its best.

"What happens when everything is the best it can be?" Glorious Pearl whispers to Curious One. "I'm curious about what we do once we create all that our hearts' desire here."

Pearl has seen a lot in her day but the idea that a world can be creatively transformed, that it is a living work of art, is a new way of thinking for her. She is not sure what comes next once that job is done.

Curious One shares, "The Old Man told me, when our job is done here, we move on."

FREEMONT AND THE TOMATO MILLIONAIRES

When Mobile Urban Center decides to become as self-sufficient in food production as possible, its citizens set about planning ways to grow and raise their own food within the city limits. They soon recognize the Mobile financial district as an ideal location for growing tomatoes; with the banking houses, its Stock Exchange, the Commodities Market and the big investment and insurance companies all situated where the air, soil and rainfall can produce some of the best tomatoes on Planet Earth. Unfortunately, very large skyscrapers are built in the middle of that ideal tomato patch and the only things being cultivated there are wealth, power, and influence.

"I like tomatoes as much as the next guy." Adriano "Wheeler" Fabriani, one of Mobile's leading financiers, tells the Urban Food Production Program staff. "I just hope you don't expect me to grow them."

They are meeting to identify what is expected of the 'suits' at the Mobile Stock Exchange and their wheeler-dealer counterparts in the finance houses of Mobile's commercial district. The men and women of Mobile's money world send Adriano to the meeting because he puts business first and tolerates nothing that will interfere with the bottom line.

"You want money? It's yours." Adriano promises. "The market is booming, or should I say blooming, since this Message thing. Cleaning up the Planet is making more work and more business, for more people in more places, than anything since humans harnessed electric power. We can certainly afford to give you whatever financial help you need to grow food."

"Unless someone has figured out how to eat money, stocks, bonds or securities, we'll take a pass on that offer." Faith Leonardo, the UFP coordinator, tells Adriano. "We want tomatoes. We don't care if you personally grow them or not. We just want them grown in the financial district, to help feed the city. If our estimates of yield are correct, we could also export them to help feed northern Population Centers during the winter months."

"What about all the buildings here?" Adriano asks. "Won't they get in the way?"

"This location is ideal." Faith explains. "If we were silly enough to turn good farmland into skyscrapers, that does not change the fact that the sun and soil here are just right for a bumper tomato crop. Your District just needs to add water and seeds."

"There's plenty of natural fertilizer around." Adriano admits. "It's been a bull market for months. Unfortunately, the only things grown in this Neighborhood are portfolios. None of us knows a thing about raising anything except interest rates."

"You're smart people." Faith tells the stockbroker. "I believe you can do anything you set your mind to. You say you can't grow tomatoes here? Find someone who can."

The last person in Adriano's family who might have had a clue about raising tomatoes would have been his great, great grandmother. She died decades before her descendant is faced with this agricultural challenge. Adriano does not even know anyone who might know anyone who might know how to grow a tomato. He knows only one man who even looks like someone who could or would do such a thing. That one man is Freemont Jackson, the small brown guy who is the clerk at the Quickie Market, located in the Mobile Stock Exchange building.

"I'll ask Freemont to find us someone to grow them." Adriano proposes.

It is true that most of the people who grow, and harvest food do look like Freemont and his family. When Adriano's family lived and worked in Italy, generations before the financier's birth, his family members, brown from the sun, looked a lot like Freemont. They were the ones growing things then. Contrary to appearances, Freemont's ancestors were not.

Freemont comes from Tiger Country and his ancestors were hunters and gatherers. They grew nothing and lived by their harvest of the Rain Forest's bounty, which Tigers were kind enough to share with them. Luckily, Adriano does not know a thing about Freemont's past and approaches the Quickie Market Clerk to enlist his help.

Freemont knows nothing about growing tomatoes, but he is able to see an opportunity to help more than the food supply, when one presents itself. Freemont realizes that this Tomato Project is a way to grow financial stability for the world's micro-economies and that most people on the Planet need economic opportunity as much as they need tomatoes.

Freemont can also see that members of the Mobile business community are more likely to become sharecropping dirt farmers than share their access to the world of finance with those most in need. They, like most people with wealth, either do not know that people in need exist or do not have a clue how to help them. Most are too busy making money to worry about such things at all.

"No problem," Freemont tells Adriano. "I'll take care of it for you. I'm an expert."

"Get whatever you need to plant the seed." Adriano tells Freemont when the clerk accepts the job as Tomato Project coordinator. "Let my Assistant know what money or help you want, to get things growing."

"OK." Freemont assures the financier. "I know I can find any number of men and women who would like to grow with the tomatoes."

"Grow tomatoes." Adriano corrects him.

"We'll take care of it." Freemont promises. "Don't give it another thought."

Adriano happily puts the whole thing out of his mind, once he sees a sign posted for a meeting of the Tomato Project team. It is a meeting worth attending but neither Adriano nor any other member of the Stock Exchange show up, just as Freemont hopes. He does not want the powers that be around while he educates Tomato Growers about the stock and bond market instead of the farmer's market, as they expect.

What Adriano and others like him do not expect is that Freemont knows more about the Stock Exchange than he does about tomatoes. He learned by watching the stock market, the currency exchange, and commodities markets, while on his job at the Quickie Market. Freemont observes the flow of the river of money on a Stock Exchange video monitor, installed in the convenience store so brokers will linger there longer and buy stuff.

Freemont watches the world of finance on that video screen, asks questions of the brokers who come in and draws on their expertise and knowledge. He gets the story behind the numbers he sees flowing by and that information causes him great concern. Freemont sees big problems in the current money flow. Though the river of wealth waters global change in both the developed and the developing world, it follows a very uneven course.

"I see trouble." Freemont points out to his wife, Betsy Ross Jackson, when he tells her about the Tomato-growing offer. "It appears that some people have built large dams for their wealth. They are collecting more and more money and resources there. If nothing changes, they will eventually turn the world into a desert, and drown themselves in their own excess."

"You'd better do something, then." Betsy Ross tells Freemont. "You've always been a problem-solver in our Tiger Country community. I expect no less of you now."

"The Tomato Project is the just chance I need to help." Freemont tells his wife. "I am not about to let my inability to grow tomatoes stop me from accepting Adriano's offer."

"I want to make sure you all understand the full scope of this job." Freemont tells people at the first meeting of Tomato Growers. "I am looking for people from many parts of the world who are smart, who like to learn, who like helping others and who would like to help as many people as possible make money."

There are some puzzled looks from those who think they are there to grow vegetables in the newly constructed roof gardens and window boxes on the Financial District buildings.

"I am going to teach you about the river of money. You can use that knowledge to make money for yourself and others. If money is of no interest to you, you'll be bored to death here. You should leave, now."

Freemont translates what he says into Spanish and Portuguese for the Mexican, Central and South Americans, into Chinese for the Chinese and into French for the Vietnamese, Cambodian, West African and Caribbean members at the gathering. Freemont could have translated his speech into Tiger and Eagle so human language variations are easy for him. Once his message is clear, about two dozen people of the sixty people get up and go.

Then Freemont adds. "It's good if you know how to grow tomatoes, too, but that is not important. We can easily get instructions from tomato-growing experts for that job. You are really here to learn to be financial advisers- to learn what's needed to make money for yourself and for people like you, all over the world."

In any language, Freemont's remaining audience is interested. Even though they are sitting in a conference room at the Mobile Stock Exchange, where some of them work cleaning windows, offices or as security guards, most never imagined getting a chance to learn how the Exchange actually operates to make money.

"You mean the man is going to let us reap and sow here?" Harold 'Wup-ass' Greer asks.

Harold is a graduate of the University of Alabama Department of Economics but is unable to get an internship or an entry-level position with any of Mobile's finance houses after his graduation. Those jobs go to graduates from Ivy League schools or to young men with relatives on the Exchange, not to folks like Harold. He is working as a security guard at the Stock Exchange and, to add insult to injury, is fired from this job shortly after The Message.

"People are too busy doing legal things to engage in crimes so, other than flood, fire, or act of God, there is no longer a need to employ me there as a guard." Harold tells Freemont the day he turns in his badge.

Freemont knows Harold will be an excellent Tomato Grower and makes a special point of inviting the ex-guard to join their team to grow financial options for small business investors. Harold is overjoyed at the prospect and also has some actual gardening experience under his belt. With his understanding of how the stock exchange works and his ability to produce a good organic tomato, Harold is soon voted Project Foreman by the other Growers.

Though he is well educated, Harold bows to Freemont's ability to make the very complicated world of finance easily understandable to the other team members. When Freemont likens the flow of wealth to the large river that bisects Tiger Country, this image is one that they understand on many levels. They have all experienced, firsthand, the desertification of their native environment. All come from places that have been drained dry, both environmentally and financially, by globalization and corporate greed. Each knows what it is to have no drop of relief in a land where others hold and kept much of the natural and man-made wealth before they send large amounts of it somewhere else for safekeeping.

"The way that river flows away from them and their nation is why most of you folks are here in the USA."

Freemont points out to the class. "You follow your nation's wealth here."

"How can we stop that drain of human and financial resources?" Harold asks. "Can people like us help?"

"We can help, and we must help." Freemont tells his students. "If we don't help the river becomes clogged with the destruction it creates as it flows and it eventually stops flowing. If that happens it backs up until it drowns all that are behind this ruination. The flood will overpower and destroy both the wealthy and the poor."

"How can we help?" Harold wonders aloud. "Most of us have nothing. Or as close to nothing as you can get."

"We must help grow new tributaries, dig new channels for wealth, nurture new and growing options for the tiny flow of money that we do have." Freemont explains. "This will help that vast river move in ways the wheelers and dealers cannot imagine. The wealthy will benefit as much as anyone, but I doubt they can do this without our aid."

Freemont outlines a plan for the Growers to develop investment options for micro-businesses. Their job is to identify small industry, shops, and service providers, to give them the financing they need to expand, through sale of part of their business to small investment groups. Group investors are often from their own community or from a like community elsewhere in the world.

"By pooling the resources of thousands of small investors, we can reduce the risk to each individual and allow citizens to profit from a real business, in their own Neighborhood or Urban Center." Freemont explains. "We help people grow with their own, local economy and I'm sure we can grow some great tomatoes, too."

So begins a program that helps people, from each cultural, ethnic, and social community in Mobile, to train as financial advisors and investment consultants to their own. When word gets out about the District 5 Tomato Project, more Growers apply for similar training. No one is turned away.

"We must train Growers for work in other cities, besides this one." Freemont explains. "We must spread out and teach others, in every urban center in the USA, and then move out to other human population centers around the world. Some Growers will return to the lands of their ancestors, to help grow new economies there."

❋ ❋ ❋ ❋

Three months after the project starts, Adriano sees *Roma* tomato plants and vines of cherry tomatoes growing past his twenty-seventh-floor office window. He completely forgot about the tomatoes and none of the other brokers give their food-supply responsibilities much thought, either. The Tomato Project carries on quite well without them because their Growers are hard at work. When District 5 is identified as a model food production program, Adriano knows who should get the credit for their much-praised efforts.

"Freemont and his people are doing a hell of a job." Adriano comments to a meeting of Brokers, as the fragrance of tomato plants fills the room.

"We sure can't take credit for a thing." Adriano admits before he moves on to the next topic on their agenda. "What more do we need to know?" he asks, not giving tomatoes a moment more of their valuable time.

✻ ✻ ✻ ✻

"All they need to know is that we are growing tomatoes." Freemont assures the graduates of the District 5 Tomato Grower Training Program in his speech at their convocation. It is eight months since the program started and graduates are there to receive their Grower's Certificates.

"We won't worry them with the details." Freemont continues. "They don't notice the small businesses you trade in anymore that they notice the tomatoes you grow here. It doesn't matter a tomato to them that you do. So, leave them to their million-dollar corporations as you handle a thousand transactions that are a thousand times smaller than the companies they finance. That does not make what you do any less important. In the big picture, you are growing the economy just as much as they are."

Freemont pauses as the graduates and their proud families applaud. They all know how workers, like themselves, are working and making money like never before. They know that people want to invest some of what they make in their own community, where the need is greatest and where they benefit, on a daily basis, from the businesses they finance. Thanks to the District 5 Tomato Project they have new ways to do just that.

In his speech to the Growers, Freemont describes some of the projects started in Mobile, with the help of members of their graduating class:

"One Mobile Neighborhood pooled their resources and bought a machine that recycles old auto tires, making them into materials to line underground power and communications lines, to make them earthquake proof." he explains. "They supply the whole city with this needed product and plan to diversify, to other materials for insulation and safety once that project is finished here. They'll finance their new equipment by selling or trading their old machinery to another urban area that needs earthquake proofing, too."

"One family in Mobile saw a need for more bees, to pollinate orchards and gardens now being grown within the city limits." Freemont continues. "The District 5 Tomato Project found them dozens of small financiers and some expert help. Two businesses were started, one for beekeepers and one to processes the soon-to-be-world-famous Mobile Honey. It has a chili in each bottle that gives the honey a special zip. People love it." Freemont tells his audience.

"Little by little, business by business, small investment by small investment, people build their wealth by providing what they and others like them really need."

Freemont finishes.

The first Growers that graduate pool their resources and open their own office in one room of the Mobile Exchange building. It is years later, when The Grower's Market Brokerage and Exchange takes over three floors at the Mobile Stock Exchange, with offices in every Urban Population Center on the Planet, that Mobile brokers finally begin to notice the Growers.

"Those new folks on the fifth floor look familiar to me." Adriano tells Freemont one day when he goes down to the Quickie Market for a soda.

Freemont still works as a clerk there, keeping an eye on the flow of the river of money. His timely updates on market trends are as invaluable to Growers as they are to Brokers who stop by for a chat.

"I could swear one of the men in that office grew tomatoes here, once." Adriano tells Freemont.

"How would I know?" Freemont responds. "I'm from Tiger Country and, to me, you people all look alike."

FBI-CAN

Who's Your Friend In The Neighborhood?

"Since The Message we do not have time to waste on pollution." the President of the United States tells the people of North America. "In the USA we have decided to turn all criminal law enforcement matters over to local, urban Police Departments where they belong. Our FBI will now be known as FBI-CAN, the Federal Bureau of Investigation of Crimes Against Nature. We hope to make FBI-CAN our international, environment law enforcement agency for the New World."

The President offers FBI-CAN services to countries bordering the United States; Canada, Mexico, and the Caribbean, and promises to expand the Agency to include all Central and South American nations should they chose to join.

"We are all in this game together, environmentally speaking." the leader of the free world explains. "Let's all play on the same team."

Citizens of Central and South America know they cannot sell a banana or elect a President without some kind of intervention, interference or intercession from Big Bro in the North and have not been able to do so for centuries. The idea of an official, US-sponsored police force is not a big surprise. What does astonish the governments and citizens of the Americas is that the US government wants them in on the enforcement of environment laws when most health and safety laws have been ignored by US companies for decades.

The change comes about after The Message, when Zones of the Human Spirit are established to turn sacred lands over to all Earth's people. After this, most citizens have a stake in how the Planet operates because about a tenth of it belongs to them and everyone else. They get behind taking better care of the place. When the US President proposes to change the *School de Norte' Americos* at Fort Bendthem, Georgia, from a killer-training academy to an FBI-CAN training school to defend the environment, the vast majority of North, Central and South Americans support his plan.

"The FBI–CAN Training Academy will be open to citizens from all nations it serves. It will train Agents who fight pollution and environment destruction, instead of wars." The US President advises his American counterparts.

"Maybe it's a typical US dirty trick." President Ramone Gonozo Sanoma of Equalito, a Central American bastion of democracy and social equality, speculates. "But since the USA has their agents in every nation, anyway, what have we got to lose? Now, at least we'll know who those agents are and have some of our own people working with them."

Each nation where FBI-CAN operates becomes a member of WEA- the Western Environment Alliance. Former FBI "G" men are now known as WEA men or 'E' men, for short. There are lots of 'E' women, too.

"The Americas need your help." FBI-CAN Director, Avery Winslow proposes to Agents as they begin their initial training. "You are here to learn but you are also here to teach one another. Each of you represents the best interest of the ecological zone you know firsthand. The rest of us may not have a clue about what's good for that part of the Planet. In addition to being a student here, you are our teachers."

While at the FBI-CAN Academy, Agents are assigned to Regional Teams and each team has a leader with an intimate knowledge of the environment neighborhood, or zone, their team will protect. FBI-CAN finds as many InDios people as possible to head up these regional teams. As the first humans to arrive in much of North, Central and South America, InDios people usually have good ideas about how to live in a place without wreaking it.

"You will be the ones to recommend what is legal and illegal in your zone." the Director explains to the team leaders. "In the past, environment laws were determined by developers, lawyers and politicians; those with the least interest in preservation. Now the policies and land use practices will be made by people who actually know what is best for the land."

Many of these FBI-CAN team leaders know what is best for the land because they hold a vision of their land healed. The vision exists in memory; in their stories, songs, and ancient ways that are not forgotten. This memory shows the ways things are when People live in harmony with a place and such memories prove invaluable to the effort to return the Planet to its healed state.

"Some problems can be cleaned up or prevented by good planning but face it, there are some real messes out there." Director Avery continues. "FBI-CAN needs to follow your lead to heal these lands and keep them safe."

One FBI-CAN Director, for the Mobile Urban Population Center, is also head of WEA's Gulf Coast Task Force. Wilhelm Brightfoot is an InDios man who knows a lot about keeping things safe. Wilhelm knows this because his InDios group has been protecting marshlands, wetlands, beaches, and coastal dunes, around

Mobile, for more than five thousand years. The fact that there are a couple of million others visiting the area, for the past three hundred years, does not stop Wilhelm and his People from doing their best to keep things secure.

In modern times, Wilhelm's People run the Stonewall Security Agency, to patrol and guard businesses and homes. Currently, most people in Mobile have no idea that Stonewall Security is there to guard the Wild places around the city; that Stonewall personnel protect homes and businesses for a living but secure the environment as their life's work.

Wilhelm plays a major part in teaching the FBI-CAN Agents about swamps, marshes, and coast environments. Many of these areas have been drastically altered by human actions over the past two centuries. He also tells them about rivers, creeks, streams, and bogs, often adversely effected in most North and South American ecosystems.

In addition to Wilhelm's extensive knowledge about the ways of water, he also has extensive experience teaching others. His job at Stonewall Security is the highest position he can hold in his tribe; teaching Youth their group's purpose, when they are old enough to help fulfill it.

"We're the guardians here." Wilhelm tells the young men and women of Panther Country. "Others may think they hold the deeds to these lands, but we hold the spirit of the place. We hold the living heart of this area in our trust- always have, always will. We are part of this. We are humans with important connections here."

Wilhelm also teaches these young People that they are members of a living Nation and that the protection of their land is the primary reason their nation still lives. Each Youth serves for a time on the Stonewall security force before they leave home to pursue other careers. Some, like Wilhelm and his son, Howard Beau Brightfoot, stay in the Mobile security game as their chosen profession.

"This land is who I am and who you are." Wilhelm advises his students. "You do what you wish with that knowledge. If you want to help in our task to protect this place, you can do so. If not, we ask only that you do no harm here; and that you find another place on Mother Earth that you can connect to, so you can protect things there."

When FBI-CAN starts to recruit for its operatives, Wilhelm is not surprised to see that many of his past students become Agents for North America. They are those most knowledgeable and best prepared to speak for the land where they reside and are used to protecting things.

"We expect to be leaders in helping restore our Earth Mother to health." Wilhelm tells Director Avery, when asked why he knows so many of the newly selected Agents. "We have been waiting for your call for three hundred years. Better late than never."

When Wilhelm gives Avery the names of other First Nation Leaders in other parts of the New World, he assures him "They have been teaching their Youth and waiting for your call, too."

Director Avery makes those calls.

Who You Gonna Call?

Next, Avery calls together the FBI-CAN regional advisors for a policy meeting. The Agency needs their advice on ways to get humans and human stuff out of the Wild.

"Most humans plan to live in urban centers these days." Avery reports to the meeting participants. "But we need to set some limits on what humans can bring into the Wild if they decide to live there. I'm sure a TV and Stereo in a fully-equipped off road camper is not what the Tiger Preservation Project has in mind."

Many of those present have lived for long periods in the Wild with very little human stuff. This is simply their way of leaving the Planet alone, as much as possible, a time-honored strategy that is now part of the basic game plan for all humans. Such a game plan will allow the Earth to heal itself as quickly as possible. To play it, humans need to leave Wild places and take their human stuff out with them when they go.

"Humans have plenty to do in their cities to make those places healthy." Avery points out. "That should keep mankind busy for a couple of generations, at least."

"But humans lived in the Wild far longer than they have in cities—millions of years longer." Wilhelm Brightfoot reminds the Director. "What do we tell humans who don't want to leave the Wild now?"

"That's what we're here to decide." Avery notes. "Suggestions, anyone?"

The guidelines that FBI-CAN Regional Advisors establish for Wild Men and Wild Women; those who choose to live outside Urban areas, are known as the Wild People Guidelines. They are best explained to the world by the US Secretary of the Interior, J. Philip Randway, in a press conference held at FBI-CAN headquarters:

"If you want to live outside a city, go ahead!" he tells the room full of news reporters and TV crews. "You just have to do it like people did it a thousand years ago, before there were many cities."

"How's that?" calls out Newsman Harrison Chambers, always the one with the tough questions.

"No cars, no electricity, no guns and no domesticated animals or modern farming." Randway explains. "Plenty of People roamed the wild like that. In fact, most of the time we've been on the Planet as humans we've lived in Wild places without much technology. Maybe that's how we're supposed to live here."

FBI-CAN recommendations are formalized and become the foundation for the Wild Humanity Treaty, signed by every nation on Earth and ratified by all human and non-human government bodies. Whale delegates think the terms of the treaty are especially helpful to ocean environments. Human water-based machines have been driving them crazy for decades.

Most humans respond to the prospect of life in the Wild, bereft of human stuff, with a polite 'No, thank you.' They stay in urban centers as more and more humans have done for the past thousand years. Some, like Secretary Randway, leave for the Wild without a second thought. He resigns his post as Secretary of the Interior the day after his speech to the press.

"I've always loved the Wild places." J. Philip tells his wife, Bisbee, when they part. "I would just die without time in the Wild."

In the Wild, Randway joins an estimated tenth of the Earth's human population. Most families have at least one Wild member. Despite their large numbers, Wild Folks seem to do no harm there. In some cases, the Wild appears to improve by having a few humanoids back in the Neighborhood.

"Maybe they are dying there and letting their human remains return to the Earth." Director Avery speculates to Wilhelm Brightfoot.

"Some spots have known human visitors for countless generations. Those places would not be the same without humans." Wilhelm reminds Avery. "Their shit might be helping, too."

Singer and songwriter Acton Maxum helps get word out about the Wild Humanity Treaty in a song "Living Free", that guides humans going into Wild areas. Sung in his unique vocal style it goes:

> No TVs, no movie stars
> No hot pretzels and no guitars.
> Live in the Wild
> Live the Wild way
>
> Leave the city behind you,
> City stuff don't play.
>
> No more cows, no balloons
> No fast food and no fast tunes.
> Live without stuff
> Living Nature's way.
>
> Leave the city behind you
> Live life the oldest way.

No more kings, no crown jewels
No more taxes, no state rules.
Life of the butterfly
Life of the bee.

Leave the city and mind you
Live a life that's free.

Most people get no closer to being Wild folks than singing a song about it.

❋ ❋ ❋ ❋

Havana, Cuba is selected as the location of FBI-CAN's international headquarters of operation because many of Cuba's citizens are well educated and speak Spanish, English and French, languages spoken by the majority of people in the Carribean, North, Central and South America. They also can communicate well with the many Spanish-speaking US citizens and with French-speaking Canadians.

Cuba has previously given technical aide and emergency assistance to many of its Latin American neighbors, in times of disaster. They also have a lot to teach the rest of the Western Hemisphere about using scarce resources well and provide for the food needs of Cuban citizens, using organic food production systems. In addition to all that, the music in Cuba is great and Agents assigned there have a lot of fun, a necessary prerequisite for any successful international posting.

❋ ❋ ❋ ❋

"With People confined to the cities, it's a lot easier to control their use of resources and their impact on the environment." Alberta Jackson Brightfoot, a visiting lecturer in Havana, tells a group of FBI-CAN Operatives.

Alberta and Howard Beau Brightfoot are the leaders of the Friends of the Planet Tiger Preservation Project, a worldwide movement for global healing, established in response to The Message. Both are in Cuba to explain their project's importance to FBI-CAN administrative staff.

"The Project provides Planetary ground rules that make the survival of a lot more than Tigers possible." Alberta explains. "Laws, rules and development planning are made on a local level, in accord with the Tiger Project's guidelines. Then local plans are coordinated by regional organizations and this helps guide continent-wide change. The UN Environment Program oversees world-wide plans for healing the Earth and its oceans and atmosphere."

"FBI-CAN will act as the watch dog for local, national and regional policies in the Americas." Howard Beau tells FBI-CAN personnel. "If each region can stick to their rules this will allow our Planet to heal and, hopefully, Tigers to thrive wherever they may be. Everything else can thrive, too."

"Is there some overriding rule of thumb we should follow if we are not sure what to do?" asks Knarl Hope the West Coast Division Administrator from the San Francisco Bay area.

As the one to first identify the 'Ten Rules of the Game' to clean up Planet Earth, Alberta answers him:

"The most important Rules are the two given to us in The Message they are 'Have Fun and Be Kind'. Of these, the most important is 'Be Kind'."

"It is the foundation of any creative change." Howard Beau adds. "Sure, you can force someone to do something or stop them from doing another thing, but you rarely have the best outcome by pressuring people."

"FBI-CAN Agents must become expert advisors on innovative ideas and offer options that are better than the old ways of doing things." Director Avery notes. "Whenever people come smack up against an environment problem they can't solve, let them know that "FBI-CAN!"

❋ ❋ ❋ ❋

Go Bust 'Em!

"Our ideal solutions are positive changes that people will make voluntarily, because they benefit from the change, too." Director Avery tells the United States Senate Environment Committee, headed by Senator Sterlin Sommes.

"Ought to bust some of them pollutin' sons of guns! Throw them in jail!" Senator Sommes rants, in full view of the TV cameras there to cover the hearings.

"Jail time for offenders is no longer an option." Avery notes. "Prisons are just big old, destructive wastes of time, energy and human potential. FBI-CAN is here to help individuals, neighborhoods and urban centers come up with plans that meet their needs and the Planet's needs, too."

"Y'all mean you're here to help people learn, not lean on 'em?" Senator Sommes asks. "How you gonna' get results that way?"

"Step One: educate the public. Many of our citizens have never seen a healthy environment. How can we expect them to know when one is being degraded?"

Newsman Harrison Chambers, there to report on the Senate meeting, knows that the mass media–TV, radio, and film, puts out the most effective teaching messages in the world. Harrison, personally, has been getting more news out to more people than any other living human for the past thirty years and knows how to get a message across. After the meeting, he approaches Avery with a suggestion.

"Put whatever you want to tell people on a TV show. Make it funny and have sexy men and women present it. Do that and millions of people around the world will watch. Make your characters environment fighters. Hey, make them E Men and E Women! No one will ignore anything you teach if they learn it from their favorite sex symbol, especially if they can get a few laughs at the same time."

Avery takes the newsman's advice and gets on the next plane to Hollywood. With the help of Acton Maxum, a singer famous for his part in Hollywood's response to The Message, Avery organizes a meeting with sympathetic actors, scriptwriters, producers, and directors. All gather at Acton Maxum's estate for a planning session.

"Why a TV show?" Acton is the first to ask.

"These days FBI-CAN detects environment crimes and arrests those who commit them, but the prosecution of such lawbreakers is up to the newly-created Environment Courts." Avery explains. "Judges come from the areas where the crime occurs and are elected by people who live there. The Court is answerable to the human population of that area, those most directly affected by environment problems."

"What about big polluters that destroy the air or contribute to global warming? "Who prosecutes them?" asks actress Gia Furrow.

"There is a North America Environment Court and a World Court for international polluters." Avery states. "FBI-CAN Agents refer cases to all these courts for prosecution and judgement."

"So, what's the problem?" Producer/Director Reb Reindeer asks. "It sounds like you got it all covered."

"The problem is that local courts often acquit polluters. In many cases citizens do not realize the harm that is being done to their environment. We want to use the mass media to help folks understand how close to home these pollution problems get."

"Not another one of those nature shows." groans actor Stream Martin. "Can't we make it funny so people will watch?"

"Funny and sexy, with lots of big stars and some dynamite plots." Avery tells the group. "That's where you come in."

Many volunteer to work on both TV and radio show scripts for 'The E Files' but Director Beary Marshfall reminds Avery, "Just because we inform the Planet, don't assume we are informed about the Planet, ourselves."

"Face it, we're as ignorant of what goes on in our environment as most folks, maybe more." Actor/Director Awren Beetree admits. "We're often so busy making up our own world we don't notice a thing about this one. Give us some help."

The Hollywood writers get that help from United States' FBI-CAN agent, Ludlow Parker, Trudy Mae Netto of the Navaho Nation, and French Canadian operative, Luis DuMond. From Cuba, the writing team of Hernando and Maria Ernesto joins the creative team, as both environment and media advisors. The Ernestos are not only tropical forest experts, but they have also been writing Spanish-language soap operas for decades. Latin Americans find North American programming very dry, and they hope to add a little gusto to the E Team scripts.

"You want funny?" Agent Trudy Mae advises. "You writers don't have to make up a thing. Just show people what's happening for real-it's as hilarious as it is ridiculous!"

Trudy gives the program team and example:

"Billions of dollars have been spent, over decades, to change the flood patterns of rivers like the Mississippi. Prior to the Message, decades of work on the river only succeed in creating floods where there were none before."

"Before FBI-CAN stopped them, some people were actually making plans to build pumps to take that redirected flood water to someplace new, which has also never flooded." Trudy explains. "Talk about passing the buck. Not only would they deliver a deluge to dry spots, BUT the US taxpayer would ALSO pay for it, big time."

"Then that buck stops here." Director Martin Landnow responds. "Let us do that story and stop those buckers. Who are they?"

"A couple of construction companies and some property developers, who stood to gain some major coin for this engineering feat." Agent Ludlow informs. "But they couldn't have done a thing without help from a US government agency, the Army Corps of Engineers. The Corps needed to approve their plans."

"Our tax dollars at work bucking us!" laughs comedian Eddy Myrrhtree. "Wouldn't be the first time. Tell me someone stopped them!"

"FBI-CAN did." Agent Dumond assures them.

"We could not actually charge them with a crime." Trudy clarifies. "But we did to sue them in Environment Court, to stop them before they spent millions of dollars on a tunnel through a mountain to divert the river's flow."

"Our lawyers represented Girl Scout Troop 25, whose summer camp would be flooded out by that relocated water." Ludlow adds.

"Judge Sigfried Tupalow presided over the case and those developers were out of luck. He made them an offer they had to refuse!"

The writers decide to title this first episode of the E-Files 'Pumpers'.

❋ ❋ ❋ ❋

"I'll give you a choice. You want to move a lot of water from one place to another, you can move that H2O to any location where YOU live or work, or where you have YOUR homes or businesses." Judge Tupalow, played by actor Wildman Doefoe, tells the rich and powerful defendants facing him in court.

"As an alternate plan, you can bid on the contract to restore the lands along the river you want to divert. When that is done, the area surrounding the present waterway can absorb more water when rainfall is heavy." the Judge adds, referring the Pumpers to an alternative flood control project, the Wetlands Preserve Program.

"The WRP, started in the late 1990s, and works with farmers and other landowners along rivers and creeks." The Judge explains. "Their program helps farmers stop growing Soya beans and other crops that are ruined when the river tops its banks, and pays them to plant native trees, like cypress or tupelo gum, along the waterways. These trees are harvested, using a sustainable timber cutting system, and provide some income to the landowners, in addition to funds they get for letting their lands return to the Wild."

None of the developers has ever considered going into such a constructive line of work before, so they have no comment as the Judge continues.

"You either get water up to your ass at your own home or business, or you bid on a multi-million-dollar contract to coordinate area reforestation and levee removal." the Judge offers. "The Wetlands Preserve Program needs all the help it can get, even yours. Take your pick."

The Pumpers, never adverse to a multi-million-dollar contract of any kind, actually know the rivers and waterways in question, from years of preliminary studies, and can underbid other contractors and engineering firms for the job. They join forces with The Wetlands Preserve team and go into the business of tree planting and levee removal, leaving the natural movement of the river water to do the rest.

"Who better to restore balance there than Mother Nature?" actor Woodman Harrythem, playing the role of the leader of the E Team, asks his co-star, Molly Huntress, in the final scene of the program's first episode.

The series attracts famous stars like Wildman, Molly and Woodman, who want to help their Planet and their careers. Since 30 million people watch each episode, actors find that helping the E-Team is as good for their public image as it is for their Planet.

❋ ❋ ❋ ❋

"There is an even better story, about a timber conglomerate that builds and operates pulp plants, equipped with huge tree-eating machines, that cut down vast areas of privately owned forests in the South East USA." Agent Ludlow tells the E- Team writers. "Their pulp mills work 24 hours a day, pulverizing trees that are otherwise commercially useless. They plow right into the skinny old pines, the brush, and the scrub that nobody but the critters ever call home. They just devastate the land."

"But why?" asks Producer Marshy Caughtthem.

"Those tree pulverizers can turn anything that looks like wood into wood chips. Their mills turn the chips into particleboard, pulp for paper, and a variety of wood-like products. Anything fed into those machines comes out money, for the corporation. Too bad not a thing is left standing in those piney woods, after they get through."

"Don't people who own that land care?" asks Director, Mellow Rooks. "That kind of clear cutting must just be catastrophic."

"People never imagine anything like it and are totally unprepared for that degree of destruction." Ludlow explains. "Many landowners are from families who harvested those forests for generations, taking out a few mature trees from time to time. They had no idea the contract they signed meant everything growing there would be clear-cut. When they do realize that it's too late."

"And you say thousands of acres are cut in this way? Why would any business operate like that? Surely, they can see they'll run out of trees to harvest, sooner instead of later." Actor/Writer, Allman Allday queries, wondering if anyone will believe this story if they tell it.

"The timber companies' figure, at the rate they are cutting, they will have nothing to cut within a hundred-mile radius of a pulp mill, in five years' time. They still kept building more and more mills, anyway, until FBI-CAN stopped them."

Ludlow sees their looks of disbelief and adds: "The factory operators, workers in the mills and those who cut the trees helped us put a stop to this, too. They all knew it's crazy to keep doing what they were doing, but it's what their bosses wanted."

"Corporate executives try to bring in huge profits to show big corporate gains over a short period of time." Trudy Mae clarifies. "People, who never see these trees push for the destruction of whole stands of forest, to benefit their bottom line."

Many of the writers, actors and directors in the room have changed their work to benefit the bottom line, even though that change is devastating to their original creation. They know what Trudy is talking about.

"That's what gets those corporate executives the mega-bonuses, with the big golden parachutes when the company they bring to ruin goes bankrupt." Actor/writer and Network Executive, Mill Crosstree, concedes. "So how did the E-Team stop them?"

"The lawsuit that brought these companies to the North American Environment Court was a brief from the Government of Japan." Trudy informs.

"Japan?" asks Director/Producer Raven Spellbird. "I thought you said these forests were in the USA?"

"The trees are there but Japan knows it will be under water if global warming isn't stopped. Trees take CO2 out of the air and stop the warming process that's melting the polar ice caps and drowning Japan, inch by inch." Ludlow puts in. "Judge Rockerfellar 'Bud' Hayes heard that case."

"Those execs were toast." Trudy Mae laughs. "Judge Hayes once hunted and fished in the forests that are now acres of naked stumps. He did not look kindly on those who destroyed so much there."

❊ ❊ ❊ ❊

"They were just following orders from their shareholders." Attorney for the Defense, screen star Westerly Sights, pleads to the Judge, who is played by character actor Charlitan Beaston, in the second E-Team episode, 'Forest of Death'.

Judge Bud is having no lame excuses from the defendants, no matter how rich they look. He convicts all of them on all counts, telling them:

"I sentence you to live outdoors in one of those once-beautiful forests, for a month." Judge Bud thunders in voice that makes the sentence sound like a pronouncement from Jehovah. "Take whatever you can carry in on your backs and nothing else."

TV audiences are in tears when these elite business executives, played by their favorite super-stars, wander around on what looks like the surface of Mars on a bad day. When it starts to rain, even the most sympathetic viewer cannot help but laugh as mudslides decimate the campers' well-equipped campsite. All the campers need to survive washes away, as though one of their giants, environment-eating machines were at work on their world.

All appears lost, until the helpless men and women reach the protection of a stand of trees. Sheltered from the worst of the storm's rain and wind, the sorry-looking bunch is literally hugging the trees that give them shelter. Then the roar of a giant pulp eater is heard, coming closer and closer, until it breaks through the trees and proceeds to eat up their poor protection, in a blink of an eye.

❋ ❋ ❋ ❋

"FBI-CAN operatives come to the rescue before there is any loss of human life." Ludlow explains to the Hollywood team. "I can tell you; those folks will never take a tree for granted, again."

"Did any of them survive a whole month in the Wild?" Actor Eddies Murky asks.

"They had their sentence revised when we took them back before the Judge." Ludlow explains.

"It will take about twenty-five years to restore the lands they ruined, and even then, they will never be the same." Trudy Mae shares with the E-Team production crew. "But clear-cutting stopped everywhere else it was being done, when word got out what happened to that group. No timber company owners wanted to chance a similar fate."

"What was their new sentence?" asks Actor/Writer Allford Brooks. "Did they do time?"

"Even worse for them." Trudy explains. "They did time and money."

✳ ✳ ✳ ✳

"Please, let us submit a reforestation plan for the forests we ruined." actor Catfish Swaytree pleads, for himself and the other corporate e-wrecks that stand before Judge Hayes.

Judge Bud tells them:

"In lieu of serving the rest of your sentence in a clear cut, you give me restoration plans that you will finance, to heal those lands. Include in the plans your personal commitment to go out twice week and plant trees there or someplace else, for the next five years. By the way, I'm freezing your personal bank accounts until all those trees are replanted."

"Reforestation plans, in lieu of certain death in the lands of their own destruction, sounds like a good deal to these deforesters." the E Team Leader, played by actress Windover Righter, shares in the final moments of E Team, episode two.

Windover stands in a clear-cut, next to a hole dug by a timber company executive, working on her real restoration project. Seen behind both is the actual area being replanted, like the surface of Mars on a bad day, but dotted with tree seedlings.

"You can see these are real places, not make-believe problems with easy solutions." the actress explains to the audience. "E-Files shows you the real thing, at the end of each episode. Otherwise, people will never believe that humans are capable of doing such stupid stuff. We are, but we are also able to help correct our past mistakes, to get smart and help our Planet, one tree, one forest and one Earth Neighborhood at a time."

THE GREAT AMERICAN REVIEW

"If I don't come up with something, and right quick, they are all going to up and leave us." Cherry Tupalow says to herself, looking over her employees.

Cherry is not relating a fear that her workers will make a career change. She is talking about the choice of death as a way out of life, taken by the unwell and the unhappy, after The Message. Three days after The Message, near all the Cherry Hill employees are semi-comatose, and appear to be fading fast. Cherry knows she needs to find the men and women who work in her whorehouse another way to make a living, before they stop living, altogether.

Cherry knows the young people who work for her better than most of them know themselves. She believes they each have something to offer the world besides their body and that The Message can help them to do that, with a little help from their madam.

"These kids have no idea of their gifts, talents and skills. If they did, they would not be working for me in the first place." Cherry admits to herself. "Most of them have such a poor self-image and such a meager knowledge of the possibilities of this world, they are the last ones able to judge whether or not they should live or die."

Many in the Mobile community would be happy to have Madame Cherry and her whores bid their city good-bye, no matter how or why they went, but Madame C is not about to have any of her bunch leave without giving life, and themselves, at least one more chance. To this end, Cherry calls a meeting to tell her staff about their future careers:

"I'm closing down the Cherry Hill whore house and we're going into another field of entertainment." Cherry explains to the group assembled in the front parlor of Mobile's largest and finest house of ill repute. "None of you are leaving us yet."

A few employees open their eyes but Cherry notes that Ernestine appears to have stopped breathing. The girl's lips are turning blue, and Cherry has to yell, "I say! No one is leaving us! We're getting out of here together!"

Ernestine's eyes fly open, and she starts breathing again and sits up. She has never been farther from Mobile than the nearest adult correctional center for women, where she visited her mother as a child. The opportunity to take a trip anywhere else has never before presented itself to Ernestine and she is not about to miss it.

"Say what?" the young woman asks. "Where we goin'?"

"We're going to put together a musical review, with my sister, Loni Cox, as the star. We'll take the show around the world as a good-will gesture to the people of Planet Earth from the people of the United States."

"Who's going to pay for that?" Gregory Garfield asks.

Greg is not familiar with good-will gestures of any kind. He learned very young that someone has to pay for anything they get, do or have. He has never had a gesture of any kind or kindness come his way that did not cost him. Greg wants to know what the deal is now.

"I have arranged funding for our show from many of the prominent men and women who've enjoyed so much with us here at Cherry Hill, and who have a strong aversion to anyone finding out about that." Cherry informs the group.

This sufficiently explains the motivation of their patrons to Cherry's employees. What they are still not clear on is what they are expected to do for the money. Most of them know only two options for work: being a whore or being a Madam. Cherry appears to be offering them another choice and they need clarification.

"We are going to put on a show." Cherry tells them.

"Like Las Vegas or something?" Pretty DuPree asks.

Pretty can relate to this option, having worked for a brief time as an exotic dancer before the only strip club in three counties is closed down. The club owner refuses to pay bribes to the local Highway Patrol officer and is busted for lewd practices.

"More like vaudeville." Cherry explains. "A little singing, dancing and some simple skits, a stand-up comic, a magician and a few other acts. Everybody keeps their clothes on."

Cherry can see the disappointment some faces.

"Dazzling costumes and fabulous hair styles, lots of costume jewelry and really tight pants." Cherry promises, as she describes what most of her group are currently wearing. "We might as well stick with what is familiar and, after all, we're representing the wealthiest nation in human history. A little glitz is in order." she assures the group.

They respond with hopeful smiles.

"What are we going to do in this show?" Alice Blue asks. "I promised my mama I'd never follow in her footsteps and do porno."

"It's not porno!" Cherry exclaims. "It's the Great American Review, for Carpenter's sake. We're talking about representing the U. S. of A., all over the world."

Cherry's crew bursts into laughter. They have never heard anything funnier in their lives.

"Us?" gasped Parker Phillips, regaining control. "We are going to represent the USA? What as, the US Olympic Trick team?"

"I know it sounds weird," Cherry admits "but you people underestimate your talents. Y'all can move six ways to Sunday and with a few dancin' lessons you can do some simple routines. My sister, Loni Cox, will carry the vocal numbers and most of you sing well enough to back her up."

They all know Loni Cox has a superb voice but do not look convinced, until Cherry further explains:

"I have a voice teacher coming here with Loni. My sister says Ms. Lillian can teach a cricket to sing opera. That should get you through the singing numbers."

"Why are we doing this again?" Paula Fitzgerald asks.

"You are doing this so you can use more of the gifts God gave you. I'm doing this because I'll be danged if I'm going to let y'all up an' leave us after all the time and trouble I've taken with your sorry butts, all these years!"

Cherry is now speaking a language they all understand. When she tells them, she wants a return on her investment in them, she is saying something they have all heard from various people for most of their lives. A couple of Cherry's employees come from wealthy families, who expect even more from their offspring than do parents who are dirt poor. The rich require their progeny to have power, wealth, important careers, and often arrange marriages for them, or require their life-long service in some family business.

"More than one way to sell yourself." Reid Worthington Smythe told Cherry when he joined her staff. "My family expects me to marry a woman I can't stand and work for her family. Not only am I gay, but can you imagine me running an elevator empire? I had to bail. Once I've worked for you here, there's not a chance anyone in my family or hers will have a thing to do with me."

All the men and women at Cherry Hill are whores for equally compelling reasons. Sometimes they are economic ones and sometimes social, but her staff hears The Message, just like anyone else. Like anyone else, they feel compelled to contribute to the planetary clean-up effort. Though their chosen profession is one of the oldest on Earth and is virtually non-polluting (with the advent of birth control and safe-sex practices strictly adhered to at Cherry Hill) they do not recognize that they have as much to offer their Planet as anyone else. Cherry is there to enlist their help.

"The show is about changes regular people in the USA make in response to The Message." Cherry explains. "We will tell stories about everyday people and what they are doing to help clean up Planet Earth, one Neighborhood at a time. It's a public relations gesture."

Cherry's group looks puzzled and concerned. They have no idea how regular people do things, before or after The Message. Most of them have little or no experience with regular people, except when those people patronize Cherry Hill. If they had a clue how to live, as average citizens do, most of them would not be living or working at Cherry Hill. They would have been out of there and on their own, long ago.

"Don't worry, we will have script writers." Cherry reassures them. "You don't have to know anything about regular people, to be in the show."

Cherry's entertainers look relieved. She hopes their leaving the whorehouse and acting like regular people might help some of them build skills to prepare them for a more normal life someday.

"We have a month to put the show together, then we start our tour in Mexico." Cherry further explains. "All I ask is that nobody "leaves us" for a month. During that time, stay here and try your best. Then if you want to bail, bye-bye and God bless."

That seems a fair enough proposition to everyone in the group, so when their singing teacher arrives, they give it all they have. Cherry spares no expense for their dancing and singing coaches and they all love the great costumes Betsy Ross Jackson designs for them. Her wearable fabric creations seem to have an energy all their own and Cherry is pretty sure she hears them singing in the prop room late at night, without benefit of human presence.

In a month's time, with Cherry driving them to rehearse ten hours a day, they are a competent group of performers and even they know it. They video tape the show's dress rehearsal and when they watch the tape, all have to admit they are goooood!

The World Premiere performance of the Great American Review is put on for the show's sponsors, their old Cherry Hill patrons. There is not a dry eye in the house when the final curtain comes down. It is hard to say if this because of the content of the show or because Mobile citizens will miss the services of the Cherry Hill employees, the kindness and beauty they experienced in the old mansion. Kindness and Beauty are the main reasons Cherry Hill patrons went to Cherry Hill but since The Message kindness is easier to come by in everyday life.

Kindness is, after all, the basic premise of the Response to The Message. Kindness is also the theme of the Great American Review's skits, jokes, songs, and dance numbers. All are about ways people come together to plan and carry out acts of kindness in neighborhoods and nations, everywhere. There is a clown act about the Tiger Summit, a skit about Wild Folks, a dance number about people saying good-bye to those who 'left us', and a stand-up comedy act called The Story of Food. Parker Phillips puts together a magic act he calls "Great Garbage Transformation Tricks", showing ways USA citizens are recycling a lot of their trash, to turn it into things people in other parts of the world need- like solar powered cookers, wind generators and cheap fuels.

The American Review is a great show but, admittedly, the Cherry Hill Tricksters are nervous about their tour. Few of them have been outside Mobile and they are about to see and be seen by the world. None of them has a clue what that world is going to show them or whether or not what they show the world will be well received. In spite of their fears, none of them 'leaves us' except together, by plane, to Mexico.

Their first performance, in a community of the working poor on the edge of the giant megalopolis that is Mexico City, is quite a surprise to everyone. Their production is staged on their elaborate portable sound stage, equipped with its own lighting system, trucked in, and set up in the only open space, the market square.

Their show is presented in South American Spanish, but they have a local interpreter along, to help translate any words or songs that their audience does not fully understand. They hope the show will delight and inform but are unprepared when it appears to be a complete bomb.

"We might as well be aliens from another Planet." Cherry admits, looking out over the sea of faces that gaze, in wonder, at the performers, looking up at the stage as though frozen by an intergalactic ray gun.

The people watching are clearly dumbfounded by what they see and have no idea what the troop is talking, singing, or dancing about. The only skit they respond to is Ramada Beaumont's parody of North American politicians. Most political leaders, from both North and South, are cut from the same cloth and the Mexican audience recognizes their absurd ways as any other audience would.

Ramada's caricatures of these political jokers are gleaned from seeing so much of so many of them at Cherry Hill. Her audience learns the ways of their own *politicos* during the very brief visits paid to their area, right before an election. Their politicians come bearing promises and looking for votes. Even without translation, Ramada's characters are easily recognized and universally funny to those watching her act.

"The fact is, politicians are not all that different, no matter where they are from." Ramada tells her audience. "Argentina to Zimbabwe, they still are selling dreams that end up being our worst nightmares.

Funny thing is, Argentina to Zimbabwe, we keep letting those fools get away with it!"

Fortunately, Cherry has sense enough to close their show with Ramada's act, followed by their big finale with lots of singing, dancing and bright costumes. Despite the fact that their audience claps and cheers, Cherry knows there is something seriously wrong with the American Review. Their translator, Father Ernesto Cruz, a priest who has worked in the community for twenty-five years and knows its inhabitants well, best explains the problem.

"Your show was the equivalent of God coming down to Earth and showing heaven to humans here." Father Enrico explains to the discouraged performers after the show. "My people were enchanted but most have no idea what you are talking about. I know this because I am aware of the existence of the things you refer to in your show. I know they exist because I read about them in a North American newspaper my sister, Carlotta, sends me from California. If I did not get that paper, I never would have seen or heard of any of this."

"That makes it tough to get our message across." Cherry admits.

"I translate, but you speak of a different universe, a different economic and social reality. You are showing a world these people have never known, even in their dreams."

Then Father Enrico shows Cherry and her troop around his part of the city. The Cherry Hill troops sees a community hanging on by prayer and a dying hope that their children will, some way or another, have a chance for a better life. They have no idea what that chance might be.

The daily struggle faced by the men and women of Father Ernesto's parish is for some work that will enable them to live. This struggle for basic necessities takes up the majority of people's time and energy. They have no land and have not had lands for generations. What skills and training they can wrest from their environment, which is their only source of education, is all they have to help them survive.

"The Great American Review is about things these people can't even imagine. Your performers are singing and dancing about people who have resources like vehicles and education. Those blessed with so much are now sharing with each other and with the world, for the first time in decades. Your audience here has almost nothing to share. What they do have they do share. They have always done so, or most of them would not have made it this far. A life based on sharing is a way that allows some to survive, and they all know this. The do not need an American Review to teach us that."

Cherry comes from Mobile's poorest neighborhood and her family was the poorest of the poor there. Compared to what she is seeing now, she and her kin were fabulously rich. They, at least, had options.

"How can such poverty be?" Cherry asks.

"These people live in a world that sucks more and more from their meager resources of strength and labor, every day they live. These citizens, like their counterparts around the world, are on the edge of extinction." Father Enrico explains. "In fact, about a sixth of the world's humans are in this same boat, and more get on board the ship of slow starvation every day."

Cherry is astonished by the scope of the problem.

"Until the world begins to share the basics for food, shelter and clothing for all citizens, the people you see here will die." the Priest explains. "Right now, they die a little at a time, weakened by gradual starvation. They could go quickly however, should there be a major outbreak of disease. Many of them are too unwell to resist serious illness."

Cherry is as speechless as their audience was earlier that evening.

"Yet they did not leave us" Father Enrico points out. "They survive on some small hope for their future, and they know their children have no future without them. Many stay because there is no way they would abandon their family."

"What can we do to help?" Cherry asks.

"Take your show home." Father Enrico suggests. "Sing about the plight of these people, so those in your nation and other wealthy countries see how so much of the world lives. I can assure you, your countrymen have no idea, even if they've traveled around the world a hundred times. They never see this."

"Such a show would help people here?" Cherry asks. "How?"

"If nothing else, it will do away with the idea that people like these have some ability to change their lives and fortunes by hard work and resourcefulness. Let's put it this way, they no longer have enough to steal from one another, to get ahead." the Priest explains. "No one can rob Peter to pay Paul, here. Both Peter and Paul are broke. Both need significant help from the rest of the world before that is possible again."

"What will rich people do with the information?" Cherry wonders. "I've met a few rich folks in my time, and they may have wealth to spare, but they are even more clueless about ways to help than I am."

"The wealthy own the economy that exploits these workers." the Priest points out. "They need to pay people enough to live, to stop this. Then, at least those with jobs will survive. As they survive, they help others around them do so, too."

Exploitation is something Cherry understands. She made a lot of money at Cherry Hill and her employees made very little. She owned the Cherry Hill mansion and her employees paid her to live there. They did not even own the clothing they wore when they were being screwed for Cherry's benefit. She owned their garments and her workers paid her for their "uniforms" on a monthly basis.

"Some things have got to change." Cherry admits. "Otherwise, all these people will 'leave us', one way or another. Then where will we be? We need them to help the Planet."

"Then help them first." The Priest explains. "It's the least you can do."

✼ ✼ ✼ ✼

On Father Ernesto's recommendation, Cherry hires citizens from the priest's parish to help rewrite their skits, work on new songs, and come up with acts to show a U.S. audience the state of affairs for most of the world's poor. Her new advisors are not lacking in talent just because they lack funds. Some of them survive solely on their talents and their lives depend on them being good. Their expert help transforms the content and the spirit of the Great American Review in entertaining, informative ways:

The Magic act becomes "The Disappearing Land and Resource Show."

Ramada tells The Story of Food but expands its scope to tell the story of Food for Export.

There are skits about an International Living Wage for everyone who works, no matter where in the world they live.

Cherry's favorite act is their opening number, a re-write of the hymn 'Amazing Grace', with these words:

Amazing Blessed
Our wealth abounds.
We've everything we need.
What others yield
Is what we've found
Or taken out of greed.

Amazing Blessed
We take from all
From People, Lands and Seas.
Our profits grow,
Surplus abounds,
But more we think we need.

Amazing Blessed
We rarely share
Our wealth and all we have.
We'll sell you some,
We'll float a loan,
You'll pay for it in blood.

Amazing Blessed
We hold the loans.
That drain the world's last stores.
And once that's gone
We'll take some more,
Your lands, your mines, your shores.

Amazing Blessed
When will we cease
To bleed the Planet dry?
If we don't stop and
Start to share,
This world will surely die.

Amazing Blessed
What will we have
If we destroy it all?
Nothing left
To own and keep.
No life left here at all.

Amazing Blessed
Let's change our tune,
Let Profit have no say.
The time for that
Has come and gone.
Let's find another way.

The lead singer in their group, Cherry's sister Loni, does a terrific job singing the song. Her voice takes the meaning of the hymn to every heart. The new version is soon being sung in every church, synagogue, mosque and temple, across the USA and Europe.

It is not long before the international minimum wage idea; presented in their skit 'Every Worker Counts' is made law by the World Trade Organization and the World Bank. Industrial nations that are members of the WTO have to comply with a policy that provides people enough to live. Many are happy to do so, when they realize that more people, with more money to spend is their dream come true.

❋ ❋ ❋ ❋

"Big business bitched and complained about it, for a while," Senator Sterlin Sommes tells Cherry one night after a show, backstage at a Washington, D.C. theater. "Then they figured out we need those workers as consumers. Poor folks are vital to the world economy, so it's best not to let them all die out. Poor people also need a lot more than rich people do. It only makes sense to promote their well-being."

By this time, the Review has played in the US for two years and comes to the Urban Center at Washington, D.C., every three months, to educate and re-educate elected officials there. Despite The Message and all the changes on Planet Earth, US Legislators are still pretty dim when it comes to positive change. Senator Sommes regularly sponsors the Review in the nation's capital, to give them a clue.

"Why did the corporate world really start paying people enough to live?" Cherry asks Sterlin. "None of your window dressing about kindness, now, the truth."

"When industrialists realized that people in developing nations would use wages to buy what their industries are making, they changed their tune." Sterlin explains.

"What did they think poor people would do with money they earn, take a weekend in Las Vegas? Of course, they use it for what their community needs. They live there!" Cherry responds.

"That new Anthem you wrote helped change some minds, too." Senator Sommes tells her. "It's your best song, yet."

"I thought you'd appreciate it, Senator."

"Appreciate it? I'm thinking of sponsoring a bill in the Senate to have it made our national song. No one can remember the words to the Star-Spangled Banner and who cares about old battles, these days? Your anthem is much catchier."

The song he refers to is known as The Smart Sharing Planner and is sung to the tune of the old national anthem:

> Oh, say can you see
> By the Message's light,
> Just how much we do keep
> For our personal treasure.
>
> All our stocks and our shares
> All our funds, but beware
> We are buying the world
> Making profit the measure.
>
> But the danger is clear
> Sell the Earth and beware.
> The foundations of all
> Will be consumed as well.
> Oh say, can't you start to share
> Part of your wealth?
> With the others of the world,
> So that all have enough.

"I like the part about all having enough, the best." Cherry admits. "I put it in, hoping it would come true, but I never imagined it would come true so quickly."

"How do you know that's happened?" Sterlin asks.

Sterlin is on the Senate Foreign Relations Committee but is never quite sure how things are going for most people outside the USA. His best source of international intelligence is Cherry. Sterlin, who knows Cherry through a distant family connection, gets updates on foreign affairs, whenever they meet. These briefings are worth the cost of sponsoring the show to him, because Cherry's reports are never wrong.

"How do you know what's going on?" the Senator inquires.

"My sister travels the world as a singer." Cherry reminds Sterlin. "She gives me regular reports on how people are doing, all over the Planet."

"Loni? It's hard to imagine her doing that."

Sterlin notes, recalling Loni Cox from her days as a waitress at the Big Ear Cafe. "How do people trust someone who looks as much like an American as Loni does?"

"She learns people's songs and then she sings them, beautifully." Cherry tells the Senator. "And she has a secret identity that helps, too. In most places, people just refer to her as 'The Voice'. She sees and hears everything and tells me all about it to keep the Review topical and up-to-date."

"Who would have thought Loni would speak for the people of the world?" the Senator marvels.

"Sing for them. " Cherry corrects. "Let's keep that under wraps, though. We wouldn't want to blow her cover."

BEHIND THE VEIL

Loni Cox Tupalow looks like she belongs in a Weight Stoppers commercial, in the "Before" picture. She weighs about 250 pounds and is only five feet two inches tall. Though Loni sounds like she should be the Diva at the Metropolitan Opera House before she began traveling with the Great American Review Loni never had a successful audition.

"People get too distracted by how I look," Loni says. "and I'm never sure if the looks on the faces in the audience are in awe of my sound or if they are gaping at my size. I get so anxious; I lose my concentration and I blow the audition."

When Loni gets the role as the lead singer in the Great American Review, no audition is required, and her sister will not take no for an answer. Loni quits her waitress job for a chance to sing full time. All appreciate that her work in the show is important to the healing of the Planet but, unfortunately, being in the Review does not help Loni's weight problem.

While working as a waitress at the Big Ear, Loni sang what she wanted to sing and kept her weight down by walking constantly. When she goes on the road with the Great American Review, she starts to add on pounds, almost daily. Though she eats no more than anyone else in the troop, Loni grows fatter and fatter and is so discouraged she threatens to stop singing and is ready to quit the show.

"I look like the USA must look to the rest of the world -like I've swallowed the whole of Planet Earth, in one bite." Loni comments. "It's as though I'm sucking up everything and am holding it all in, fit to bust."

"I think you are gaining weight because you're not singing the songs you want to sing." drum player with the Review, Abu Akbar Mohammed, proposes. "You're keeping your own songs inside and they're making you swell like a balloon."

"That's exactly how I feel." Loni admits.

"You must sing what you want to sing, all the time." Abu advises. "Even though the Review's message is important, it may not be your message. Perhaps you can help the Planet in another way."

"Singing is what I do best. I tried to sing on my own, in the past, but the way I look got in the way." Loni tells him. "American audiences can't handle my size. If anything, I look even heavier now than I did then."

"I think you look more beautiful now than you did before." Abu admits, then explains to Loni that most people in the world regard her size as the ideal form of beauty.

"That much weight means wealth." Abu tells Loni. "Don't change a thing about yourself, as far as I'm concerned. I treasure every kilo of you."

"Romantic as that is, Abu, I'd still like to keep singing." Loni says. "How can I do that if I leave the show?"

Abu hands Loni Cox what looks like a shroud that covers her from head to foot. There is a place for her to peek out to see the world, but beautiful, voluminous folds of cloth cover the rest of her.

"Not seen but heard?" Loni speculates. "Sounds liberating!"

When the Great American Musical Review goes back to perform in the USA, Loni leaves the troop and begins a tour singing songs for peace and personal liberation, everywhere else. Abu joins her as Loni's accompanist.

"We will never be able to bring our act to the USA." Loni tells Cherry when the sisters part. "You know if I sing shrouded from head to foot, Americans will make more of a stink about that than they do about my weight. I like singing like this and I'm not about to give it up to please an audience."

On tour, Loni finds her unique voice and sings many of her songs as free-form vocalizations or spontaneous, vocal poems. Music seems to flow through her, finding voice for a spirit that comes from the hearts and souls of all who hear it. No song is ever the same twice, but a part of each song's beauty enhances the listener, so her songs are never completely forgotten by anyone who hears them.

Three months into their tour, Loni marries Abu and goes with him to honeymoon in Palestine, his homeland. There, they are both instrumental in finalizing peace talks still in progress with Israel. Though the city of Jerusalem was made an International Zone of the Human Spirit seven days after The Message, there are endless other real estate and administrative details that still need to be worked out to finally bring Peace and stability to the Holy Land.

After six thousand years of fighting, bickering and numerous all-out wars over the territory, it is about time.

When the newly married couple arrive, negotiations over the territory are still in progress. It is no surprise to either side that, again, talks are bogged down in disputes. Israelis and Palestinians are starting to look at each other with the hate and mistrust that characterized their interactions for only Jehovah/Allah knows how long. All looks as though it is lost, yet again.

Then Abu shares a secret with his new wife. It is a piece of information known only to a person raised in a family with both

Arab and Jewish members. Unfortunately, such families are as rare as Allah's teeth in modern Jerusalem. Thank Jehovah's bunions, in the case of Abu's family, his father's Aunt Sheba is a Jew and lived in his family household for a time, when Abu was a child.

The secret Abu shares with his wife is that both Arabs and Jews sing their children to sleep at night with the same song. Loni brings this information to the negotiating table by positioning herself at a window across the street from diplomatic headquarters, late one night. Rumor has it that both sides are on the verge of giving up on the talks when Loni begins to sing that bedtime song.

The sound of her voice, so pure and so lovely, reminds each negotiator of their own mother, and of a time when they know nothing of war and everything about kindness. The song also reminds many of them it is their mother's ardent wish, sometimes her last wish before she dies, that they reach a settlement for Peace. Mothers are important in that part of the world, so they work something out and finalize the peace plan before everyone goes home to sleep as soundly a babe. In this way, the last remaining, unresolved human conflict on Planet Earth is settled and world peace is declared.

It is throughout this peaceful world that Loni and Abu make their way, doing their part to make sure things stay peaceful. They become Wanderers who travel from one urban center to another, where they make harmony and, as such, are welcome wherever they go.

Loni and Abu usually show up in locations that are having some kind of problem or dispute and people are having a hard time settling things themselves. They are always found where bad trouble is brewing. It is never clear how they manage to get such timely intelligence, but no matter how they get there, Loni and Abu bring harmony to places where they make music.

"We don't like discord." Abu explains. "It's our job to help do something about it, before the ugly noise of war starts playing a gig here."

In one instance, the couple gets the government leaders of both sides of a dispute together, as a choir, and has them sing. Each vocalist gains respect for the voice of the others and each realizes that in unity they can be heard with far greater effectiveness than when solo.

"The world will really listen to us, if we sing the same song." one Leader tells another, before all sit down to make a concerted effort to settle their differences. "Divided there is only discord. That makes all of us easy to dismiss. In concert we can't be ignored."

In a city divided by generations of conflict, Loni sings love songs to the young people of two warring factions. The sons and daughters who attend her concert fall in love with one another and get married. Their parents are forced to settle their quarreling, or they will never see their grandkids.

Abu and Loni are once asked to perform by Loni's third cousin, twice removed, Preston Sommes III, when they meet him in East Africa. There, at Preston's request, Loni sings fish to the surface of a river so two groups arguing about fishing rights can see that there are plenty of fish there for everyone.

When Loni removes her veil, Preston III is astonished to find that the one people call "The Voice' is none other than this third-cousin, Loni. She is equally surprised to learn that Preston is the world-famous 'Fish Man', and that both of them are Wanderers, homesick for Mobile. The sight of a Neighbor from childhood, plus the sound of another lilting Alabama accent, causes each to welcome the other with open arms, before both Wander on.

Next Loni sings a grizzly bear out of an Urban Center and back into the Wilds where it belongs. The creature thinks her voice sounds just like golden honey and would have followed her anywhere.

In addition to the hit Loni makes with fish and bears, the performers become world famous among human audiences. Major media moguls never hear them, but street people and crowds of urban folk flock to their concerts on street corners and then in parks, stadiums, and arenas, as their fame grows. They usually make music for free or charge so little that all can afford their performances. No one is ever turned away from a concert for lack of money.

It is estimated that during their tours, three quarters of the world's human population hears the plenty that Loni has to sing about. Though they never do a concert in the USA, from time to time they send the American Review the songs they write about peace, harmony, and international solidarity for workers. In this way their work is heard in the USA, even if they are not.

Still, as far as Abu can tell, Loni is as big as ever under the veil she wears for her concerts. That is fine with him, but when Loni returns from a visit to her family in Mobile, she is noticeably thinner.

"I don't think your country agrees with you." Abu tells her. "You must be half the weight you were when you left."

Loni is even thinner a year later when she presents Abu with a fine daughter. After the birth of baby Jasmine, Loni weighs in at 160 pounds and is shrinking fast.

"Promise me you will not disappear altogether?" Abu requests.

"Not much chance of that." Loni assures him. "I'm having too much fun here."

Their daughter never recalls her mother being heavy. She does remember her being happy. Jasmine also recollects her mother being very, very smart. When Loni sings, wearing a veil in her public concerts, she is world famous. When her mother takes that veil off, she is completely anonymous, and no one gives her a second glance. In this way Loni can live a normal life, just like any other woman, between concerts.

"All people see of my public image, is my veil." Loni explains, when her daughter asks why she still wears a traditional, Islamic covering at a time the rest of the world's Muslim women are taking off their veils.

"There is an advantage to the veil." Loni explains. "When I sing from behind the veil, it's not just me singing. I am singing the song of Mother Earth. I am its voice and People listen."

"And she never sounded better." Abu comments, giving his wife a kiss.

THE FISH MAN

His family and friends never could figure out why Preston Sommes III became a Wanderer. In fact, they were not even sure he had become one when he disappeared a couple of days after The Message. Preston's relatives feared he 'left us', until his mama found his note stuck on their refrigerator with a magnet shaped like a salmon. It read: 'Gone fishing. Love, P.III'

Since fishing is what Preston most liked to do, Cora May had hope that her son still lives. Preston's father, Preston Sommes Jr., hopes that Cora May is right and that his son is not food for the fish, himself, at the bottom of some pond, lake, river, or estuary.

"That boy had everything in the world to live for!" his brother, the Senator, tells Preston Sommes. "He could have been President of the United States!"

The Senator long had his eye on P.III as the only male Sommes capable of a career in politics, after he retires. Sterlin had plans to launch his nephew's political career, shortly before the youth's disappearance. His father knows his son hates politics as much as he does, so Sterlin's words bring Preston Jr. some measure of comfort.

"No wonder the boy left town." Preston tells his wife. "His choice to disappear into the Wild may be the only way to get Sterlin off his back. No one can oppose the Senator when he is determined to have his way."

"I just hope our boy finds what makes him happy out there." Cora May responds.

Right about the time his Uncle Sterlin gives up hope of ever seeing his nephew again, Cora May has a visit from a distant cousin, Loni Cox. She reports having seen Preston III in East Africa. Cora May is happy to know her son is alive, well, and is actively pursuing his interest in fish, as he wanders the world.

By that time, being a Wanderer is a well-accepted lifestyle of choice, for those who do not want to stay put in any one Urban Center. PIII's parents decide not to let Sterlin know their son has been sighted, fearing the Senator will track the young man down and have his way with him.

"If a person decides they don't want to settle in one place, they should not have to do so." Preston tells Cora May. "Even if Sterlin is their Uncle and that place is the White House."

"Our boy's gifts and talents are in big demand, now." Cora May admits. "I'll miss him, of course, but the fish need him more."

P III has more than an extensive knowledge of fish and riparian habitats. He has an instinctive feel for what is needed for water-based communities to stay alive and well, and how to keep a river, stream, pond or ocean, and its inhabitants healthy. It is not clear who first starts calling Preston III "The Fish Man", but he uses the name when writing his Internet web page. If there is a problem with water or fish, people write to him and he responds to try to help. Sometimes Preston shows up in person to do so.

The young man speaks for fish when The Message calls for restoring Wild places to the way they were two hundred years before The Message.

Many places were under water, before humans drained swamps, built levees, and dried up the creeks, ponds and pools that were once part of the landscape. They need to be so, again, and Preston often enlists the aid of InDios people to restore waterways to their former aquatic glory.

"Who better to get the place back to the way it was?" Preston admits. "They lived here a thousand years before foreigners came to displace them. Unfortunately, a lot has happened to places near water since they've been gone. The new arrivals have done just about everything one can imagine, and a few things not even God could have conceived, to their lands."

It is by working on projects, like the reforestation of the Mississippi valley, that P III's reputation is made. Some of these streams and rivers are so polluted there are more fish-shaped magnets on his mama's refrigerator than actual fish in the water. The advice of someone like P III, with guidance from local environment groups, InDios citizens and others, helps heal riparian zones and restore land that has been turned into farms in the past century.

"Everything that once lived near the rivers and supported the fish is needed, too." Preston points out. "The trees that shelter the banks and hold the soil are needed. The land plants and insects that die and fall into the streams are needed. The tiny plankton and other creatures fish eat are needed. To support them all, we need a water supply that's pure enough not to kill all those other things. Then, when fish are reintroduced to those lakes, streams, and rivers, they will have a chance to survive."

"Sorry Fish Man, most of what is needed here is long gone." his helpers point out, discouraged by what they find.

"Then we start by getting the people and their animals out and the water flowing back in." Preston advises. "Once that begins, the rest of nature takes its course."

"How can we ever bring it all back to health?" the discouraged workers ask. "We wrecked a lot of places before we even found out what was there. We have no idea what to do now."

"It would be impossible for people to turn lakes and streams, rivers and swamps into healthy waterways." Preston agrees. "Don't be discouraged, though, the Earth can do it. Once the water is clean enough to support the return of life to its shores, the fish, birds, and insects will follow. We have some good ideas about what is needed and enough people who want to help. The rest is a matter of patience."

"What do we do besides wait?" asks the gathering of artists and airplane mechanics, beauticians and butchers, cabbies and cooks, drivers, and dry cleaners (and so on down the alphabet), who are eager to respond to the call of the Wild and come out to help with the cleanup.

"We lower these dikes and levees enough to allow natural flooding, and then replant some of the trees, bushes and grasses that do best in wetlands and swamps." PIII advises. "If we start these projects in natural creeks and rivers that feed into a larger body of water, the web of life spreads downstream from the healthy Wild spot and will gradually help restore the whole ecosystem."

"You mean nature does all that without us?" ask these incredulous helpers.

"Once our cities and factories stop pouring polluted water into the rivers and shorelines and we let waterways return to ways they were in the past, there are a few things we can do to help." PIII notes. "Mainly the Earth heals itself, as it always has, with or without us. It will take time, but eventually a healthier ecosystem is bound to develop in and along our waterways. Our job is to be as kind as we can to the place, and to each other, while we wait for that to happen. One jump up that fish ladder at a time."

With the help of The Fish Man, and others like him, a game plan for fish in the thousands, fish in the millions and, eventually, fish in the billions comes into play. The streams and ponds, then the rivers and lakes and eventually the coastlines and the marshes, swamps, wetlands, estuaries, and oceans, begin to recover from centuries of human interference. What went on for a thousand years before The Message and put an end to sea life in places like the Mediterranean Sea, begins to be reversed.

"You got to be patient with fish." Preston III explains to a group working to liberate a river that was resigned underground, confined to pipes and culverts, and paved over two decades before The Message. These urban citizens want access to its waters for community fish farms and to plant wild rice and native food crops, like Miner's Lettuce and watercress, along its banks.

"Patience." the Fish Man advises.

While the group is being patient, they go to work and remove the concrete and replace rocks, soil and some plant cover needed to return the waterway to normal.

"We don't need to breed mosquitoes here, they seem to show up without any help from us, at all." Project Coordinator, Luis Fredrico Bolla, comments. "Everything else needs to be replaced or replanted."

They have their work cut out for them, but Planet Earth helps, too. Once the mosquitoes come back, so do the birds. Birds bring tiny spores on their feet and feathers, and seeds in their droppings. There are also seeds and roots that wash downstream that help replant and replace some of what was there before. Patience.

Once the water sees sunlight again, tiny plants, algae, and microscopic animals, which need light to live, begin to thrive there again. With them come small insects, then crustaceans and beetles, frogs and snakes and even tiny fish, which live on the tiny plants and animals. Patience.

Once the water slows in some pools and inlets, and rushes faster through other parts of the waterway, channels are created by the flow of water over rocks and soil. These variations in the flow of water allow sand and soil to silt to the bottom in some areas and wash up on the banks in others. This creates both hiding places and shelters and some fast-moving currents, for a variety of different plants and animals to get established. Patience.

When rain falls it is slowed by bushes, rocks, grass, and trees and no longer feeds directly into the flow of the waterway. More water is stored underground, to reappear as springs that feed the swamps and marshes, which once bordered the area around the river and now appear there again. Patience.

People along the river are able to start raising ducks and fish, freshwater clams and herb crops, which all thrive in these marshy spots. They eventually need to put their houses on stilts, in the flood plain areas along the river, as the marshes expand. In a few years, folks living there can fish from their back porches, just as their ancestors did, generations ago. Patience.

❄ ❄ ❄ ❄

Preston III moves on to help other Wild places and other waterways. It seems when anything important is happening with water or for the creatures that live on, under or near it, Preston III is there. When asked how he always seemed to be present to speak up for the water world, the Fish Man points out:

"This planet is mostly water. There is never a time that water, and those living in it, are not an important part of the picture. If anyone is talking, anytime, about anything important, someone needs to speak up for the water world. I'm always in the right place to do that, no matter where I am."

THE HOLY ROAMING EMPIRE

Zones of the Human Spirit are designated at an International Conference of Religious Leaders, shortly after The Message. Holy guys and gals approve sites around the world as belonging to all man and womankind. These sites are so approved because of their international, and sometimes inter-dimensional, religious significance. The zones are many and varied but prove to all humanity that one does not have to own a thing to be in possession of about a tenth of the Planet. For the first time, all humans on the Earth know they have a real stake in what goes on here.

"The Zones are little embassies of the heart, in every Nation on Earth." Ike 'The Preacher' Ham explains upon his return to Mobile, after attending the Conference that creates the Zones.

"All will be accepted there." he tells the tens of millions of humans who watch Ike's last, live broadcast from the Tower of Salvation, his tele ministry headquarters.

"All will find refuge in the Zones of the Human Spirit," Ike promises "as long as they mind their manners."

Many are surprised that it is not the ministers, imams, priests or priestesses, rabbis, swamis, or shamans who take off to visit the International Zones of The Human Spirit, after The Message. It is not the Holy Ones, the Religious leaders, or the clerics who leave all behind to travel from one Zone of the Human Spirit to another. It is regular people, most of whom belong to no organized religion or religious practice, who begin pilgrimages that take them from one Holy Zone to another, all over Planet Earth.

The general public thinks this is because clerics and religious leaders already have the answers, Creator-wise, and have no need to go so far afield to discover religious truth. Not so. Most religious leaders are the first to confess they stay put because they already spend too much time contemplating holy stuff. They readily admit they cannot imagine themselves doing any more of that than they already do. In fact, after The Message, many of the planet's religious counselors and guides look for other work, themselves.

It turns out there are a lot of interesting career options for clerics, after The Message. Many former religious leaders take advantage of this and change professions. Not a few of them become stand-up comics since they are already used to presenting outlandish material to crowds of people. A few become actors because they are excellent at pretending to large audiences.

"Hey, this stuff is truer than a lot of what I was preaching." one Minister-turned-Thespian admits, though the play he is currently in is about a village whose citizens are all abducted by aliens from outer space.

"I once taught that an alien, in the form of an angel, told the founder of my religion how to live on Earth. Our entire religious teaching is based on that conversation, as recorded by the founder who took notes on what was said in writing only, he could read. As a result, our scripture is actually a lot crazier that this script is." the actor admits.

Citizens who make the rounds of the Zones of the Human Spirit are known to the rest of the world as Holy Roamers. Clerics know that most Roamers never go to churches, temples, synagogues, or shrines, anyway, and their leaving town makes the construction of more houses of worship unnecessary, which is a good thing. Those running religions realize they could never find the man or womanpower to staff new congregations with spiritual advisors, if all the Roamers started going to regular places of worship. Many doubts the newcomers would find answers in conventional religions if they did show up there.

"Creators bless these pilgrims, and may they find what they seek in the Zones." most clerics say of those who do hit the road in search of a Holy Zone.

"It is many of these irreligious, the ones who believed in nothing but the almighty dollar or who valued only earthly power or prestige, who are the first to become Roamers. They are trying to find something of value beyond their wealth and influence." the Pope tells Newsman Harrison Chambers in an interview. "They probably tried conventional religion long ago. Now they go to look for another source of enrichment, and many go to the Zones in search of it."

One of these Holy Roamers is Combi Witherspoon, stockbroker, and financier from the Mobile Stock exchange. Another is a man from the same city, Merriweather Marion Jenkins, a contractor, and construction tycoon who built half of Mobile before The Message. The last of the trio is Lobelia St. Thomas, a Dean at Hardwood Law School. The three meets by chance on the train headed for the Zone of the Human Spirit nearest to Mobile, known in the Mobile community as The Abiding Light.

Lobelia is back in Mobile after her mama "left us" and she does not have the heart to return to her position at the Ivy League School once she makes her escape from that prison of irrelevancy. Unlike her mother, Lobelia decides to change, rather than die, to switch.

Combi is there because his devotion to acquiring money has robbed him of any shred of joy in life. He spends every waking hour, and some of his sleeping ones, worried about money and has to leave all that behind for an opportunity to Have Fun and Be Kind, the basic rules of the Game as indicated in The Message.

After a serious attempt at an attitude adjustment, in the swamps around Mobile, then while working with the folks at Neighborhood 7 & 7, Merriweather Marion Jenkins heads for the nearest Zone. He hopes to get the racist nonsense he believes out of his head, before it does him and his world more harm. Once sentenced to a stay at the Abiding Light Sanitarium for trying to kill the President of the United States, Merriweather now goes in voluntarily to give the Zone a try.

When these three wealthy, famous and powerful people spot each other alighting from the train at the Abiding Light station, they recognize one another at once. Most people from Mobile know Merriweather Jenkins on sight, and most people on the Planet know Combi and Lobelia on sight. The three go into a huddle on the station platform, to check things out with their own, before taking their next step through the Abiding Light gates. It is not that any of these three lack courage. In fact, each is considered a Tiger of their profession. They consult one another because they know the value of checking with a "we" group, before making any major move.

All know, from long experience, that any big change needs to have the backing and support of others like themselves–the powers that be.

"Others might think we're movers and shakers," Merriweather is the first to admit, "but we know we're only a success because we go with the status quo. Sure, we used our considerable power, wealth and influence to support that status quo right back, but Creator only knows who or what the status quo is these days."

"On the nose, Merriweather." Combi agrees. "The status quo has changed completely. We aren't supposed to be concerned with money and power now, only with kindness. I, for one, need some new coping skills."

"I know nothing about being kind." Lobelia admits. "I've spent my life studying the law and that has little to do with kindness. Heck, most of it doesn't even have much to do with fairness or justice!"

"At least we realize we're clueless." Merriweather admits. "That's a start."

"You think this Zone of the Human Spirit place will help?" Combi asks, surveying the high stone gate before them.

"The three of us have covered all the usual bases of power and influence." Lobelia surmises. "Merriweather controlled vast amounts of land and property. You are a leader in the world of money and finances, Combi, and I'm an expert in the world of law and government. If we know nothing about Kindness, with all that under our belts, then this must be the place for us."

The three look up at the sign above the gate they are about to enter. It reads:

'The Abiding Light Sanitarium for the Mentally Ill'

"We don't have to stay here if we don't like it." Lobelia reminds her two companions, as they travel up the garden path toward the sanitarium's door. "I hear there are other options, like prisons that take in Fortunate 500 executives, for retraining in creative change."

"There's hope for us, yet." Combi notes, as he knocks at the door. "But let's try here, first. There must be some reason they nominated this place as a Zone of the Human Spirit. I'd like to start my quest by finding out why they made a nut house a Zone."

"Wasn't always a nut house." Merriweather shares, as they wait for someone to come to the door. "I know about most of the land in and around Mobile, and I know that this land has been occupied by humans for almost three hundred years, and maybe, for centuries before that. Something in this Neighborhood makes people stick around."

"Have humans been in Mobile that long." Combi admits. "Who was here three hundred years ago?"

"Founder of the Sommes clan, for one. This old place was the first settlement built by a white man, when Sommes ancestors came over from England." Lobelia recalls, having studied Mobile's long history of human power plays.

"Right, Lobelia." Merriweather agrees. "But I bet you didn't know that Dr. Sommes built his place smack dab in the middle of the land most important to the humans who were living here when he arrived. His first homestead was built on their holiest spot."

"Smart move." Lobelia acknowledges. "Nobody would attack him there. His next smart move was to marry a Medicine Woman from that group. They weren't about to attack her, either."

The door to the Abiding Light opens and they see Freda Tarkel Phillips on the other side of the threshold, exiting the Sanitarium. Freda is being discharged.

"But what makes this a sacred spot?" Combi asks.

"People come here to die." Freda answers. "They been doin' that ever since anyone can remember."

Freda gets the attention of the people on the steps with that remark. None of them have any intention of "leaving us."

"You're leaving here." Combi points out. "So, not everyone comes here to die."

Freda pushes past them but calls back. "Some come to be reborn. You don't have to leave your body for a transformation to take place." she adds, as she runs down the path toward the train station.

"Relieved to hear it." Lobelia puts in.

"Don't you mean re-lived?" Betsy Ross Jackson asks, as she opens the door wide for the new arrivals.

Betsy is cleaning the front entry hall but waves them on down the hall toward the Admissions Office.

"Is what she said true?" Lobelia asks Betsy Ross.

"Have a lot of people Gone to God from here?"

"Not only do people go to God," Betsy Ross assures them. "God comes to them."

"What?" Lobelia asks. "Creator here?"

"It's been known as a Holy spot for generations." Merriweather reminds Lobelia. "That implies a certain amount of direct communication with the Lord."

"And the Lady." Betsy Ross points out and then goes back to washing the floor.

"The Sommes family moved out of this location around the turn of the century because they were dying off, fast, in this old house." Merriweather explains. "They got out but turned it into a TB Sanitarium where people are expected to die."

"Another smart move." Combi admits. "Give people what they want and you're sure to be a success, even if what you're selling is death."

Combi has been in on enough arms and weapons deals to know that humans spend a lot of money on death. Prior to The Message, many governments went bust trying to match weaponry with their foes, and that did not even count the cost for the actual combat, started to justify the use of all their money and resources on weapons of war.

"Why is it a mental hospital, now?" Combi asks.

"Once a cure was found for TB, it was politically correct to have big mental hospitals instead of TB Sanitariums. There's always a need for some kind of long-term problem, and craziness became pretty popular after World War II." Lobelia explains. "We built big warehouses, usually outside city areas, to house our crazy people. We also developed all kinds of ways to make money, for county and state, for taking care of them in those warehouses."

"But most of the mental hospitals closed in the 1970's and 80's." Combi reminds Lobelia. "The Abiding Light must be one of the last of its kind. What are we building these days, instead?"

"Prisons." Merriweather puts in, having built many of the state and federal prisons in the area before The Message. "Crime was called the plague of the 20th Century, and our prisons were our big, expensive, isolation units."

"Too bad the patient almost died." Lobelia notes, well aware of how the twin cancers of wars and prisons drained the US economy, prior to The Message. "Thank Creator for The Message."

"From what I hear, you can thank him in person." Merriweather reminds her, as they reach the Admissions Office door.

Merriweather remains at the Abiding Light for many years, moving on when he leaves his physical body. Then he becomes a cloud over the rain forest of the Congo. In that form he is in charge of minor rainstorms and significant, near-Earth, rainbow events, finally able to allow a little color in his life. You can learn more about Merriweather in the next book in The Message series, '*The Gospels According To Reverend Ike.*'

Combi leaves the Abiding Light after a stay of a few months, to become a nursery school Teaching Assistant for the Neighborhood 9, District 12 Boston, Massachusetts Urban Center Department of Education. Combi decides that learning to play again will help his personal evolution most. To do so, he studies with the experts, the three- to five-year-olds at the Play Way Nursery School and ChildCare Center.

Lobelia leaves the Abiding Light after ten days, to pursue her studies at the Dan and Don Academy of Self Defense and Clown Training, in Washington DC. She enrolls in the course taught by Dan White and Don Bo, former Secret Service Agents for the First Family. Before Lobelia can defend herself and others from dangerous and deadly injustice, she needs to find a sense of humor about politics and power. Once this is accomplished, she becomes a true warrior for laughs and justice in the US political arena.

"We're lucky Dan and Don located their school in Washington, DC." Lobelia acknowledges, gratefully. "Our elected representatives are constantly vying for the title of most ridiculously powerful and that certainly can be powerfully ridiculous."

Lobelia learns to laugh at much of what goes on in our nation's capital and, armed with her clown training and her legal-eagle reputation, she soon has many of the world's most powerful people laughing at themselves along with her. She does a standup comedy act, 'The Rise and The Fall of the Roving Vampire' regularly for Congress. It never fails to slay them.

"You think you'll get us to die laughing?" Senator Sommes gasps, barely able to catch his breath as he recovers from Lobelia's testimony before a Senate Finance Committee meeting. "You're tryin' to get us all out the picture that way and take over the government?"

"Were it only that easy, Sterlin." Lobelia shares.

"You call me in as an expert witness to speak on the impact of defense spending, so you get my comedy act. I can't help it if what you want to do is so ridiculous."

"So, you try to get us to laugh at ourselves, before someone else can?"

"Then everyone's laughing with you, not at you. Politically that's a whole different ball game." Lobelia shares. "In the words of the High Clown, our teacher to the world's leaders: 'Nobody's perfect, but that doesn't mean we can't have fun with that.'"

"Words to laugh by." Sterlin agrees. "But wasn't Don and Dan's school started to prevent domestic abuse? That is surely no laughing matter."

"I try to teach our government officials to stop beating up on the voters who put them in office." Lobelia answers. "I think 'Assure the domestic tranquillity' is the way the US Constitution puts it."

"Sign me up for those classes." Sterlin concedes. "I was once told to do battle with the self-serving jackass in me, as the way I can best help the world. It's nice to know there's a school, right here in our Nation's Capital, where I can have some fun while I learn to do just that."

DREAMING CLEAN

Reid McCullers Benson once joined Dan White and Don Bo, as a member of the team guarding the President of the United States and the First Lady, at the historic Tiger Summit. The meeting took place five days after The Message and is where plans were outlined for the transformation of the United States and much of North America, in light of The Message. It is at this meeting that Reid admits he beats his wife and begins to transform himself.

Reid has been trying, for years, to control the violent outbursts and reactions he has when the bathrooms in his home are messy. At the Tiger Summit he sees this is just plain crazy; insanity from his own childhood that has nothing to do with his wife or her housekeeping skills. It is clear to Reid that he better clean up his own act before he kills Ramona over a towel left on the bathroom floor, or a water spill by the bathtub.

As soon as Reid leaves the Tiger Summit, he tells his wife he will never hit her again. Then he offers her the option of leaving him if that makes her feel safe. Ramona is out of there in fourteen and a half minutes and Reid does not blame her a bit.

Always a conscientious Sheriff, whose stated career goal is to 'Clean up Mobile Come Hell or High Water', Reid spends fifteen to twenty hours a day at work. After his wife leaves him, the Sheriff moves right into Police headquarters and takes up residence in one of the jail's empty cells. The Sheriff keeps the door of his cell open and his cell spotless. In fact, he keeps the whole jail clean, putting the inmates there to work on their areas.

He supervises and advises them endlessly on the finer points of scrupulous cleanliness and by the time most are ready to leave, they vow never to return to jail again. Reed trains them so well they are qualified for high-paying jobs in the computer industry, as technicians in clean room environments. Thanks to Reid, they no longer want or need a life of crime.

Cleaning up the criminal element is still not enough to satisfy Reid. He worries not only about the cleanliness of the jail, but about the cleanliness of the water that comes out of the jail plumbing. When the Sheriff begins to patrol the local water treatment plant, testing the water daily, complaints are made about him to the Mayor.

The Mayor is quite aware of Reid's cleanliness problem because Mayor Trueblood Benson is Reid's eldest brother. Trueblood is quite a bit older than Reid and left their family home just about the time Reid began to agitate to install indoor plumbing there. Trueblood will never forget the fuss Reid made, nor can he figure out why an indoor toilet and shower meant so much to the boy. He just knew his youngest brother's requests for a bathroom drove their daddy wild. Whitacre Benson used to beat the shit out of Reid for bothering him about such non-sense when he was about killing himself just trying to feed them all.

"Don't we have enough shit going on in this house with all you children? You want to bring more in here?" their daddy would yell, as he hit at Reid with his belt.

Fearless or foolish, Reid persisted in his requests and Whitacre in his violent response to them, until their daddy had a stroke and died during one of their arguments. Reid took the pitiful bit of insurance money from his father's estate and built the family an indoor bathroom with it. His brothers always though Reid was a little crazy, but that indoor privy and the absence of those frequent beatings seemed to straighten Reid right out.

Always a clever child, the boy went on to do well in high school and Reid joined the police academy right after graduation from Mobile High. Reid got his college degree while working his way up the chain of Command in the Mobile Police force and is elected Sheriff after ten years on the force. Reid remains a clean, upstanding individual who has done their city no end of good since he joined the Mobile Sheriff's Department.

Trueblood owes his own successful career as Mayor to his brother's influence. No doubt Reid could have been Mayor, himself, if he had a mind to it. Politics never held an interest in Reid. He only wanted to clean up their town.

"You're going a little too far with this clean water campaign, though." Trueblood tells Reid after a meeting of the City Council. "You sound like a damn nut case out there, going on about pollutants in the lifeblood of the Mother. Get a grip Reid!" his brother warns. "You need help."

Fortunately, the helper Reid finds is a former psychologist, Sunny Leonardo. Before The Message, Sunny gave up his mental health practice to become a professional painting and home repair contractor. Sunny got to talking to Reid, when the Mayor engaged Sunny to renovate the plumbing in the jail. Trueblood made a special request that the workman start their work in the cell where Reid lives.

"Do you think someone is nuts because they believe something you don't?" Reid asks Sunny, as aware of the plumber's mental health background as he is of the life story of most of Mobile's citizens.

"If what you see and believe does not bother you, why should it bother me?" Sunny responds.

"Can't I take a pill or something?" Reid asks.

"If you want to take something to change the way you think that option is always open. Changing how you act in the world can be a little more complicated." Sunny admits.

As they speak, Reid has a vision of his own mother, so unhappy and ashamed of what she believes, she kills herself when Reid is only five years old. Though he was very young when he last saw her, Reid can still recall the look of pain on her face. It is the look he sees in his own eyes when he looks in the mirror.

"My wife, Faith, thinks that water is the life-blood of the Mother, too." Sunny assures Reid. "She tells that to people, all the time, in connection with her job with the Urban Food Production Program. Sometimes people think ideas are strange because of who says them, not because of what is said."

"So, you think she'll know what I'm talking about?"

"She'll know. She's a mother herself."

Faith has no problem with Reid's obsession with clean water and Reid shares how his own mother used to pine and sigh, crying the purest tears, because she could not keep a household with seven children clean.

"My bothers tell me that mama got really depressed after her eighth child died. Her only daughter, Lilly, was born when I was four years old, but the baby died from an infection. Mama was never the same after that, no matter how we tried to tell her it was not her fault. The woman needed help."

Faith tells Reid; "She is gone, but the Mother of All is still here. Mother Earth can use your help to clean things up, too."

Reid joins Faith and her crew to construct water catchment systems, on rooftops and above parking garages and public buildings, so rainwater can irrigate all food grown in Mobile. Reid has little else to do, as most people are so busy working to repair and rebuild their Neighborhoods; few have time to commit crimes. Rather than dismiss another on his police force, Reid turns his own law enforcement duties over to his Chief Deputy and goes to work each day with the Clean Water Development Task Force.

"It's the only way we can assure that chemicals and other pollutants in our ground water are not going to continue to poison our children." Reid points out to the City Council, when he updates them on the group's work.

Listening to his brother's report, Trueblood realizes that Reid sounds completely rational and normal for the first time in ages. Reid also seems more at peace with himself, since he got out of law enforcement and began to actively work on water purity problems.

"Reid is as obsessed as ever with things being clean, but he is putting it to good use these days." Trueblood tells Reid's ex-wife Ramona, when they meet for coffee at her request. Reid had called her and asked her out to dinner, but she is not sure meeting him again is such a good idea.

"He's in charge of assuring that water in all garden and rooftop storage tanks is not contaminated and that project sure has benefited from Reid's attention to detail." Trueblood tells his former sister-in law.

"Reid still living in a jail cell?" Ramona asks.

"Afraid so." Trueblood admits.

"Then I don't think he's ready to date yet." Ramona responds, "The man is still deeply disturbed."

For the next six months, Reid continues to benefit from time spent in the gardens of their city. He always feels better in the open air and sunshine.

Faith Leonardo tells Reid, "If anything can help you, it will be letting go of what you no longer need and giving it back to the Mother. A garden is a great place to do that."

Reid is confused by Faith's comment. He knows he lost his father, his wife, his home, and his career in law enforcement because of violence. All he has left is his ability to clean and he is putting that ability to good use. Reid asks Faith to explain what she means.

"The Earth Mother always knows just what to do with that which will hurt us or someone else. If we keep it inside, it can do us harm. Give it to the Earth and it goes to good."

Reid does feel as though there is a toxic waste dump inside him. He is astonished Faith suggests give anything to the Planet, who has problems aplenty of Her own.

"I thought we are supposed to be cleaning things up to help our world?" Reid asks. "What can the Earth possibly do with more human pain?"

"Mother Earth has ways of turning all we give Her into something positive and Beautiful." Faith assures him. "She works miracles with all kinds of energy, even the sorrow and pain we feel. Take a look at Spring if you doubt me."

"Did my mom return her sorrow to the Earth when she died?" Reid asks, as he recalls a vivid memory of his mama's homemade coffin being lowered into the ground.

When she killed herself, her church refused to bury her in their churchyard, so mama's funeral was in the wood behind their home. Reid was secretly glad she was buried there and continued to visit her gravesite well into adulthood, even after his brothers had her body moved to a public cemetery, years later. He was sure her spirit was in the cool, clean depths of that wood.

"Perhaps in her own way she did return her sorrow to the Earth." Faith answers. "But you do not have to die to do it."

"How else?"

"First, give yourself permission to let go of anything you no longer need. Give it to the Earth." Faith proposes. "Then, make room for something better to take its place."

"Oooh Kaaaay." Reid responds, more confused than ever. "I'll try."

Reid has more ideas how to fly than he has how to try what Faith suggests. Fortunately for Reid, what happens in the process Faith described has very little to do with ideas. Soon after their talk, as he works in gardens and orchards of the city, Reid is struck by a series of unusual physical sensations that have him doubting his sanity.

On one occasion, the entire world turns shades of blue, as though a pair of huge blue sunglasses covers the sun. A few minutes later Reid's vision returns to normal, but he feels as though he is freezing cold for the rest of the day.

Another time, strange odors reach Reid's nostrils. First, he smells a stockyard odor that lasts for hours. Then everything smells like a field of spring flowers. Shortly after that occurs, all Reid's hair falls out.

Reid's hair grows back strawberry blond, the way it looked when he was a kid, and he often hears snatches of songs he heard sung as a child. Memories of his childhood continue to rise in his mind's eye. From some hidden reservoir of experience, he sees a detailed vision of his mother, pregnant with his sister Lilly. She looks radiantly happy and is washing the family clothes.

Faith is the only one Reid talks about the truly weird stuff that is going on.

"I could not have been more than four years old then." Reid marvels to Faith. "Mama was so happy when she told me she was going to have a girl child! She was sure of it… said my sister talked to her."

"It's not unusual to have dreams about those we love." Faith reminds Reid. "What are you worried about?"

"One day, I swear to Creator, I saw Penguins walking around, everywhere." Reid laughs. "It wasn't funny for those ten minutes, but I laughed like a maniac afterward. I got a few worried looks from folks then."

"What did you tell them, to put their minds at ease?" Faith asks.

"I told them I just got the joke."

"Are the strange things still happening?" Faith inquires.

"Not since I started remembering my mom." Reid admits "Before now, when I tried to remember my childhood, it was like looking down a dark, empty well. Now I see my mother. At least I think it's her." he speculates. "She's so kind, she must be my mama."

Reid's memories of childhood are a revelation to him because everything that happened as a child had been blocked from his recall. Details of his childhood were learned from his brother's stories, not from his own memory of them. Prior to his work with Faith, Reid recalls only the time he was a teenager, building the indoor bathroom in the family home after his father's death.

"I hope you're enjoying the time with your Mother, now." Faith replies.

"I am, but I'm afraid I'll get to the part when she gets really sad." Reid admits, starting to shiver, despite the fact it is quite warm outside.

"You might get to those sad memories if you need to let go of them."

Reid tells Faith, "They are just memories. I don't know what you mean by letting them go."

"It's not a knowing thing." Faith assures him. "It's a doing thing and you are doing it. That's real, even if it happens only in your own mind."

"I don't pretend to understand any of this." Reid admits, giving up on a logical explanation for what is happening to him. "I'll keep working for the Earth and the rest will just have to take care of itself."

"By Goddess, I think he's got it!" Faith exclaims and gives Reid a big hug.

It is a long time before Reid trusts what Faith tells him, but despite his doubts, more and more memories come back to him. For a while, most of them are in the form of terrible dreams. During this time, he asks to be locked in the cell he still occupies at night.

"Otherwise, I'd not let myself get a wink of sleep, for fear I would kill anyone who comes near me." Reid admits to the Night Deputy, who is happy to oblige.

"I think these are the memories of things that happened to me when I was growing up." Reid tells Faith in the light of day. "Fortunately, I don't recall a thing the next morning."

"It sounds like you had a hell of a time as a child." Faith acknowledges. "Do you wake up feeling better?"

"The dreams are terrible but at the end of every dream I see my mother. We walk through the rain, a regular summer downpour. The rain is warm and light shines through it and the air is full of rainbows. It makes me forget everything else that happened. That wonderful water washes away every fear, every hurt and every care. At the end of the walk, I feel completely clean."

"By remembering it so clearly, you have started reprogramming your past."

"Say what?"

"When you remember something and surround it in that light of love and kindness that you see at the end of your dream." Faith informs.

"I can change memories?" Reid asks.

"They are your thoughts and dreams, Reid." Faith points out. "Who else can change them but you?"

❋ ❋ ❋ ❋

"Mama, can I still see you at the end of the dream if I start to change my memories?" Reid asks his mother that night, during their walk through the rain.

"You can do anything you want in your dreams, just like you can in the waking world, Reid. It's all yours to do with as you wish. Always has been, always will be."

"You make it sound so easy. I'm afraid to let go of the pain. It's how I hold on to you."

"You don't have to hold on to fear and pain, Reid. When you leave the fear behind, you will see me in your dreams and you will know me when you are awake, as well."

Then the Mother's face begins to change, and she looks just like Reid's ex-wife, then like Faith Leonardo, then like many of the women, girls and elderly women Reid knows in his daily life. Then his mother's face begins to look like his own face, washed clean in his kindest dream.

Five Years after The Message, the world has changed a lot. Things are different enough for people to begin to get ready for Union.

THE WAY SCAN SCHOOL

Bobbie Turner looks out over the sea of faces beyond the windows of the PetroChem building. It is still early, but thousands of people fill the PetroChem Plaza, there to apply for admission to the Way Scan School. For the most part, the crowd is made up of parents and their children, but some children come without their parents and there are a few adults who have no child with them. Many are obviously grandparents with their grandkids.

"You got to wonder what would have happened if we'd advertised this." Emaline Hawkins Purcell notes. "One brief announcement on local public access TV and a mob turns out. People must be as unhappy with public schools as we imagined."

"Things weren't going well at most schools when we graduated." Winston Brightfoot comments. "From what I hear from my younger brothers and sisters, schools have gone rapidly downhill since then."

Winston comes from a family of seven children and five of his siblings are still in public schools. Some of them are doing OK but his brother Knowland Luigi is having a heck of a time. As far as Winston is concerned, Knowland is the smartest kid in their whole family, yet the boy is finding it almost impossible to make it through the seventh grade.

"The problem is that schools are still twenty years behind, in almost everything they teach and, in the ways, they teach it." Ruth "the Flame" Feinstein explains. "That was never a good thing; but the rapid evolution of almost every human system in the past five years makes schools about 100 years behind times."

Ruth just finished student teaching, as part of her state requirements for a teaching credential, so she knows what she is talking about, firsthand.

"I almost went nuts from boredom." she explains. "They had me teaching stuff that nobody had any reason to learn. Personally, I couldn't see any reason to teach most of it, either."

"I hope you explained the concept behind that to the kids." Toni Leonardo put in.

"What concept?" Ruth asks. "You mean there's a reason for that waste of time and human energy?"

"In our old education system students are supposed to fill their minds with irrelevant trivia and propaganda, so they have no energy left to think an original thought." Toni explains. "That method came into fashion after World War I. Before then people mostly taught themselves whatever they wanted to learn."

"Why propaganda?" Ruth asks, astonished.

"When most people started attending schools, most governments figured that people make less trouble, as workers and as citizens, if schools operate that way."

The Way Scans look at Toni in shocked surprise. She usually jokes about things, but she seems serious now.

"Hey! It worked for generations!" Toni explains. "Especially for newcomers to a system. How else could you get them to believe all the non-sense that people here are supposed to think about the modern, industrialized world. Most of it make no sense, in human terms, or for the Planet."

"That just colonizes people's minds!" Bobbie protests. "Their new masters are big business interests, instead of an occupying army."

"It also means a third world education for everybody, here and elsewhere. No wonder the world was such a mess before The Message." the Flame admits. "People were so misinformed!"

"Since The Message, people have started to think for themselves and do creative problem solving." Bobbie points out, taking another look at the crowd outside. "I guess that explains why we've got ten thousand people here today. They know schools are a problem we need solved."

Toni agrees. "Most people can see that conventional schools are not helping. They may be misinformed, but they're not stupid."

"That's what LeDean Winslow said when he gave us money for the Way Scan School." Bobbie reminds the other Way Scans. "He knew that something different is needed to educate people. He has degrees from our top Universities, and he thinks those places do not teach people in the right way, either."

"We're supposed to start a school that will allow kids and adults to use the brains God gave them." Emaline reminds the others. "But how?"

"That's not all he said." Toni reminds them. "He also said 'Don't let schools turn out a bunch of jackasses like me, anymore.'"

The Ways Scans laugh at Toni's perfect impression of the multi-billionaire's honest appraisal of himself. LeDean appealed to the Way Scans as the head of PetroChem, a multi-national corporation that once turned Tiger Country into green goo with a chemical spill. PetroChem had significantly cleaned up its act and wants to help the rest of the world to do the same. His company leads a worldwide ecolution in science and technology and he wants new schools to meet his, and the Planet's needs for creative innovators.

✳ ✳ ✳ ✳

LeDean first meets the Way Scans in the year 2000, when they were a youth collective; a group of kids who hang out together, known for the sunglasses they wear. They are also known as a weapon of mass instruction and work as a team to stop trouble and support positive growth in their community.

LeDean has no idea how they do what they do, because he is not raised or educated to have a clue about that kind of stuff. He is raised and educated to know how chemistry works, not how people work. He is raised and educated to know how a business works, not how the environment around that business works. He is raised and educated to have power and control over people and things, not to be kind to people or to a Planet upon which he lives.

LeDean is smart enough to be one of the world's richest and most powerful men and, at age 75, is still smart enough to realize he knows little of value. When he meets the Way Scans, at the Tiger Summit meeting shortly after The Message, he sees they know a lot of value and he decides to support them in whatever they want to do.

LeDean goes to the Way Scan's High School graduation and is impressed not only by the five-part Valedictorian speech they all give, but also by the entire Mobil High Senior Class. The whole Class puts on sunglasses to show support for the Way Scan viewpoint, and all have Tiger stripes painted on their mortar boards, in support of the recently inaugurated Tiger Preservation Project, a world-wide effort to save Tigers and everything else.

As he is one of the richest and most powerful men on Planet Earth, the school Principal is astounded when Le Dean approaches him before the ceremony and asks to address the graduating seniors. LeDean's reason for doing so is even more of a surprise.

"I come, today, to give full college scholarships to your five top students, the Way Scans." LeDean states to the crowd of students, families, and teachers.

The crowd responds with polite applause.

"Heck! All you kids are pretty impressive." LeDean admits. "I'm gonna' give scholarships to you all! In fact, if any child in Mobile can finish high school, I'll give them a scholarship, too. Why stop with you guys? Go on, young people of Mobile, learn anything you want. It's on me."

The audience sends up a wild cheer and there are a lot of college graduates, four years later. If you count the numbers who finish trade schools and non-academic career training courses, at LeDean's expense, more than 95% of the Class are graduates of a school of higher learning. Unfortunately, this does nothing for the public school system and LeDean is worried about that.

"The number of kids graduating High School each year has declined sharply, every year" LeDean tells the Way Scans sadly, when he meets with them a few months before they are due to finish college. "Let's talk about new kinds of schools."

"I want the Way Scans to start the kind of education system that the kids will stay in, maybe even LEARN something in." LeDean explains. "The public schools are not changing fast enough to meet the needs of our times. Think up something else, and I'll pay for it."

The Way Scans want to work together to promote positive change in their community. The prospect of actually starting their own school, so soon after they finish college, is their dream come true.

❋ ❋ ❋ ❋

"This dream could become a real nightmare, with so many kids and adults asking for a change." Emaline Purcell voices, as she notes the growing numbers of people outside the PetroChem building. "There must be fifteen thousand in the crowd out there. Do we say "No" to anyone who wants into our school?"

"No one should be denied the opportunity to attend the Way Scan School." Winston reminds them. "LeDean was very specific on that point. He said we should spend as much as we need on the school. We should take all comers."

"But how will we teach them all?" Ruth asks.

Winston brightens as he shares, "Betsy Ross Jackson once told me; 'Learn as much as you can about the gifts and skills of each student, as the first step in helping to teach them.' She was Head of the Board of Education in Tiger Country, the one in charge of planning the learning program for all the human children there, so she knows a thing or two about education."

"We need to devise an entrance exam that will exclude no one and will help us learn about each student. If we can't find out what they know and what they want to learn, we're just doing educational business as usual." Bobbie observes.

"So how do we learn from them?" Emaline asks, voicing what the other Way Scans are wondering.

Each of them, as usual, has a part in the answer to that question:

Toni Leonardo, clowns, "I want to see who can do good stand-up comedy. Teachers will need a sense of humor, as a lot of so-called "facts" turn out to be fiction. I'd like to know who could get a good laugh out of that. They might be our best teachers."

"Figure out a way to test for that gift." Winston proposes. "Remember, we have to find ways to develop the skills people have, so they can use their gifts to teach and to learn."

"I want to know who thinks differently from others, who has a different kind of mind." Bobbie Turner states.

"We will have to encourage people to see things in whole new ways, if we are going to meet the challenges of the future."

Bobbie, always the lookout for their group, decides to hunt for students with different ways of knowing and to track their unusual ways of solving problems.

"Same deal." Winston tells Bobbie. "Find a way to test for such gifts and then see if you can come up with a plan not to change those different minds once you have found them. That may be our biggest educational challenge."

"I want to work with people who can operate on other levels of being" Ruth the Flame acknowledges.

"Why would you want people who do that?" Winston asks.

"Because you never know." Ruth answers. "Like Bobbie said, there may be a whole lot we need to teach and some of it may not exist yet. Maybe, some of the people out there can help with that."

"Ho!" Winston agrees.

As a member of the Brightfoot family, Winston has always been into new ways of understanding things. Seven children, with seven, different views of reality (nine ways if you count his parents) teach Winston not to discount anyone's take on what is real. Winston hopes he can work with students to realize their own point of view, while living in harmony with others around them. The Ways Scans do not call Winston "Bridges" for nothing.

"The point is not to get another to change their mind, but to help them clarify their view of self and, perhaps, share it with others. That kind of learning gets dialogue going, to begin to solve problems with positive solutions." Winston agrees. "I'll help you with that talent search, Ruth."

"I want to start a school for fun." Emaline Purcell voices. "This whole world needs to train people to be professional party animals. When we learn how to plan, execute, and orchestrate all kinds of fun, even for doing the stuff people don't usually want to do, problems will be fun to solve."

"I get it!" laughs Toni. "Have potholes on your street that need repair? Have a dance event to fill them in and fix the road. It's an audience participation thing."

"Sounds good to me." Winston concedes. "Help people be happy, positive people and you have a happy, positive city. Learning how to play as we work together sure should be part of that game plan."

"I've already thought of a fun way to screen perspective students." Emaline tells them. "They have to identify what they most hate doing and then come up with ways they can make it fun and interesting, like a party event for at least two dozen people. Heck, they get extra credit if they can make something the whole urban center can have fun with!"

"That party idea might be a good way to do our initial testing, too." Bobbie foresees. "We could hold a big, day-long event and invite people to try all kinds of different contests and games. We'd learn about the people there and what we need to organize to include them in our school as students or teachers."

The Way Scans agree that playing is just about the best way to do anything and decide to take that news to the crowd waiting outside. They have no worry about getting people's attention to do this. They just use the Way Scan method of relating to others, which never fails them:

First, Ruth 'The Flame' Feinstein walks out the door of the PetroChem building and all eyes are on her, immediately. That always happens, no matter where she goes.

Then Emaline Purcell sings out with a voice so compelling as to bring people out of their offices, from buildings surrounding the PetroChem Plaza. As usual, Emaline's sounds focus all attention on the Way Scans.

Toni Leonardo comes out next and tells jokes. In keeping with the occasion, she shares a story from her own school days.

"When I was growing up, my parents taught me the importance of learning from my dreams. So, when I started kindergarten, I thought my time in the classroom was for sleeping. I would have graduated with honors, except that my snoring made the teacher angry. She said I was keeping her awake!"

Tony went on long enough to put their audience in a good mood and to allow Bobbie a chance to move through the gathered crowd for a closer look. He is surprised to find so many young adults there.

"I never made it in school." Abubakar Tang Suharno, age 20, tells Bobbie when asked if he is the prospective student. "I figure maybe I'll give school another tries. I like to keep an open mind."

"Student!" 70-year-old grandmother of six, Jessica Trimbeau, exclaims when asked. "I want to teach at your school! I raised a bunch of kids who really know how to live. They help anyone they can, no questions asked. I must have done somethin' right. I want to teach a class on kindness."

Bobbie knows a good teacher when he meets one and takes down Ms. Trimbeau's phone number to contact her later. When Toni finishes Winston gets up to speak. The audience is in a great mood and his proposal of a party the next day puts them in an even better one.

"There'll be lots of great games to play." Winston assures them. "The Community Access Channel will give you details on time and place. Don't worry, no one will be turned away. If you want to go to a Way Scan School, a place will be found for you there, for as long as you want to learn."

There is a collective sigh of relief from the waiting crowd. Kids who have been kicked out of every school in the city will now have another chance. Parents of kids who have been kicked out of every school in the city will now have a moment's peace of mind.

"God knows what they've been learning out there on the street, by themselves." the mother of a habitual truant, Alexander Farquar, tells the father of Lupe Henry.

Alexander's problem is that his head is in a different time zone from the rest of the local population. He cannot get up in the morning to save his life and fails all his classes.

Lupe was asked to leave every school she went to because she writes on every classroom wall she can and has done so since the age of five. Lupe's mother hopes the Way Scan's new school will be more understanding of her daughter's compulsion to beautify classrooms.

Both parents leave the PetroChem Plaza hoping their problems will be solved by an alternative to the old system that ejects their children from schools because they are too different.

After the crowd clears the Way Scans get busy planning their Getting To Know You Game Day. They decide to use the Mobile Civic Sports Complex for the event. It is the home of the Mobile Tigers basketball team, led by Rodolpho Mantubo, a Nigerian giant known in the NBA as "Roar" Mantubo for the sound he makes whenever he makes a three-pointer. The Civic Sports Center is large enough to accommodate both Mantubo's fans, and his roar, so the Ways Scans figure it should be big enough for their event and they invite the whole Urban Center to their party.

As creative as they are, even they are amazed at the variety of ingenious contests and events they devise to get to know their students and find effective ways for all to learn. The (con)tests they plan, with the help of a gifted gamesman, are destined for use in the Way Scan school system as both teaching and learning tools.

Roar Mantubo is one of their especially helpful game advisors. When they go to check out the space for their party games, Emaline finds the player practicing at the Sports complex. Mantubo is shooting baskets from various spots in the stands to make his workout less boring, and when Emaline tells Roar about the educational games the Way Scans plan for their party, he volunteers to help.

"I grew up in the Nigerian countryside and we invented games all the time, to enlighten our lives and connect with the Earth and the Ancestors." Mantubo explains. "We could use this Game Party to identify the true party animals in the group, by making up the Game as we play along."

"That sound like life, since The Message." Emaline voices. "Rules about so many things changed when healing the Planet became the endgame. If we can find expert players, when rules and circumstances are ever-changing, we find our leaders of the future."

"We can find out who is best at thinking up new game plans, who can come up with rules they can explain to others and who masters new physical and/or mental challenges easily. We'll also see who is flexible enough to have fun when there are no rules or when the rules change during the play." Mantubo ads, more excited about the challenge of this game than about being the world's most famous gamesman.

❋ ❋ ❋ ❋

Mantubo is delighted when 'The Game Game' participants come up with dozens of games people can play, alone or with a group. They come up with a game a whole school can play, and a game a whole urban center and then a whole nation can play. It is not long before they devise a game the world can play. It has to do with saving the species Homo Sapiens from extinction. When humanity plays it, they have fun worldwide.

The Game Game, however, is not the only game in town.

The 'It's Your Story Game', designed by Ruth Feinstein and Winston Brightfoot, challenges participants to come up with their own story about a world they create, or would like to create. Their world can be any way they want it to be. The storyteller must believe in their vision enough to share it with others, in some fashion. They show or talk about their world in any way they can; to identify who has the eyes to see, or the ears to hear other worlds, and good enough organizational skills to tell that tale.

"If we can find people who can express a different reality to others, they might make good teachers." Winston proposes.

The results of the 'It's Your Story Game' are phenomenal. Some people play the Story Game by themselves, as solo affairs, others tell stories in groups of two or more. One tale involves all humans on Planet Earth though, admittedly, some do not yet know they are part of the 'Big Story', as it is called.

One epic is told by seven-year-old, Dorothy Partridge Palmer, whose tale has an atomic scope to it. Hers is the saga of a world created when one fork hits against another in a cutlery drawer, as it is slammed shut. Her audience of over three thousand people is spellbound, as she becomes the forks, at an atomic level, and shares that experience with others.

One group imagines they land on a planet where nothing grows except rutabagas. Now there is a tale. Another group enacts the tragedy of a wasted mind. They have the audience in tears. Yet another family-size group acts out ways they communicate with a member of the family who is deaf and blind. The whole play is done from the viewpoint of that deaf and blind member! What the audience learns! Another couple uses symbols they paint on the body of the other to tell their story. It is an intense tale, which draws a standing ovation from those watching.

"These people are gooood!" Ruth tells Winston. "Tell me again who the teachers will be and who the students?"

"I think we are going to have to throw concepts like that right out the window." Winston admits.

"Maybe we should set up computer programs for basic reading and math skills and let everyone learn those skill at their own pace. The rest of the time we all just learn together." Ruth proposes.

"The rest of the time will take a lifetime," Winston admits "but if that fork girl will be one of our teachers, I'd take her class, myself."

Bobbie comes to the same conclusion about the teacher/ student relationship in his game arena. He is trying to identify children and adults with scientific abilities and the group response to his 'Olympics of the Mind' Contest is blowing him away.

Bobbie starts his game by explaining the basics of Newtonian Physics to his participants. Then he asks them to make up games to prove that some of the stuff Newton talks about is a bunch of hooey.

"Take gravity," Bobbie tells the group. "please! Gravity is another name for a good guess. We don't really know what causes it or what it does, and when you go away from Earth all our theories about it get shot to heck. Can any of you come up with a better explanation for why this happens?" Bobbie asks, as he drops a book that crashes to the floor.

He speaks to a group composed mainly of kids under age twelve, except for that Abubakar guy with the open mind. Bobbie recognizes Winston's brother, Knowland Luigi Brightfoot, when Knowland raises his hand to comment.

"I think we've been taught to see it going down." Knowland proposes. "It may be a function of time as it relates to our movement through space, but we should have a chance to discuss other options for that book."

"No wonder the kid is having trouble in school." Bobbie marvels to himself. "He is speaking in alternative universals."

"Well, here's your chance to discuss those other options, Knowland. See what y'all can come up with, when you keep an open mind." Bobby adds with a nod to Abu.

That day, the group invents a theory of matter, time and energy that will lead to the development of propulsion through time and space, based on the power of intentionally. None of them are quite ready to do the math for that yet, but at least they get the right perspective on the problem.

"We found out the questions." Knowland Luigi tells his family later that night over dinner. "Finding the answers should be a cinch."

Toni Leonardo's game, "The Fix-It Challenge" involves her group in repair of something that is broken, using humor and enthusiasm as a part of the healing. The group is assigned to undertake both physical challenges and emotional repairs- to try to fix all kinds of problems, from a broken toilet to a broken heart. Sometimes broken lines of communication are healed, as well.

All participants at the Game Party have a chance to play any game they wish, but 'The Fix-It Challenge' attracts the largest playing group. This is not a surprise to the organizers. They know that most who are interested in the Way Scan School are told that they are broken, by their school system.

"It seems natural that many of you would want to play a Fix-It game." Toni tells the players "Remember, not only are you not broken, but you are also going to be the ones who fix what's wrong with this world. If anything gets done, you are probably the ones gonna do it! First, start with your own problems and then you can help with those others."

Those who had the most trouble with the old system are the ones who solve their problems that day:

Lupe Henry and her father come up with the idea to paint classroom walls with water-soluble paint. Then all kids can create, right there in their classrooms, and wash the walls off each day to be ready for the next day's artwork.

The habitual truant, Alexander Farquar, admits he does not function, at all, before 11am. He and his mom devise a school schedule for him that starts at noon. He plans to lock up at night when he finishes learning stuff. Alexander goes on to be a world-renowned astrophysicist, once he stays awake long enough to do the math, so his plan is a good thing for all.

By day's end, it is obvious that most of Mobile's school-age children and most of their teachers want enrollment in a Way Scan School. You did not need to be a genius or a Way Scan to see that.

❋ ❋ ❋ ❋

"So, you think we need to turn all the Urban Center schools into Way Scan Schools?" the Chairman of the Board of Education, Jethroe Franklin Cartwright, asks the Way Scans at a special meeting of the School Board, the day after their Game event.

"That would be wise." Emaline voices to the Board. "If you don't, you'll have so few students in your system's schools, the District will go bankrupt."

"LeDean Winslow offers to pay tuition at alternative schools, for any students that don't want the Way Scan system." Winston shares. "We would never force anyone to learn with us if they don't want to."

"That would be completely against our policy and the Rules of the Game as identified in The Message." Ruth the Flame enlightens the Board.

"How do you expect to handle so many students, with so many diverse needs and backgrounds?" Una Prentice, newly elected School Board member asks. "Your plan could destroy our educational system, completely."

"That is the basic idea, Una." Toni Leonardo whispers under her breath.

The Way Scans recall how Una ran the Robert E. Lee Junior High School before Betsy Ross Jackson started a process that made the school a model learning environment. Elected to the Board, based on her successful career there, Una still has no idea how or why Robert E. Lee works so well. She would have been astonished if presented with the fact that her students are the ones who turned their school around, with a little help from some Beauty.

"Teaching that many people mean reorganizing buildings, teachers and students. It could be a nightmare." Bobbie tells the Board. "Fortunately, one of our students, an eight-year-old girl name of LuLu Kuwendi, came up with a solution that should work quite well."

"She figured it out while we were playing the Fix-It Challenge." Toni Leonardo explains. "She suggests we organize schools the ways students and teachers want them."

"LuLu recommends we let people move around until they find a group they can work with, or a way to learn that best suits them." Winston further explains. "She suggests each person find a teacher that they want to learn from, inside or outside a school building, and that such learning count, even if no one else recognizes what they are doing as educational. If it educates them, it works!"

"Anyone can teach?" Jethroe Cartwright asks.

"Lulu's plan actually describes the way that most people have learned since we started walking on two legs." Winston points out to the School Board. "Now, the education system won't get in people's way while they do the learning they need to do."

The School Board has their doubts, but they really have no choice but adopt Way Scan schools as their official school system.

"I move we give it a chance for a year and then review the outcome." Una suggests. "If more kids stay in school, we count that as a success."

The Board supports Una's motion, and the Way Scan School opens for the next school year. By the end of that year, not only do all the Ways Scan students stay in school, many of the students who dropped out decide to return. As is predicted, the school eventually has most of the city's human inhabitants as pupils and/or teachers. In some cases, they are both.

As foreseen, the Way Scan school includes the Mobile elementary and secondary schools and, within a year of its startup, becomes an official part of the University of Alabama. There are multiple campus locations, including Senior Centers, small industrial workshops, Recreation Centers, and some buildings on the grounds of private homes. Within five years, the School is also a campus of the University of Tokyo School of Agriculture Research, and the University of Brisbane, Australia, School of Urban Planning and Ecology. It is also Mobile's adult school.

Each Way Scan School Learning Center is connected to ISIS, the Information Sharing International Supercomputer, when it comes online. This allows each location to both send and received information, in a free flow of knowledge between each school and the rest of the world. Not since the invention of the Internet has so much information been available to so many. The Ways Scan school system pioneers many additions to the ISIS system; to allow students, of all ages, to access almost every other school, library, and information source on Earth.

The Way Scan Schools revolutionize education when they prove, beyond a doubt, that the age of the student and how much prior education they have does not make a bit of difference when it comes to deciding who teaches and who learns there. All learn and teach at the Way Scan schools, all the time. What helps this process most, is that there is no discrimination when it comes to access to resources for learning. Little kids and advanced post graduate students all can use the same libraries, labs, and classroom resources.

One day a top scientist can see a science project done in a sixth-grade classroom and can realize they have found the answer to providing clean water purification systems at virtually no cost, that can be replicated worldwide.

Another day, a nine-year-old asks an astrophysicist about dark matter and comes up with the exact reason we cannot see it from Earth. The reason is the same as why a large truck cannot see a car in the next lane, at times, except it has to do with time, not with position.

In this way, the school allows for an endless variety of possibilities to be introduced to perhaps. This flexibility is endlessly creative and helps humans all over Planet Earth solve their many, tough, complicated, and complex problems. An added bonus: a good time is had by all.

At the time The Message is heard, people are told they have one or two generations to clean up Earth before a return to Union. People get real busy with the Clean-Up Game and forget all about Union. At least they think they forget. A part remembers— the part that always remembers what is important.

-Betsy Ross Jackson

THE STAR QUILT

Many say the Way Scan School owes its success to the fact that it makes dreams come true for most, if not all, of its students. This aspect of the school curriculum can be attributed to one of its first students, Winston "Bridges" Brightfoot's sister, Ramona Star. Ramona attends the Way Scan school as one of its first students but is also one of its most influential instructors.

Ramona Star is in the eleventh grade at the time the first Way Scan school opens in an old barn behind the Bidewell Mansion, Neighborhood 7, District 7 of the Mobile Urban Center. At that time, she is on the verge of getting kicked out of Mobile High School. If she goes it looks like the Star will take at least a third of the Junior Class with her. She is the one they dream with.

When Anna Marie Brightfoot gets a call from Principal Alberto Piccolo, advising her that Ramona Star will be expelled from school if she cuts another class, Ramona Star explains:

"When I found out that most of the kids have no dreams for their future, I had to do something. I have a dream-sharing meeting at lunchtime and most of the students involved never go back to the class after lunch. Sometimes they don't show up for the class after that, either."

Ramona Star learns her dream skills from her parents and family. They always talk about their dreams of the night before, at the breakfast table. Each child is encouraged to keep a dream log as soon as they can write and before that, to draw pictures of what they see, hear, and feel in their dreams.

"Otherwise, you end up living out someone else's dream." their father, Wilhelm, warns. "There are plenty of powerful and influential people who would be mighty happy to have you living and working to make every one of their dreams of wealth and power come true. Just don't count on their dreams being anything like your own and don't count on their dreams being in your best interest, either."

This kind of dream work is not a Brightfoot Family invention. It is a tradition of most InDios People. The Brightfoots are of the InDios group that settled around Mobile thousands of years before it is called Mobile. They have been dreaming there for a long, long time. Other First People have similar dream-sharing practices to realize what is important. In some groups this dreaming is the most important thing they do.

"We're learning too much of importance to leave our group and go to class." Ramona Star's friend, Yolanda Tavarez tells Anna Marie. "Sharing our dreams is the only thing happening at our school that's real."

"Students share what they dream the night before, learn what their future holds if they follow a path that knows no limitations." Anna Marie tells Ramona's father, that evening. "They're planning what could be in the land of possibility, the kingdom of perhaps and the playground of their own potential."

"It is holy work they are doing, right there at the picnic tables under the trees," Wilhelm acknowledges. "but we better find another school for Ramona Star."

"I think Winston and his friends have some good news for us." Anna Marie tells her family after talking to the Way Scans about their new school. "Ramona can teach her dream class there, as well as complete her High School education."

✻ ✻ ✻ ✻

Ramona and ninety-five percent of the students at Mobile High sign on for immediate transfer to the Way Scan school, making Mobile High the first Way Scan High School. Principle Piccolo is required to take Ramona Star's class or lose his job as their school administrator. In just a few weeks he is dreaming with the best of them and convinces the School Board that dream workshops are needed in the whole Mobile school system.

"Though Ramona Star's class is a part of the first-year high school curriculum, we must recognize the importance of dreams for all our children." Piccolo tells the School Board. "We need to start these classes in pre-schools and include them in work done at each grade level.

"Say what?" is the general reaction from the School Board members, who have no idea what Alberto is dreaming about.

"Dream Realization is one of the most important things students do." Piccolo explains to the still incredulous Board Members. "If students do not realize their dreams, they will never come true. If they can't use school to make their dreams come true, they will leave the place in droves. Who can blame them?"

The Board still has questions but figures that Piccolo's plan probably will not hurt anyone. They agree to make the Dream classes a part of every School's Guidance and Counseling system.

"People will train to be their own guides and counselors." Una Prentice summarizes. "Then the school counseling staff can help our Students identify what they need to study, to do what they dream."

❋ ❋ ❋ ❋

"Dream big, Piccolo!" Ramona Star tells her Principal, when he shares what happened at the meeting of the School Board Curriculum Committee.

"If there is a way, we can get people to take this class in uteri, we should shoot for that." Principal Alberto tells Ramona and the others in their dream group. "Students at our school can train to lead these Dream Workshops for other schools. We'll be sending dream workshop facilitators all over the city, for both adults and children, as soon as possible."

Ramona stays in High School, teaching and learning there, for another two years. Her work provides Dreamshop facilitators for the rest of the city and, eventually, their Urban Center provides dreamers for the rest of the nation. As the Way Scan School movement grows and spreads to Urban Population Centers all over the US and around globe, Mobile dreamers are instrumental in their success.

By the time Ramona graduates high school she is ready for a college level course in dreaming. No such course exists at the University at Mobile. No such course exists at any school in North America, except in the Inuit Nation. Ramona can either study at the University of Ice and Snow, or she can start a Department of Dreams at the local institute of higher learning when Alabama State offers to hire her to head their new department.

"I'll take the job if I can study quilt-making at the Department of Domestic Science here." Ramona tells the school's Dean of Admissions, Ms. Ludlillo Ticker. "I think that quilts are the closest thing to dreaming, in material form, I've ever seen."

"They're what?" Ms. Ticker responds.

"Quilts are one of the oldest art forms. They probably came over the Siberian land bridge, with people from Africa and Asia when they settled the New World." Ramona explains. "Stories, music and dreams, embodied in the quilts, are the bridge between this world and other worlds."

"You think that people brought their stories and dreams along on their textiles?" Ludlillo asks.

"Quilts have been holding the patterns of their dreams and stories ever since humans began making stuff."

"Is that so?" Ludlillo responds, as she signs Ramona Star up as a Domestic Science Major and arranges for her to head the Department of Dream Science of University of Alabama Worldwide Extension Program on the Internet.

"There must be more to the art of quilt-making than meets the eye and I bet you'll be the one to find it." Ludlillo predicts, as she signs herself up for the quilting class with Ramona. "This I got to learn."

❋ ❋ ❋ ❋

Ramona ends up co-teaching the quilting class, pointing out again and again the Beauty of the quilts made by women and men, down through history. Ludlillo and the rest of the class learn how quilts are made almost everywhere. If people wear no clothing, they do body painting, scarification and tattooing to decorate their exteriors. For humans, bodies and things that cover bodies are the most universal forms of dreams in material form.

"Almost as soon as people start to use their hands to do things, they start making quilts or quilt-like objects to cover themselves." Ramona Star points out to the class. "Sometimes their quilts turn into tents or blankets. An item that is layered like this also has a much greater ability to keep people warm. It may have enabled humans to spread North and South from the equatorial zones they first inhabited."

"So, humans who can quilt live where no other humans can?" her class co-teacher, Sumtree Boatright, asks. "How do you know that?"

"These quilts hold the patterns of the dreams, songs and stories that tell those tales. They are the first books that tell us all about it. Sometimes they sing it, too." Ramona Star shares with the class.

Ramona can often hear People singing when she looks at quilts made with a singing message.

"Quilting is a universal form of expression for Planet Earth and people put their stories, dreams and songs into quilts. Quilts accomplish a myriad of tasks. "

"People make all kinds of quilts; from that gigantic quilt made to commemorate thousands who die of AIDS, to the tiny leaf quilts children make for fairy beds." Sumtree points out.

"The Hopi People talk about the Spider Grandmother, the Goddess and guide who comes down from the sky on a spider's web. Creator of humans she fashions from the mud of the Earth, Spider Woman teaches us to spin and weave. Quilting is not far behind. The patterns and designs humans weave into their cloth, pottery, rugs, and quilts hold their stories to this day. The question is, where do they come from?"

✳ ✳ ✳ ✳

"If the quilts, like the clothes, really make the man, then where do the patterns come from?" Ramona queries in her doctoral thesis proposal. "Why the decoration? Why the colors and the symbols? Why the power of the patterns, shapes and why the songs that sing in your mind when you see them? Where do these forms come from? Do People devise them or divine them–are they messages from elsewhere?"

At the end of the written proposal for her dissertation Ramona Star adds: "Maybe the dreams and visions are not from within us. Perhaps we are little radio receivers, getting info from someplace else, and making a quilt about it. I want to understand the dreams that come to us, not from us."

"Far out, Ramona!" Knowland Luigi comments after reading her Ph.D. proposal. "How will you do the research to write your thesis?"

"The answer is out there in the fabric of life and I'm determined to find it." Ramona assures her brother.

"Will you keep teaching at the University?" Knowland asks.

"I'll keep studying quilts, but I'll do a TV show about them that will take me to other urban centers. That will pay the bills while I see quilts from all over the world."

"That sounds pretty Global." Knowland observes. "There must be millions of quilts out there. You'd best narrow your search a little, or you'll be a hundred and six years old before you finish your dissertation."

Ramona Star takes Knowland's advice and specializes in studying star quilts–a common pattern throughout the world. She has a lot of fun finding these patterns, meeting quilt makers and produces a fascinating TV show.

Her audience is privileged to see quilts from attics and storage boxes that are very old, previously shared with few outside the families of their makers. Ramona shares them with the world.

❋ ❋ ❋ ❋

"How did they know that?" Knowland Luigi queries, looking at a photo of a quilt that is five hundred years old, made by a slave in Georgia before the American Civil War.

"Know what?" Ramona Star asks, looking at the interesting patterns on the quilt. Though each quilt she sees is a revelation to her, Ramona Star attaches no special significance to the quilt pattern Knowland finds so fascinating.

"It's the Periodic Table of the Elements. You know, the building blocks of matter–showing how they're constructed from electrons and protons. Here's oxygen and hydrogen–then on to the more complex atomic particles. There's gold." Knowland adds, pointing to a star pattern in the middle of the quilt.

"You're kidding me." Ramona Star responds.

Knowland Luigi is a serious kid but he can pull some far-out practical jokes when he sets his mind to it. Ramona takes the photo from Knowland, as he moves on to look at other snapshots in her collection.

"This one." he comments as he picks up a set of photos of another quilt showing the work of a Polynesian woman who lived and quilted on the island of Hawaii, in the 1930s.

Her great grandchildren took her quilts with them when they moved to mainland USA, after The Message, to leave the islands to return to the Wild.

"What about it?" Ramona asks.

"It's the DNA helix." Knowland Luigi points out. "You know, the building blocks of life...genetics...all that stuff."

"Wow!" Ramona says. "Do you mind looking over these other photos and telling me what else is here?"

Knowland looks through her album of pictures and finds the following:

A quilt that illustrates the chemical formula of the benzene ring, created by a Caribbean quilt maker in 1815.

A quilt that appears to be a detailed picture of a computer chip, invented in 2002, that makes the cheap manufacture of Super Computers possible. On the same quilt is the chemical formula for the new compound that makes it possible to manufacture that chip for a penny each. An Appalachian woman in the mountains of Tennessee made that quilt in 1940.

A series of quilts, made by an Amish woman in Pennsylvania, shows patterns of 'X's and 'O's that document the mathematical formulae for Einstein's General Field Theory of Relativity. Knowland discovers this when he puts photos of the quilts into his computer's scanner and converts the quilter's "X" and "O" patterns into binary computer language, then into numbers.

"Do you think humans always knew this stuff?" Ramona Star asks Knowland. "Is it in us, waiting to come out when we dream it, then work it into the patterns of our lives?"

"I don't know." Knowland Luigi admits. "Maybe this stuff comes through whenever human minds are in the right frame for it."

"Like a quilting frame?" Ramona Star observes.

"That information is realized if there is a frame of reference for it." Luigi notes. "The information is understood, just like I understood the patterns in these quilts, because I know science."

"You also have a computer to read those 'X's and 'O's for us, now." Ramona Star adds. "It converted the signs into numbers we can recognize. It's like the pattern of prophecy; the stories the Old Ones talk about the future."

"They see the information in their dreams and give it the form of stories, according to the frame of reference they know in their day and age. Those prophecies foretell the end of this world." Knowland reminds his sister.

"I thought our old world ended with The Message." Ramona replies. "A lot of humans left us then, to move on to Union. Those of us who remain on Earth work to clean the place up for Tigers before we leave, too."

Knowland Luigi is confused. He was only six years old when The Message is heard, and he does not remember much about it.

"Where are we supposed to go?" he asks.

"To Union." Ramona answers. "That's what The Message said."

"Sounds like Prophecy all right." Knowland admits. "You better keep studying these quilts, sister. See if you can figure out what Union is."

Ramona hits Knowland over the head with a quilted star-pattern pillow and he responds, in kind, matching her star power admirably. Star war is declared as brother and sister duel it out in a big pillow fight. When their mother intervenes and their giggling subsides, they tell Ann Marie what Knowland found in the quilt patterns.

"I'd be happy to help you study these quilts for clues." Anna Marie offers. "I always wondered what "that back to Union" stuff in The Message meant. A lot of people thought it was about uniting

People on Earth. No more wars, cleaning up the environment, all that. There could be more to it, though." she admits. "There could be an actual journey involved."

Anna Marie picks up the quilt she made for Ramona Star, when her child was born. She made similar quilts for each of her seven children, all showing the story of Noah's Ark.

"Who knows what truth these old symbols hold." Ann Marie states, rubbing the soft, well-worn quilt against her cheek. "Maybe there is something here- a Message that we already know, just waiting to be found."

Later that night, Ramona Star looks up at the sky from the rooftop observatory the Brightfoot children built onto their house, accessible from the crawl space in their attic. The platform is large enough for three kids, or one almost-full-size adult and Ramona Star fills that bill. She observes the pattern of suns and planets above her, a giant quilt in progress.

"I think I'm going to study astrophysics next," Ramona promises herself. "to see the Beauty in the Universe and know the quilt dreamed by stars...."

Most of those who survive in the Wild have lived there for generations. This is the story of one such Wildman, and how he shares his gifts with the world.

- Stillpoint Sommes

SON OF THE LAND

LeRoy Fryer's great, great granddaddy received forty acres and a mule, at the end of the Civil War during a brief period called Reconstruction. Officials of the US Government sought to help those whose life had been blighted in captivity by giving them land, and some means to work that land, as recompense for slavery and injustice it sanctioned for generations.

LeRoy's great granddaddy, a keen observer of human nature, declined the good bottomland offered him by the occupation government running his State after the war. Instead, Elam Fryer chose remote, insect-infested swampland, as far away from a city as he could get. He knew that those who chose the good land would either be dead or dispossessed of it, as swiftly as night follows day.

"I'll take what no right-minded white man would even want." Elam said to himself. "I'll make it into something, or die trying, and you bet it will be so far away from the eyes of white folks they won't know enough about it to take it away from me, ever."

Elam was gifted with knowledge of the land from generations of African and New World farmers. He also had the strong back and iron will common to every captive he ever worked beside. Using these skills Elam made a go of his farm, even though the mule died of old age soon after they arrived. He hunted the bounty of the swamps to stay alive until his first harvest.

Elam's first trip to town to sell that harvest confirmed his worst fears about reversal of laws that had, in any way, benefited people like him. Even worse, prisons to re-enslave him and lynchings to kill whoever survived those prisons, were in the planning. Elam saw the writing on the laws and got out of town, as soon as possible. He did stay long enough to get himself a wife, Arilla. and disappeared from the powers that be.

Elam chose Arilla for his wife because she could read and write. Arilla chose Elam because she had more than common sense. Upon these capable foundations and his own, considerable, gifts and talents, Elam built his life, his family, and his farm. Over 150 years later, the Fryer farm still exists, and young LeRoy Fryer plans to keep it that way.

"Says here we got to return the farm to the Wild and all move to an Urban Center." Daniel Fryer told his son, as he read a letter from the Alabama Farm Board. "They've offered us a good price for the farm and a place to live in the city." he shares. "Says they want us to help the city folks out with their urban food production system."

"What if we don't want to go?" LeRoy asks.

LeRoy knows the Fryers never borrowed money on their land, so they do not owe anything to a bank or anyone else. No one can force them to leave their farm against their will.

LeRoy's mother, Calypso, states. "We've never really had a chance to sell, in the past, but seems to me we should take them up on this offer."

"You're the last son left on the land, son." Daniel reminds LeRoy. "I'm not getting any younger, so you got to decide. After all, you practically run this place yourself, these days."

LeRoy knows he wants to stay. He is born on the land and the place speaks to him. He is almost eighteen years old but never has the dreams of leaving the place his other brothers and sisters share. Years before The Message, LeRoy begins to institute ways to run the farm with fewer and fewer people, as his siblings leave. He also thinks up all kinds of ways to do without the inputs and machinery that other farmers view as essential to their operation. LeRoy knows he must work with the diversity of life on his land, much the same way his great, great granddaddy did. It is the only way to succeed as a farmer and harvester of the natural bounty there.

LeRoy floods areas that once had been drained by Fryer ancestors and plants wild rice, a disease-resistant crop he harvests by boat and sells for top dollar to gourmet restaurants in Mobile. He also builds a bat roost that brings hundreds of bats to an area near his fields. The bats eat the insects that would have attacked his crops. They also keep down the mosquito population that would have swarmed around the Fryer house, making life near the newly flooded marshes unbearable. LeRoy used the bat guano for fertilizer for his organic garden.

LeRoy grows all the food for his family, raises the chickens and small livestock they consume and has beehives that produce the Tupelo honey, for which the area is famous. LeRoy has eager buyers, year-round, for the harvest of his farm and his hives.

The young farmer also cultivates wild herb and swamp plants, sought out by a growing number of alternative medicines practitioners. They cannot get many of the plants he harvests anywhere else, especially when humans are barred from the Wild after The Message. In addition to the plants, he brings them, LeRoy passes on some of the secrets of the swamp plants to these healers, getting his information from an old diary kept by his great, great grandma, Arilla, and by each generation of Fryer women, since. Decades of healing knowledge are passed on to practitioners who pay LeRoy well for his help. He never lacks for customers.

LeRoy also "leases" some of his lands to an environment group; with the agreement he will replant the areas with Tupelo gum and Mangrove trees. This is done to help with flood control along the river and to promote sustainable harvest of the forest in the future. The organization pays the Fryers to plant the trees, then leave the land alone until the time is right for some of them to be cut for human use.

Though he and his family have developed a sustainable farm on their family land, LeRoy encourages his parents to take the offer of a house in an urban area, when they are too old to work the farm. They agree, to be nearer to their other children and grandchildren, even though LeRoy has no plans to join them there.

"That urban area needs Fryers farming there." LeRoy tells his father, who hesitates to leave his youngest son. "You can share all the great things we've done here with your new, Urban Neighborhood." LeRoy points out. "They'll be trying to grow enough food for a whole lot of people, on areas about the size of our farm. They need to know what the Fryers know."

Daniel and Calypso can see the wisdom of LeRoy's argument but are concerned that their son will be lonely there, all by himself.

"Now all I got to do is figure out how to grow me a bride, and I'll have everything I need." LeRoy jokes when they express their reluctance to leave him without human companionship.

"I'll find a bride for you." his mother promises.

Calypso knows if anyone can find the right mate for her son, it will be her. She is an excellent judge of character and has three daughters in the Urban area that will help her look.

"Sure mom." LeRoy responds, but is resolved to live a solitary life in the Wild.

He vaguely recalls once meeting a Wild man, who lived out there all alone. LeRoy reckons if that old white man can do it, so can he. He is astonished when Calypso returns to the farm, two months later, with Viola and the Reverend Tony Smallwell to marry them.

Along with Viola, come her computer, a crate of electronic gear, some solar electric panels, and a cell phone. An earth-orbiting satellite connects her to a telephone network and Viola's computer connects her to the Internet. This combination of humanity and technology effectively brings LeRoy a bride and all she connects with on and around Planet Earth.

"She's a computer freak." LeRoy whispers to his mother.

"But a lovely girl." Calypso responds. "She's the right age, completely healthy, and it doesn't matter to her where she lives. She's perfect for you."

"Instead of working out at a gym and running every day, I'll just work here on your farm." Viola later tells LeRoy. "I always felt all that sweating on those exercise machines was a waste of energy. Now, I'll accomplish something for the calories. Just show me what you want me to do. I'm a quick study."

The Reverend Smallwell is reluctant to perform the marriage ceremony when he realizes that this is an arranged marriage and that bride and groom have never laid eyes on one another before. Then Calypso points out that the entire Fryer lineage is founded on the same kind of relationship, between Elam and Arilla Fryer.

"They knew each other less than a day before they got hitched." LeRoy's mom advises the Preacher. "It worked for them. Before that, the folks who thought they owned humans like us paired us up, like cattle, or got us pregnant by raping us." she adds. "Compared to that, these young people have all the choice in the world."

That point taken, and doubly assured that neither of the young people is being forced into it, the Reverend Smallwell performs the ceremony with LeRoy's mama and many other relatives as witness. Generations of Fryer ancestors are present, though dead, buried in the family cemetery on the hill overlooking where LeRoy and Viola tie the matrimonial knot. The young people also jump over a broom there, as is a custom among Viola's people- brought with her ancestors from Africa on an involuntary trip in 1760.

Then Calypso and The Reverend Smallwell leave the happy couple to enjoy getting to know one another. The rest of the ancestors stay put, and do not bother the newlyweds a bit.

Calypso's belief in her ability to size up appropriate mates is proven true by their match. Viola and LeRoy are both easy to get along with, are kind and polite human beings, and both serve to provide each other with knowledge and experience that make both their lives more complete. They are different people, but each might have been made for their union with the other.

"I know almost nothing about the natural world, firsthand." Viola admits. "I was raised in a city and have spent the majority of my life in a classroom, then a computer lab, but I'm willing to learn."

Viola is painfully shy and rarely says a verbal world to anyone, so this conversation with LeRoy shows how much she likes and trusts him, already.

"After the Message, I couldn't imagine how I might help the world return to the Wild, and I was pretty depressed about that." she shares. "Until our marriage provided me with this chance."

LeRoy admits, in turn, "I know nothing of the world of technology but I'm happy to share all I know about the natural world with you. I'll teach you all about this farm and the Wild places around it."

LeRoy is a natural storyteller and teacher, but rarely writes down anything he knows and never has touched a computer in his life. He sees an opportunity to help others with Viola's assistance.

"You can tell others about what you learn here, if you want." he suggests. "Some of what I know might help restore the marshlands and swamps if you get the information out on the Internet. I can also help people create sustainable farms in swamp areas."

Viola's web site, 'Swamp Farming', provides helpful information when humans try to return places along rivers, coastlines, and lakes to their natural state. She and LeRoy spend a couple of hours each evening responding to questions that come in, by email, to their web site.

"Who would have thought I'd reach more people here, way back beyond no place, than I'd reach living in the middle of New York?" LeRoy muses.

"Who'd have thought I'd ever be doing something that helps the Wild?" Viola marvels.

Both are happy to help, and LeRoy and Viola are the first to admit they are better together than apart. Viola takes the greatest delight in everything she learns about LeRoy's world, and is quick to recognize that the intricacies of nature are far more complex that any computer she ever used. LeRoy is grateful that Viola is so happy and enjoys the times she helps him reach beyond the boundaries of his farm, to others all over the Planet. They make a good team.

The only cloud on the Fryer horizon is the fact that they have no children, after years of trying to produce an offspring. LeRoy hopes there will be at least one Fryer child to inherit the farm after he dies but what Viola gleans from the Internet is not encouraging.

"A lot fewer babies are being born these days." Viola shares. "Of course, that only makes sense, what with people's needs being met now, even into old age. They don't need a family to support them when they get old. No need for many children to work their family land, either. People do that with their Neighbors, now, and the less people a Neighborhood has to feed the easier it is for everyone."

"But what about people's gifts and their heritage?" LeRoy asks. "I'm not even talking about inheritance here. I'm talking about family traditions and knowledge; the part of human history that really matters."

"People seem to be sharing that with one another, more than ever before." Viola responds, seeing this clearly when surfing the Net. "Humans seem to be crazy for each other's food, each other's stories, each other's styles of building, fashions, and just about anything else of lasting value, that human beans ever came up with. We're sharing our passions and our prayers, heck, we're even sharing our inside jokes. It's global!"

"Humans have become a human family, at last. There's just a lot less of them, than there was twenty years ago, when The Message is heard. Is that what The Message calls Union?" LeRoy asks recalling The Message in detail, though he was only a kid when it is heard. "If I remember right, The Message promises Union in one or two generations."

"If there's supposed to be two generations to get to Union, shouldn't we be having kids, to do that?" Viola asks, worried that at age forty her biological clock is all but ticked out.

"Seems to me we're trying our best." LeRoy puts in. "You think we're doing something wrong?"

"We'll have children when they want to come, according to almost every religion ever devised or defined by humans." Viola shares. " I've checked out religious teachings from around the world on the subject of conception. In fact, most religions say it's up to the kid when they want to come, and who they want to come to."

"Then we better get to calling a child." LeRoy tells Viola. "Maybe they all think we have other fish to fry. Why don't we invite one of them here?"

"Couldn't hurt." Viola admits. "It certainly would be an improvement over that brew of weeds, bark and roots that you've had me drinking for the past six months. I know that recipe for fertility came from your great, great grandmother's diary, but it looks like a swamp, and tastes like bat shit. I sure don't relish drinking any more of it than I have to."

"You're the one who said your years for having healthy children have almost passed." LeRoy reminds his wife.

"I'm not getting any younger and giving birth as an older mother can have serious complications for me and the child, the longer it's delayed." Viola admits.

"You go into Mobile Urban Center, to give birth to our child." LeRoy insists. " I'm not taking any chances."

When Viola got pregnant later that month, she reminds LeRoy of his suggestion that they go to Mobile for the birth. "All those Holy books also say that children decide where they want to be born, too. Maybe this child just wanted some assurance of being born in Mobile."

"Something calling the child there?" LeRoy surmised. "Wonder what that could be?"

"I guess we'll find out." Viola responds. "What about the farm?"

"While we're gone, the trees will just keep growing, and the Wild will keep on doing all the things it does. I doubt the old place will miss us much, until we get back." LeRoy speculates.

"I hear that Mobile is a mighty nice spot, but this place is heaven, LeRoy." Viola admits.

"Maybe every place else is, too." LeRoy proposes. "Let's go see."

THE GOSPELS ACCORDING TO REVEREND IKE
By
Karen LaMantia

"What's next?" Betsy Ross Jackson shares. "The next book in The Message Series, ***The Gospels According to Reverend Ike,*** is the further adventures of those you met in ***The End Game*** and ***Mobile Tales***. You'll find yourself back at the Abiding Light Sanitarium for the Mentally Ill and will see how the Residents there enlighten Reverend Ike 'The Preacher' Ham. Ike learns about the changes needed before humans can move on to Union. Then he tells the rest of the world all about it in a new set of Gospels."

Betsy Ross continues, "Here's some of what's in store(y):

- You'll travel through time with me and the Abiding Light Staff
- You'll find out what happens in a police department that loves, honors and cherishes
- You'll see how two socialites change business as usual
- You'll rejoin Cherry Tupalow at the Sisters of Perpetual Motion Strip Club and Homeless Shelter
- You'll see how Merriweather Jenkins cleans up his act at the Abiding Light and you'll watch as Mobile continues to transform itself, to be ready for those Different Minds."

DIFFERENT MINDS
By
Karen LaMantia

The fourth book in The Message Book Series, is a fascinating and funny book available from EarthNeighborhood.com

EARTH NEIGHBORHOOD ONLINE!

If you can't wait for more news from Mobile, check out the Earth Neighborhood web site, for on-line environment and social justice news from your favorite Message Book Series characters. You can buy all The Message Books online at the Earth Neighborhood Store. Come to the hood any time at: www.earthneighborhood.com

See you in the hood!"